OUR MAN IN THE DARK

OUR MAN IN THE DARK

A NOVEL

RASHAD HARRISON

ATRIA BOOKS

New York   London   Toronto   Sydney   New Delhi

ATRIA BOOKS

A Division of Simon & Schuster, Inc.
1230 Avenue of the Americas
New York, NY 10020

First Atria Books hardcover edition November 2011

ATRIA BOOKS and colophon are trademarks of Simon & Schuster, Inc.

For information about special discounts for bulk purchases, please contact Simon & Schuster Special Sales at 1-866-506-1949 or business@simonandschuster.com.

The Simon & Schuster Speakers Bureau can bring authors to your live event. For more information or to book an event, contact the Simon & Schuster Speakers Bureau at 1-866-248-3049 or visit our website at www.simonspeakers.com.

Design by Esther Paradelo
Title page art based on *Homage to Martin Luther King* (1996) by Xavier Medina-Campeny

Manufactured in the United States of America

10 9 8 7 6 5 4 3 2 1

Library of Congress Cataloging-in-Publication Data
Harrison, Rashad.
  Our man in the dark / by Rashad Harrison.
    p. cm.
  1. King, Martin Luther, Jr., 1929–1968—Assassination—Fiction.
2. United States. Federal Bureau of Investigation—Fiction. 3. Civil rights workers—Fiction. 4. Informers—Fiction. 5. African American men—Fiction.
6. Race relations—Fiction. I. Title.
  PS3608.A7837O97 2011
  813'.6—dc22   2011000114

ISBN 978-1-4516-2575-2
ISBN 978-1-4516-2577-6 (ebook)

For Jennifer

". . . being invisible and without substance, a disembodied voice, as it were, what else could I do? What else but try to tell you what was really happening when your eyes were looking through? And it is this that frightens me: Who knows but that, on the lower frequencies, I speak for you?"

Ralph Ellison
Invisible Man

AUTHOR'S NOTE

The FBI campaign against Martin Luther King, Jr., and other black activists (known officially as COINTELPRO) has been well documented. Among the most sinister tactics employed were surveillance, wiretappings, disseminating false information, and the use of paid informants. These informants came from all walks of life—they were accountants, policemen, church folk, itinerant preachers, and photographers—all compelled by different motivations, and, in these instances, all African-American.

While the plot of this book is inspired by this factual backdrop, it is a novel. The conversations and thoughts of real people such as Martin Luther King, Jr., Ralph Abernathy, Andrew Young, and J. Edgar Hoover are fictitious inventions (except for those known and documented), created to set the atmosphere of the novel and meet the demands of the narrative. The character of John Estem is fictional, born from my imagination, and not intended to portray any real person. Therefore, his dialogue and actions with respect to persons real and imagined are wholly fictional, as are his family and associates, such as the characters of Candy, Gant, Count, and Mathis and Strobe.

OUR MAN IN THE DARK

Night has come, and so have the shadows that once pulled me in against my will. I believed the promises made by those exaggerated figures that followed me, but I am no longer fooled by illusions. Their lies must stay outside. Up these darkened steps, and past that door, is the truth.

My flashlight leads me to the file cabinet. It isn't locked. There are many files inside, but one in particular intrigues me. It's labeled **JEST** in bold letters followed by a sequence of numbers. I open it to reveal a series of black-and-white photos. They show a man leaving a building, crossing a street, and alone inside a telephone booth. At first, I assume they are random individuals of no importance. But then I look closer. They are pictures of me.

I turn to cast my light on the doorway and then back to the photos. I scan them, imagining the clicking of a camera's shutter as I view each one. I try to make sense of them by placing them in order. The booth, the street, the building. It's the last one that's the most telling—it was taken as I left the bank. They were watching me from the beginning.

Atlanta: Summer 1964

I sit at my desk at the headquarters of the Southern Christian Leadership Conference, mulling over accounting records and figures. A few years ago, Martin was accused of tax evasion—which is comical, since most of what he earns goes back into the movement. The man lives like a pauper. But we are trying to make sure it doesn't happen again. Gant has me sifting through the financial records to ensure that Martin hasn't received any compensation that cannot be accounted for.

I work with a particular column of numbers and notice the sum: fifty thousand dollars. A flash of warmth surges up my neck. This figure is an anomaly, but I don't suspect any wrongdoing—at least not immediately. Though it troubles me to do so, I feel compelled to bring this to Gant's attention.

I'll have to persuade him to see things as I see them, and that is a difficult task. His judgment of me is ruthless and immediate. Anything I question results in a questioning of me. I am exhausted by our exchange before it even begins.

He walks past my open office door in a well-scented hurry. He is one of those handsome men who know they are handsome. Tall, with a face sculpted out of Georgia clay, he has a strange way of using his looks to make you feel inferior. It does not help matters that, as I approach his perfect image, I am slowed by a permanent hobble—my reward for surviving a childhood bout with polio.

I watch Gant and his secretary walk swiftly down the hallway, but before I approach them, I go through my usual ritual of checking that my pant leg has not ridden up to reveal the stirrup of my brace; it creates an unattractive bulkiness under my trousers that annoys me to no end. I adjust my pants and smooth out the fabric so that it falls properly. I don't want anyone to be uncomfortable in my presence. Even FDR went through strained efforts to appear unaffected by polio. My coworkers shouldn't feel guilty about their ability to take gallant, even strides as they march alongside Dr. King, while I lurch through the corridors of the SCLC.

I struggle to catch up, asking the back of Gant's head for a moment of his time, but he insists that he's in a hurry.

"Mr. Gant. Please . . ." I say, "just five minutes."

They pause briefly; he asks Susan to grab him some coffee and then turns to me. "Five minutes, Estem. If this is about your Chicago proposal, I haven't looked over it or discussed it with Martin."

"No, it isn't about that. It's—well, sir, I was going over the figures for the donations . . . and while I'm sure this is probably minor—"

"Your point?"

"A large sum of money, Mr. Gant. And I can't trace it to any source."

"Perhaps an old friend of King's who wants to remain anonymous?"

"There would still be a receipt of some sort."

"John, the problem? I don't see it."

"Mr. Gant, it can't appear that we—"

"I don't have time to chase numerical phantoms. Estem, you should remember that we are looking for Martin's personal transactions that might warrant attention."

"Sir, it is my responsibility to—"

"I know *exactly* what your responsibilities are. I made them very clear when I hired you."

"Yes, Mr. Gant. Yes, and I'm very grateful—"

Susan returns with his coffee. "Mr. Gant, Dr. King is waiting for you in the conference room," she says.

"Tell Martin I'll be there shortly. Are we finished here, Estem?"

"Maybe Dr. King could shed some light . . ."

"I'll try to mention it to him."

He enters the conference room, and I briefly peer in after him. Martin gives me a knowing nod before Gant quickly closes the door behind him. Muffled sounds soon follow—greetings, laughter, and friendly banter.

It's fine. This is the way I'm used to being treated. I float around the SCLC like inconsequential vapor, only a vague innocuous presence, giving nothing and taking nothing. I crunch numbers. I stack paper. Occasionally, I move the stack from one end of my desk to the other. If it were not for the creak of my brace, I doubt anybody would know that I'm here. When the secretaries and volunteers gather to form huddled islands of gossip and chatter, I foolishly linger at the edges, hoping to be invited ashore.

My conversation with Gant has left me desperate for a drink, but I need to see her just as much as I need the liquor. After work, I head to my usual nightspot, a bar called Count's.

The place is a red velvet Ferris wheel of any vice imaginable.

Drink. Drugs. Sex. All of them unifying lures for this mixed bunch of seedy characters and squares searching for the cool. I have to hand it to Count: for a place run by a Negro, it does have a certain cosmopolitan feel. Mirrors, tinted Byzantium gold, surround the stone tables and leather booths that are better suited for sipping absinthe than bourbon. Count's is also marked by integration—but it's inchoate, one-sided, and gender-specific. You'll find colored girls with white men, most of whom are policemen. Their presence is meant to keep us safe, but the only things safe in this place are the secrets.

I used to wonder how a man working for the saintly organization of the saintly Dr. King could find himself in such a sinful place. But I'm no saint although I'm a good Christian, and even the best Christians are more familiar with sinners than saints.

The floor vibrates from the dancing patrons and the rolling beat coming from the band on the small stage. I walk along the bar, hoping that my limp appears to be more swagger than stagger. The woman singing with the band is Miss Candy, also known as Candice. She looks just like what her name implies—bad for you, but oh so good. Her singing is awful, but she's not up there for her voice. She's like a sepia-tinted dream with fiery red lips flickering in the darkness. Her tight, knee-length dress covered with glittering amber sequins reminds me of a freshly poured glass of champagne. Her hair is pulled back into a tight chignon on the top of her head, à la Josephine Baker. I like it that way.

I watch her hips sway to the final notes of the song, and the crowd applauds as she finishes. They clap for the band, for her hairstyle, and even for that dress—for everything except her singing. However, as she descends from the stage and makes her way through the crowd, some of their cynicism fades. She carries a good portion of her talent behind her, and the men nod appreciatively.

I raise my drink, a signal to her above the noisy gathering. She sees me at the bar and comes over.

"John?" She looks me over with the careful eyes of a fawn. Beads of sweat still linger on her flawless skin.

"Great set tonight," I say.

"Right. Thanks." She averts her eyes, looking away from my lie.

"No, really. The crowd seemed to dig it."

"John, I got the flowers you sent. You've got to stop doing things like that. We've already talked about this."

"You didn't like them?" I'm not looking at her anymore. I stare down into the shadows by her ankles.

"They were fine, but that's not the point . . ."

Suddenly, white tapered pants and the shine of black patent leather interrupts the darkness. They belong to Count, the owner of the club.

"Candy," he says.

I don't look up; his shoes are pointing at me in provocation. Count has warned me before about talking to Candy, and I don't want to press my luck. I can feel him hover over me, holding his cigarette as if it were a weapon.

"How's your job going?" she asks.

"Fine . . . making the world better for colored folks everywhere." I peer up at Count, but I miss his eyes and meet three circular scars on the side of his bald head. He's proud of them. He must be. At least three times he has made a fool of *death*.

"It must be exciting working so close to Dr. King."

"True. I do work closely with Martin. Martin and I are close. I'm the liaison to the financial assistant—"

"Like a bookkeeper or something?"

"Right. A bookkeeper."

"C'mon, Mama . . . my sugar's gettin' low," Count says, sending a cloud of smoke toward my face.

She gives him an unpleasant look. "I've got to run," she says to me. "It was good seeing you." After placing a kiss on my forehead, she turns away, and Count guides her by the back of her neck through the crowd.

I turn back to the bar and order a martini, but the bartender gives me a shot of bourbon. It takes six more before I feel man enough to face the room and leave.

I return home that night, drunk and alone. I stand in front of the mirror talking to myself, practicing, awaiting my transition into a superman. It's a tough feat because of the brace—a strange hybrid of leather and metal, a network of buckles and straps, like stirrup meets straitjacket. I notice, between the open spaces of leather, that the skin of my leg has taken on an ashen hue from the day's wear, but I do not feel like going through the trouble of removing it just yet.

I go through this ritual after every defeat she serves my ego, analyzing and thinking of ways to improve myself, or at least my appearance. What is Candy's attraction to Count? It can't be physical. His expensive clothes can only help him so much. I'm no matinee idol, but with that pockmarked skin, he must shave with broken glass. A vain fellow like Count must have a roomful of mirrors. Someone as ugly as Count should only have bare walls. The torture she must endure, being mounted by that animal.

I go over to my nightstand and pick up evidence of Candy's ill-fated attempt at a recording career: a dance single called "Do the Gumdrop." She smiles from the record sleeve holding a large gumdrop the size of a melon above her left shoulder. Count had indulged her by starting a label where she was the only act. I place it on my phonograph, the needle hits the groove and, in a weak tinny voice, Candy instructs me to "Do the Gumdrop, baby. Do it . . . Do it . . . Do the Gumdrop." I love her and have played her song many times, but I still find it hard to listen to.

Count has created an amusement park full of funhouse mirrors, a place where she can indulge in make-believe and see limitlessly different versions of herself. Trying to decipher what is real must make her dizzy and any attempt to escape futile.

The allure of money and its hold are undeniable. I would love to strut for her and let her have a glimpse of the man I've been hiding away. I have tried persistence, but never money. I've never tried it because I've never had any. This is tragic considering that every day I track its movements. I know money's habits, I know where it breeds, where it rests, and where it feeds, but it remains elusive. Like a frustrated hunter, I lose its scent somewhere. I look around my meager surroundings. No sign of it here. My apartment is almost unbearable. A simple one-room box. I've made no attempt to decorate it. Part of me still senses that there are better things in store for me, and this is not where I want to leave my mark.

Money—no; but power, or something like it, may be within my reach. My idea for a march in Chicago makes sense. Martin, Abernathy, and Young would bring me into the hierarchy once they saw that I was thinking about the long-term advantages for the movement and not just the colorless duties required of my job. I'm just a hopeful pledge, but it could be my opportunity to join their exclusive fraternity. But obviously, I'm being foolish to harbor such aspirations and optimism; Gant would never allow that to happen.

It'll be morning in a few hours, but I'm not quite drunk enough to sleep so I go to work on my own supply.

I walk my scotch over to the window and light a cigarette. Looking out into the Atlanta night, black with heat, I take a drag and notice that the smoke has taken on a new characteristic. Behind the charcoal and stale tobacco mingled with the bite of menthol is a fourth note: the earthy smell of hand-worn bills.

2

I sit at my desk, disheveled and nursing a hangover, when Gant calls me into the conference room. There's a strategy session with some volunteer law students and Martin's executive staff, and Gant needs me to pay attention while he dedicates himself to charming the room. As I stand, I feel gravity weigh on my brain.

Andrew Young, executive director, leans to his left and whispers something intently in Martin's ear, talking emphatically with his hands. Young has the good looks of a soul singer, and his loosened tie gives him an air of detached cool. Ralph Abernathy, SCLC secretary-treasurer, has the unfortunate luck of being seated in close proximity to Gant. Abernathy nods lazily, his hound dog cheeks swaying subtly as he struggles to appear interested while Gant recalls a story about running into Adam Clayton Powell, Jr., in the Caribbean. The rest of the group discusses the horrific attack on two people, a white woman and a colored man, killed savagely on the outskirts of the city.

Martin picks up that thread of conversation. "What do we know about those two?" he asks, addressing his staff. "Were they romantically involved?"

Abernathy ponders the question while Young gives his ready answer. "Not sure. The details are sketchy. The talk is that they were headed down here for Freedom Summer, but we should stay silent on it until we get more info."

My mind drifts through a foggy attempt at understanding Candy and her unwarranted attachment to Count. Do civil rights activists hold any sway in afterhours juke joints? If she could see me now, here, with the prominent leaders of the movement, challenging America to live up to its promise, she might aim her adoration at me, the more appropriate target.

My attention shifts back to the meeting when I hear Martin mention the president and the plans for an aggressive push for voter registration among Negroes in rural areas. Martin looks at me but quickly shifts his eyes when I nod at him. He leans back in his chair, unbuttons his collar, and puts his hands out in front of him as if preparing to frame an argument. He is about to speak when I interrupt him. "Since we are on the subject, I think it may be a good idea to have a march in Chicago. Housing and job discrimination are horrific there. We could organize and split costs similar to the March on Washington. CORE and NAACP could—"

Gant's eyes grow wide. "Estem, please . . ."

Martin gives me a pitying smile. Then Young jumps in. "We're not on that subject *exactly*, but the idea has merit," he says, his voice trailing off.

"It's John Estem," offers Gant.

"The idea is sound, John, but CORE and N-double-A-C-P are out of the question—that'll be a three-way fight for control. And we really can't afford to take on a solo project up North, especially in Chicago. With Daley's machine? No. We don't have the resources politically, and we definitely don't have them financially. . . . You'd think the bookkeeper would know that."

Everyone laughs.

"Well, Mr. Young, actually, there is a surplus—"

"Hold on one second, Estem," says Gant. "Could you start working on those contributors' statements of deductibility? I think we have it from here."

My headache shifts to my pride. "Of course," I move to rise, and my brace rattles as I stand. I know everyone has heard it, but suddenly I am invisible. I leave the conference room, turning to peek inside one last time. "There's a *surplus*?" Martin asks before I close the door.

I head back to my office and look at the form letter waiting to be sent to past contributors: "*Dear So and So . . . Thank you for your*

*contribution. This letter is to remind you that your donation may be com-
pletely tax-deductible, but please check with your financial advisor . . ."*

I open my desk drawer looking for names to match with donations,
when I notice a check. It has already been cleared by the bank. It's written out to one of the charter companies we use for buses. The signature
line bears the imprint of Gant's rubber stamp. I am the one who applied it.

Gant taps on my door. It's partially open, and I reflexively tell him
to come in before I realize that I am still holding the check with the
delicacy and admiration of a stamp collector.

"Well, Estem, I guess you're full of surprises, huh?"

"I'm sorry, sir. I was out of line." I place the check back in the
drawer face up on top of everything so that I can see it.

"There's a pecking order you have to respect here, John. The archi-
tects don't want to hear design strategies from the bookkeepers. That
sort of thing requires subtlety and finesse. You should learn it, Estem.
I admire your ambition, but you have to trust me. I know how these
things work."

"I understand perfectly."

"There's something else I need to talk to you about. I want to
apologize for the other day."

"Apologize? That isn't necessary."

"No, it is. You were just doing your job. So I hope there are no hard
feelings."

"Sir, there were never any hard feelings."

"You've got an eye for detail. I like that. Which is why I need your
help."

"Help? Of course."

"First, I need you to close that account. Discretion is key here,
Estem. We'll bring it into the fold *gradually*. Martin may tell them what
they should do, but the balance sheet tells him what he can do."

"I'll get right on it."

"Estem, what I really need you to do—and this is very important . . ." He looks concerned.

"Yes, sir, I'm listening." Maybe I've been too hard on him. He's finally realized that he can no longer neglect my talents and usefulness.
He needs me.

"I need you to pick up my suit from the cleaners. Martin's giving a press conference at First Baptist. The pants should have a sharp crease and a one and one-quarter-inch cuff. Here's the ticket. Can I count on you?"

"Why can't Susan take care of this?"

He looks down at his breast pocket, adjusts the fold of his handkerchief, then looks back at me, "This sort of thing needs a man's eye."

While alone at night, I often hear a ringing in my ear. I thought it was just a case of tinnitus, but now I realize that it's the sound of some sort of internal alarm clock designed to snap me out of my complacency. What would it take to set up in Chicago? Nothing fancy, just an office and a few donations of food and clothing to impoverished children and the sullen men on the unemployment line. That would get some attention, wouldn't it? Then Martin, impressed with the groundwork I've laid, would see the pressing need to come to Chicago and assist me.

Gant leaves. I wait for his footsteps to become faint before I open my desk drawer. There is nothing suspicious about this check. Nothing at all. I have many more just like it. At some point, all of the checks written on behalf of the SCLC end up in front of me. This check has many brothers and sisters resting undisturbed in my office. I begin to wonder if they would be bothered by the addition of one more.

I turn the radio up. Otis Redding should be heard nice and loud. I think the purr of her engine adds a nice accompaniment. She's not brand-new, but she's new enough, and the strong smell of the leather seats has already prompted me to reminisce about how I acquired her.

The bank teller was a mousy little thing. Her eyes bounced between the check and my face long enough for the gentleman behind me to begin clearing his throat. She told me to wait a moment while she went up a set of stairs that led to an office with large windows for walls. It was a clear box with a dapper old man inside, who seemed to hover above us, deciding who did and did not receive their money. The mouse's white horn-rimmed glasses tilted toward me, as did the old man's double chin. I considered making a run for it—then I remembered that I don't run. A fast-paced limp is unforgettable, and I imagined I wouldn't have too much company in the lineup. I decided to stay put and learn the old man's verdict. She descended the stairs and returned to her station. She nodded, smiled, and said my name, "Mr. Estem," with a tone of approval that extended the sound of the last letter. I don't blame her for being concerned. Ten thousand dollars is a lot of money. I don't know if it was the amount of the check, the fact that I am a Negro, or a problematic combination of both. She was Negro as well, but no one judges like family.

The experience was far more pleasant when I bought my new car, a Cadillac Fleetwood, only slightly used. It was previously owned by a doctor who rarely drove. The salesman was a young Negro with a broad smile and processed hair that was parted on the left. He insisted upon calling me sir, but he wasn't pushy. He only laughed knowingly as I stared at an ad featuring a white-gloved woman seated in the front seat of their latest model. She stared back seductively as the tiltable steering wheel, shot with the blurred effect of motion, reminded me of a wagging tongue.

He talked about the engine and directed my attention toward the body and its aesthetics. The grille looked like a smile of menace or pleasure or both, and the car's long lines conjured the image of a woman's fully extended legs upon a sofa. Yeah, she could make it to Chicago just fine. I thumbed through the brochure, having already decided on a name for my new baby: Black Beauty.

She rides smooth as I drive down Auburn Avenue. I pass the Royal Peacock and slow to the speed of a parade float so that the patrons waiting to see Ike and Tina can see me first. I drive past the Palladium and La Carrousel and repeat my stunt, even though I know my final destination is Count's.

I pull up in front of Count's and notice the neon lights reflecting on the car's hood. A poster outside reads: COUNT'S, FEATURING CANDY. In the picture below, she covers half her face with a lavishly ornamented hand mirror, revealing only a heavily mascaraed eye that shines with lupine brightness.

My visit to the tailor has blessed me with a midnight blue suit: single-breasted and narrow-legged. I think the gray trilby adds some dapper mysteriousness. Inside, the shadows of the energetic crowd leap from wall to wall, and some men watch me with jealousy and admiration as I approach the bartender.

"Candy around?" I ask.

"Nope."

"When will she be around?"

"Don't know."

I reveal a roll of money, pull off a twenty, and hand it to the bartender.

"So, when will Candy be around?"

"I said, I don't know."

Listen to those bar toughs chuckle.

"Keep it," I say. "It's only money."

Hours go by and still no sign of her.

I was a fool to call and tell her I'd be here tonight—she probably skipped out to avoid me. I think of Chicago, driving down Michigan Avenue in the Caddy with enough room for her to stretch out those long brown legs. But that's a fantasy; here's where reality sets in, making itself nice and comfortable. I feel ridiculous in this suit, drinking alone. I'm stupid for even thinking that she'd come with me. Like so many nights before, I pick up my bruised pride and start for home, but this time I'm stopped by a vision.

The beautiful woman approaching me is obviously a working girl. She says she's seen me in here before. It embarrasses me to think of all the humiliating scenes she must have witnessed. I too have seen her before, on the dance floor, with the men who come in after work, seducing them with moves designed especially for payday. My focus has always been Candy, although out of necessity, I have occasionally solicited the company of other women; but I have never approached her. She compliments me on my change and evolution, and she makes it easy for me to reconsider. She has the kind of dark brown skin that takes in light and sends it back to you with an extra layer of polish and shine.

We talk. I tell her about work, and she seems genuinely interested until I run out of things to say and reach my limit of what the bartender has to offer. She whispers in my ear while caressing my chest, inviting me to the room in the back. Her torso is small, but taut and athletic and anchored by wonderfully wide hips that, for some reason, invoke the excitement and frustration of an aimless journey. I follow her to a dimly lit hallway in the back of the bar. There are only two ways to enter this passageway: be chosen by one of the girls or offer a secret code at the door that faces the alley. She manages to nibble my ear, even as I limp down the corridor. Talented girl. There are alternating colors coming from the room up ahead—a color wheel of red and blue, spinning in front of a light bulb. Inside the room, she is engulfed by color, and though it's hard to believe, the man with her, shirtless and smiling, is me.

I stand alone under the changing colors. Once the money is spent, the party must end. As I struggle to get dressed, the girl flees the scene. She's been paid, so there is no reason for her to stick around. I came here for Candy, for her to see me in a different light, but that's not how things turned out.

I leave Count's feeling a little ashamed of the desperate episode that occurred in there. Women, when I am lucky enough to have one, are the source of so many of my troubles. I have hoped to be more complicated than that, but then I think of the company I keep, and the guilt doesn't last long. A few weeks ago, Martin and I had an encounter that began to shape my perspective.

I was working late one evening when I heard the sound of a man crying. This startled me, to say the least, since I thought I was working alone. I entered the hallway and discovered that the sound was coming from Martin's office. The door was open and the lights were off, but I could still discern his unmistakable frame. "Dr. King?" I flipped on the light switch, and the fluorescent bulbs flickered and dimly illuminated the office, changing the contours of his face from light to dark. His eyes were red with sadness and fatigue, and a cloying, sweet fragrance seemed to emanate from him. He'd been with a woman, not in the office but somewhere else, and not that long ago. In a way, it made sense that he returned to the office—that place has a way of punishing you and absolving you of your sins.

He motioned for me to have a seat, and I eased myself into a chair facing him.

"It's Martin," he said leaning forward to offer me a cigarette. "No need for the formalities."

"Thanks . . . Martin," I said, taking the cigarette and immediately feeling uncomfortable. Two buttons of his shirt were undone, and he had draped his tie around his neck like a sleeping snake. A silence followed that did not seem awkward, but completely appropriate. I lit my cigarette, and Martin just nodded.

I wanted to tell him I was proud to be working with him and the organization. Even then, and for some time before, I saw him as a kindred spirit. I considered saying so, but ultimately did not.

The last of the lights finally came on. The smoke drifted up toward them, creating a sheer curtain that covered Martin's face and the dying scent of perfume.

He hasn't been the same since that crazy woman in Harlem stabbed him in the chest with a letter opener. I once overheard Gant and Abernathy talking about the incident, and soon after, I too noticed a change. When you talk to Martin, he's engaging and effervescent. His mastery of such an array of weighty subjects and his interest in you can be both impressive and overwhelming at times. He'd be blind not to see how much people expect of him. Even the most innocent of interactions demand that he charm, impress, and enlighten and prove himself worthy of such adulation. But when the conversation's over, and the spotlights of admiration are dimmed or cast elsewhere, I can almost see him fading, moving through the SCLC like a gauzy semblance of his public self.

For him, danger lurks everywhere. It was this way from the beginning, but he seemed to be aware of the romantic quality of his adventures, accepting his responsibility to the movement like some gallant knight savoring not only the victory but also the significance of the battle. You can see it in the footage that accompanied his arrival on the national stage, in that first mug shot following his arrest in Montgomery, or when the police officers slammed his shoulder into the counter of a booking station right in front of Coretta—there's still a roguish glint in his eye. Like the photos of World War II vets broken, beaten, bloody, but *smiling* from the scorched rubble of Gothic ruins.

Something changed after Harlem. He must have looked down at that blade in his chest, its ornamented handle snapped off and staining the autographed copies of *Stride Toward Freedom* with his blood, and thought how trivial it is to put your life on the line for a book signing. No blistering water hoses or prodded dogs and their angry masters, no marchers, no protesters—just an endless parade of stargazers. Yes, after that, he was different. Every day, every hour, every second—all of it was borrowed time.

3

It's just a few days since I helped myself to the money, and I've already made some big mistakes. My reformation has drawn too much attention from my coworkers. Because of the car and the much-needed visit to the tailor, I have stirred up an unusual level of commotion at work. In this suit, even a man with a limp as severe as mine can look graceful and authoritative. They see the fitted, perfect silhouette of my jacket, the tie, rakishly dimpled, and the shoes shined to a high gloss—it's all too perfect. I should reel some of it back, but part of me resents having to play the harmless hobbler. It's as if they are offended that I chose to improve myself.

I decide to ignore them, even though I know they are still watching as I enter my office. The walls of the SCLC are thin. I can hear the murmurs, those envious voices encircling me. *Did you see him? Strange . . . where did he get the money for that getup? What is he up to?*

I stand at my desk, looking around my office. It now has the unearthly tranquility of a taped-off crime scene. I hear footsteps, and then Gant passes by my open door. The sound of his footsteps stops, then starts again. Only his head appears in my doorway. He looks me up and down and lets out a whistle. "Nice, Estem . . . *nice!*" His head disappears and his footsteps fade down the hall.

Throughout the day, I continue to have an overwhelming feeling that someone is speaking poorly of me. The walls of the SCLC really *are* thin, and hostility has no trouble penetrating them. Regretfully, I long for a more receptive audience.

———

I'm starting to sober up from the drunkenness of easily acquired money, and I'm feeling anxious. I have to see my mother. I need her approval.

I arrive in my brand-new Caddy at my parents' house, a cottage-style one-story on the tree-lined end of Auburn Avenue. Little colored children play in the street, chasing a ball and each other. Briefly, I see them looking my way as I get out of the car and give the finish a quick buff with my jacket sleeve. The children grin and wave, their faces lighting up when they see my inspiring visage.

I return to reality and begin to brace myself before I see my father. Too late—my parents have seen me drive up and are already coming outside.

I climb out to greet them, and my mother, practically dancing, smiles upon seeing me. As always, my father dons his mask of stone. She says the car is beautiful, and I offer her a ride. She runs to the car, giddy with excitement, while my father stands still with his arms folded.

"Kind of a fancy car for a bookkeeper," he says. "How you pay for that?"

"God! Leave the boy alone. He probably got a raise. All that hard work."

"Yeah, Dad. I got a raise . . ."

"Seems a bit soon. For what?"

"Probably for organizing all those marches," my mother says, "and helping Dr. King with all those speeches and getting all those ballsy Negroes out of jail."

"I see. Is that what you do? Get ballsy Negroes out of jail? *You* help Martin Luther King write speeches?" The old man has a strange way of riling me up. Maybe it's envy. He's the son of a sharecropper, a former bootlegger, and a retired gardener. I'm the first member of my family to go to college. When I went away, his biggest concern was whether all the reading and lecturing would do a fine job of turning me into a pansy.

Mother strokes the car's interior. I get back in and turn the ignition. The car doesn't start. I look at her and smile. I try again, but it refuses to start.

"Looks like those marches will come in handy," my father says, " 'cause you gonna be doin' a whole lotta walkin'."

I stare at his face, his features, searching for a sign that would prove that we are not related. I've played this game before, and it's led to the usual disappointment. When I was a child, the man thought that my acquiring scarlet fever and developing polio was somehow my fault, that my weakness taunted the disease to attack me. Once it was clear that I would live, but never walk normally without the support of a brace, my father didn't believe it. He would tell me to take off my brace and make me walk around without it. "The boy will walk normal when he gets tired of falling," he'd say. I don't know if he truly believed it—maybe it's an old Negro superstition—but most of his actions are laced with an element of cruelty.

I say a silent prayer while tracing the steering wheel with my open palm. I turn the ignition once more and it starts. I notice a car across the street. There are two men inside. White. I would not have paid any attention to this had they not looked at me with the intensity of hunters in a blind.

I sometimes struggle with the fact that I actually have parents. I often think of myself as suddenly emerging from the shadows fully formed— some sort of nocturnal creature that withdraws during the day, only to resurface as the sun sets and darkness falls.

I want the visit to be over as soon as I turn the corner. The chit-chat is tedious. I make an effort at seeming interested, but I can't stop checking my rearview for those two men. Mama must see that I am troubled, because she asks me to pull over. I put the car in park, but keep the engine running. I stay silent, eyes on the mirror.

"Can I ask you something, son?" I bring my attention back to her. I can already tell this is about money. That's how family is. They see all that you have done for yourself, and then they start thinking about what you can do for them.

"What is it, Mama?"

"They put a lien on the house."

"Who put a lien on the house and why?"

"Taxman. I haven't paid the property taxes."

"What did Daddy say? Is that why he's in a bad mood?"

"He don't know about it. . . . Haven't told him."

Of course he doesn't. My father is the kind of man who breaks his back to earn his money but refuses to crease his brow figuring out the best way to spend it. He leaves it to her to take care of all the taxes and bills. Those things just confuse him.

I want to ask her where the money went, but I already know. My mother is a good Christian woman, so some of it went to tithing—the choir needs robes and the preacher needs wheels—and even more of it went to those custom-made church dresses and hats. Segregationists in this state love to harangue anyone who will listen about how Negroes contribute ten cents for every dollar a white man pays in taxes. Those numbers are dubious, but I can't help but feel embarrassed—for us both.

"How much do you owe?"

"Five hundred. . . ."

About half of what I have left. "Jesus, Mama. . . ."

"Don't use his name. . . . I didn't want to bother you with it. I know money is hard to come by, so I prayed on it. I asked Him to give me a sign. And then you come by in this car, and I knew everything would be okay. . . . Well, can you help me?"

I think about giving her the money, but to be honest, I don't trust her with it. I'd rather handle it myself. Besides, I didn't even think of helping them when I got the money. Maybe this good deed will give it a good rinse.

"Don't worry about it, Mama. I'll take care of it."

After taking a short drive around the block, I drop my mother off at home. She's disappointed that our time together has ended so quickly, but she tells me to keep our conversation to myself. I promise her as I drive away. I don't know if she heard me, but I'm eager to get out of here. I have a strong feeling that the two white men were following me. They are no longer around, but something inside tells me not to go home—anywhere but home—so I head to the assessor's office to take care of the tax bill.

Thank God, there are no stairs. The directory leads me through a maze of doors with frosted glass and freckled beige linoleum until I find the right place. The office is appointed with file cabinets, venetian blinds, and dust. Their caretaker is a large woman with bifocals that seem attached to her unconvincing wig. She hears me rattle in and looks at me. "What do you need?" she asks.

"I'm here to pay a tax bill."

"The girl will be back in fifteen minutes. She deals with the delinquencies."

"I didn't mention that it was delinquent."

I stand at the counter and she stays at her desk.

"Well, is it?"

I don't answer.

"Fifteen minutes," she says again.

I take a seat on the hard bench next to the entrance and watch the back of her wig move subtly to the rhythm of her typing.

Fifteen minutes pass and I tap on the counter again. She only blinks lazily at me. "Can't we take care of this now? I'm sort of in a hurry." That makes her neck stiffen and the wig shift. "Excuse me, ma'am. . . . I don't mean to be rude. I'm just in a hurry."

She calms down but still offers more of the same: "The girl isn't here yet."

I wait another fifteen minutes and a young, skinny colored girl enters from the back holding a brown paper bag that presumably contains her half-eaten lunch. "You're late," the woman says to her.

"Sorry, ma'am," the colored girl says. She looks at me as if she's surprised to see me. "How are you?"

"Fine. . . . And you?"

"Oh, I've been fine." She looks back at her wigged supervisor who has now decided to focus all of her attention on the two of us.

"Well, I'm here to pay a bill that's a bit past due."

"Okay. I can help you with that."

"The name is Estem."

"Of course it is," she says smiling. She shuffles through some papers looking for my parents' house. "Oh," she says when she sees how much they owe. "You're going to be taking care of this . . . all at once?"

"Yes." I pull out a roll of twenties, and the scratch of the currency narrows the eyes of the fat woman. I keep my eyes on her wig and ask the girl for my receipt. She gives it to me and I thank her for her time.

Once outside, I look to see if those two men are around. They're not. I must be getting paranoid. Maybe it showed back in the assessor's office. I start the car and turn the corner—and pass the two men in a parked car. It's strange, but now I realize that I know the girl. We went to school together. Samantha DePlush.

I drive for a long time, frequently glancing at the side mirrors. Eventually, I pass the Royal Theatre, and its faux-Egyptian columns offer me an immediate sense of security. This seems appropriate, given the relationship I had with movies during my early years with polio. Even then, they were a sort of safe haven and appealed to my innate sense of adventure and romance. They were amusing friends that did not taunt or tease, only solicited my approval. Maybe the child inside me still watches all those montages of seductions, cracked cases, double crosses, and car chases. Maybe he watches from the darkened theater of my mind.

It seems like a good place to spend some time. It'll give me an opportunity to lose those men on my tail and clear my head.

Although movie theaters have been desegregated for two years, the Royal Theatre is still the theater of choice for Negroes of respectability and a discriminating nature. There are gilded murals depicting the raising of the pyramids, and balconies embossed with violet scarabs. Above the screen hangs a large curtain with the bird-headed image of the sun god Ra. Quite the spectacle. I take one last look around as the theater lights start to dim.

The movie was about some international spy, a resourceful fellow who always managed to light a cigarette whenever his life was in danger. I wonder if such a thing would work in reality. It seems to buy you crucial thinking time.

As I leave, I notice two white men seated at the rear of the theater. The Royal is nice, but it's still quite strange for a white person to choose to patronize a Negro theater. I'm not sure if these are the same men from earlier, but I begin to fear the worst. *The money?* Maybe they're just two light-skinned Negroes and I'm imagining things. I walk along the purple runner that leads to the exit, peering out of the corner of my eye. As I get closer, they don't seem so interested. Their heads do not turn to follow me. I'm relieved, but not convinced. The money. Was I being too flashy? Police? Whoever they are, they give off a vibe that is neither cop nor criminal, but something in between.

I make it to my car. They aren't behind me, but I hear that voice again—the one telling me I can't go home. So I don't. I drive, floating through the city, just trying to keep the strangers and the sun off my tail, waiting for the night to come and hide me safely so I don't have to run anymore.

4

As night approaches, it dawns on me that all this may be ending, yet Candy has never seen the new and improved version of me. Wasn't she the reason why I did this? The fear of regrets, not knowing what could have been, offsets my paranoia. I'll go to her and face the consequences. Right now, I have the detached acceptance of an inmate before execution. If only she would be kind enough to honor my last request.

The place is crowded. Immediately, I feel the press of flesh. Some local rhythm and blues man yelps and strums at his guitar as I look for Candy through the dancing crowd, over bobbing heads and through the narrow spaces between swaying bodies. I find her in Count's arms on the other side of the bar. I take a seat at the bar and order a drink, keeping an eye on them both. At first, her body is rigid in his embrace, but then she relents. He nuzzles her neck with his wide mouth. She does not move. He lifts his head and looks at her. She sees me. I lift my drink and nod to her. Then, and only then, does she smile.

Why is she smiling? he must be wondering. He follows Candy's gaze. He sees me, but I don't avert my glare. He makes a motion toward his two men in a far corner. They seem to be practically identical: both are large and Negro and dressed in brightly colored zoot suits, one purple, the other yellow. They walk over to Count. He seems agitated, and then he points in my direction. As his men walk toward me, a path slices effortlessly through the crowd. Suddenly, I feel compelled to light a cigarette.

"Hey, little man. You buyin' or just window shoppin'?" questions the yellow suit.

I sip my drink and then puff my cigarette.

" 'Cause if you ain't buyin', and you just window shoppin', you need to do that shit outside."

"Yeah. Count don't like you starin' him in the face," says the other.

I feel a surge of reassurance, power, if you will. I have my drink, my cigarette, and a pocket stuffed with cash. These are the only weapons I need. I pull out a fistful of money and place it on the bar. "You tell Count that as long as I'm spending money in this dive, I'll look wherever I see fit. Now why don't you fellows take a few dollars and buy yourselves some real clothes." I wad some cash and toss it at them.

They look at each other and laugh. "Oh, we'll take the money, chump. But it's gonna be a *lot* more than a few dollars!"

I think I see his yellow shoulder twitch. My instincts take over. Before I realize, I've thrown my drink in the man's face, followed by my lit cigarette. He does not burst into flames. Movies have misled me. The cigarette extinguishes itself with an uneventful *sssst.*

They carry me out into the alley behind Count's.

Almost instantly, I receive a punch to the stomach. I feel my intestines forcing their way into my scrotum. I double over and fall to my knees, gasping for air and looking at their cheap shoes: faux alligator, worn and creased. I vomit all over their shoes. One of them boxes my left ear, the other kicks my intestines back into place. My glasses fall from my face and land in the vomit. I'm dazed; I see stars . . . then I see headlights.

I hear car doors open at the end of the alley. Two figures step in front of the headlights and cast what seem to be pistol-wielding shadows along the sides of the building. I can't discern their features. I'm still stunned from the attack and somewhat blinded by the brightness of the lights. I look up at my assailants. They too are looking in the direction of the two figures. I know it is not an apparition.

"What the fuck you crackers want?" demands one of the goons.

They cock their pistols in response.

"Okay, okay, we get the picture." My assailants raise their hands and back away from me.

The unknown men approach me and help me to my feet. They walk me over to their car, not saying a word, with guns still pointed at those violent Negroes.

One of them opens the car door and quickly pushes me into the backseat. The car starts and slowly backs out of the alley.

"Don't worry, Mr. Estem. We're not going to hurt you," says the man in the passenger seat.

I wipe bile from my glasses with my handkerchief. "I know," I say calmly. "That's easy to see, given your display in the alley. I mean, you're obviously not policemen. If you were, then you would have made yourselves known back there."

The passenger turns to me. I can't distinguish his features. The brim of his hat shadows his face, and he is only briefly illuminated by the passing streetlights.

"I don't know who you are," I continue, "but I'm sure this has something to do with the money."

Simultaneously, the two men look at each other. The eyes of the driver appear in the rearview mirror.

"I see . . . you didn't know about the money. I guess I've let the cat out of the bag, and she's gone and scratched me." I think of the mouse at the bank and who she may have called.

"No, Mr. Estem," the driver says, "We're well aware of the money. But it represents only a small portion of the matter."

"You see, Mr. Estem," continues the passenger, "we need your help."

"My help?"

"Do you consider yourself a patriot, Mr. Estem?" the driver asks. "I mean, despite the race problem—is there any other country more deserving of your allegiance than the United States?"

"No. But—"

"Of course not. Mr. Estem, this country is under attack. You may not see it on the surface—our enemy is cowardly and attacks from the shadows—but every day, foreign interests threaten to unravel the very fabric of American society. This is a matter of national security. Our agents can't do it alone. We need help from the public, good Americans, men like *you*. We are at war, Mr. Estem, and the FBI—America—needs your help."

A few days ago, apathy and anonymity defined me, and now the FBI is asking for my help. I have remorse about the money, but maybe taking it has set into motion something bigger than I could realize. I'd be a fool not to hear what they have to offer.

They drive me to an office on Peachtree Street. It's narrow and easy to miss, as if its sole purpose is to fill in an alley—one of those places where the address number ends in "½." Inside, the place is practically empty. We climb the stairs to the second floor; the agents are patient with me. We pass dark doors of textured glass and stop at one at the end of the long, narrow walkway. It has the word "Insurance" painted on it, but the *I* has faded away.

There's a chair in the middle of the room, a file cabinet in the corner, and a foldout table with a coffeepot and a hot plate resting on top of it. A badly worn corkboard stands at one of the walls. Whatever was on it has been removed, but the tack holes remain.

The agents offer me the seat, and introduce themselves as Mathis and Strobe. Their names surprise me. The physical features of these two men suggest something more exotic. Mathis, the older of the two, has very dark, sun-beaten skin, and though his hair is short and anchored with Brylcreem, there's still a suspicious curliness that is apparent. I suspect his real name may have a considerable number of vowels. The same with Strobe—maybe "Strobinsky" or "Stroberg"? He's younger, maybe close to my age, fresh-faced, with a broad athletic build. I suspect that he is only second-generation American.

"Communism," says Mathis. "The Soviet Union is using America's race problem to further its evil agenda."

"Members of the Communist Party," says Strobe, "are aligning themselves with groups and leaders of the Negro movement in order to influence and manipulate them."

"I'm listening," I say.

"Mr. Estem," Mathis says, "we believe that the SCLC is one of these groups and that Martin Luther King is one of these leaders being corrupted with communist ideology."

"We know that King and the SCLC are being corrupted," says Strobe.

Mathis walks over to the file cabinet and pulls out a folder. "Our sources have confirmed that, in a previous life, Aaron Gant was a high-profile member of the Communist Party."

I lean forward, elbows on knees.

"He introduced King to another high-ranking communist, a lawyer, Stanley Levison."

"I'm familiar with him. Loosely."

"Of course you are. King is becoming increasingly dependent upon him. Every speech, every sermon, bears Levison's mark. Even after Attorney General Kennedy warned King about Levison's threat to the civil rights movement. The money you took? An instrument of persuasion obtained by Gant from Levison's sources. Levison claims not to be a communist, but this is false. Similar to the way that Gant denies being a communist . . . and a homosexual."

Homosexual? The word makes me dizzy. It took a moment to deal with the possibility of Gant being a communist, but now I feel nauseated while I try to grapple with all of Gant's personas. I feel foolish for underestimating him. I've always been suspicious of Gant, but now I'm suspicious of myself, of my ability to read people.

Mathis hands me two photographs from the folder. In the first, Gant is in a parked car, touching the chest of a very pale and muscular white man. In the other, he's much younger and seated at a small desk in the first row of a classroom filled with other attentive Negroes. In bold stencils, a sign behind them reads HARLEM COMMUNIST PARTY. Now I see why Gant acted so strangely about the money.

"Not only did Gant introduce King to this wicked ideology," Mathis continues, pacing now, as if remembering lines from a script, "he exposed him to moral degenerates as well. Bayard Rustin, another advisor to King, is also homosexual. We haven't determined with certainty whether or not he's a communist, but he's definitely a homosexual."

I hold the photos casually, trying my best to appear indifferent.

"John," Strobe says, "we need you to alert us of any suspicious activity within the SCLC. Conversations, meetings, interoffice memoranda—we need it all. The future of your race and your country is resting on your shoulders. Are you with us?"

I don't respond, but I can see that this may be my opportunity to become an asset to Martin. If Gant is compromising the success of the movement, don't I have an obligation to try to stop it? Maybe I've been silent too long . . . or Strobe reads something from my face; before I give him an answer, he says, "I hope that you are. It would be disappointing to us—to everyone—if the SCLC found out about the money you stole."

Mathis throws a look at Strobe, and he seems to back off.

Strobe's clumsy hint at intimidation isn't necessary. Suddenly, I am a Negro, moments away from being draped in the American flag. To move forward, I only need to echo their line of thinking, and if it means protecting Martin, then I am happy to do so.

"I mean it when I tell you I consider myself a patriot." I do my best to recline in the flimsy chair. "The success of this country and the Negro are intertwined. If communism threatens one, even when befriending the other, then communism must be stopped."

Strobe bites his lip and squints at me. "Are you sure, Mr. Estem? This is a big responsibility."

"Strobe . . . Thank you," Mathis says while keeping his eyes locked on me. "We just want to be sure you understand the seriousness of what we are asking."

"Of course I do. Don't mistake my eagerness for foolishness. It's just that I know the deceptive nature of communism firsthand."

Mathis folds his arms. "Go on," he says.

"It's nothing really. I had a cousin—a bohemian artistic type—who lived in Manhattan. He came to visit one summer when I was in high school, anxious to educate us backward colored Southerners. He'd gone to meetings and brought some literature with him—"

"You have communists in your family?" asks Strobe.

Mathis clears his throat, and Strobe stifles up.

"He wasn't really a communist. He was just going through a phase, and that's exactly how I saw it—a phase, fleeting and temporary. I could see no permanent solution for the Negro in communism. It meant giving up capitalism and, most importantly, individualism. Those are

American ideals. What Negro in his right mind would turn his back on those ideals and run toward a collective identity?" Feeling pleased with my presentation, I cross my legs as the chair creaks ominously.

"You make your country proud," says Strobe.

"A great citizen," echoes Mathis. "You'll be compensated for the work you do for us, John. We'll start you with a stipend of one hundred dollars a week." He gives me a business card with no name and only a number. "Call from a pay phone, never the same one twice in a row. You're active immediately, so we'll be in contact at the end of the week."

I hold the card between my thumb and index finger, thinking how no one has thought enough of me to give me one before.

"One more thing, John," Mathis adds, "It's important for you to remain as inconspicuous as possible. Don't draw attention to yourself. So you'll need to be prepared to return that money, however dirty it may be. You understand that, don't you, John?"

Of course, I understand. I am an accountant. I can do the math. And the sum of my actions equals a problem.

5

I don't know what to make of the agents' claims. They say that Gant is a communist. Maybe he is, but I have my doubts. Would he really be willing to give up those tailored suits for gray coveralls? And I think they are overstating his influence on Martin. However, something about the conversation I had with Martin that night has begun to swirl around in my head . . .

I was fine, sitting there with nothing but smoke and silence between us, but Martin had decided to speak up.

"So, what are you doing here at this time of night . . . ?" He seemed to be searching for what he should call me.

"It's John. I'm working late."

"Well, you've got an admirable work ethic . . . John."

"Thank you. And you? Why are you out at this hour keeping me and the shadows company?"

He grimaced. Smoke came from his nostrils. "I didn't feel like going home just yet."

I glanced down, ashamed. I already knew the answer.

"Gant isn't being too hard on you, is he?" He was eager to change the subject.

"I can handle Gant—I mean I can handle the work."

He smiled as he tapped off his cigarette into an ashtray. "You went to Morehouse, didn't you, brother?"

"That's right."

"Guess we have that in common."

"Yes, indeed."

"Did you ever have political philosophy with old Elerby?"

"I took the class, but I can't say I stayed awake through much of it."

"I don't blame you. Elerby really knew how to put 'em to sleep. Did you read much Marx?"

"Would you hold it against me if I said I didn't stay awake through most of it?"

He let out a staccato laugh and smiled in a way that made his cheeks rounded, high and firm. It made the good reverend look quite impish. "No, brother. No. I will not hold it against you. Those shoes, yes. But Marx, no."

This was how men bonded: calling out each other's weaknesses for the sake of humor. I knew that, but maybe I gave the impression that I didn't, because Martin quickly became serious.

"There's something about asking for money that really irritates me," he said. "Always seeking the largest contributions. No sum is too large. Always searching for a new benefactor. . . . I don't think I have the taste for it—money, that is. You understand what I mean?"

I didn't, so I remained silent.

"Why do people love money so? More than they love people. The royalties from my book—I'd give them away if I didn't have a family. Doesn't seem right to profit from a message that doesn't belong to me alone but to all of humanity. I often worry if my house is too big. My wife thinks it's too small. I don't know . . . while I reject the godlessness of socialism, my present feelings are so . . . *anticapitalistic*. Maybe I am, to some degree, a Marxist."

Money did not tempt him. Greed was not a weakness we shared.

The day following my meeting with the agents is a troubling one. I don't know where to apply my efforts best. I've spent a great deal of time dreaming about revealing Gant for the fraud that he is. Though I never knew what that meant concretely, my hostility toward him is real and well deserved.

It's hard for me to admit it, but I am here because of him. I followed him to the SCLC. Gant is something of a star among Negro accountants, one of the few black CPAs in the country—forty-ninth, to be accurate, out of one hundred. I wanted to be on that list and join that exclusive club of the first hundred Negro CPAs, but you need three years of apprenticeship before you're allow to seek certification—"darky rules," as my father used to call them. Few white CPAs would grant a Negro an apprenticeship, and there are only a handful of Negro CPAs, effectively guaranteeing that fact in perpetuity.

I took Gant's classes at Morehouse. We seemed to hit it off. He appeared to admire my ambition . . . but that was then. Now I see that he was toying with me. I told him my dreams, what I wanted to do, and when he was asked to help Martin defend himself against erroneous accusations of tax fraud, he brought me along.

When I arrived at the SCLC, Gant's attitude toward me seemed to change. He would go out of his way to punish and make things difficult for me, as if he couldn't stomach the idea of sharing the same profession with me. I know he saw me then, and sees me now, as a threat. It was then that I realized that I'd been setting my sights too low. I wanted to be a CPA like Gant; the power, respect, and exclusivity were enticing, but it was a fool's errand. Their power is limited. I wanted to join a list of colored accountants, while Martin was on the most exclusive list of all. He was in a club with only one member: that's the kind of power and sway that I want. Being Gant's apprentice for three years won't get me that.

It was hard for me to trust him from the beginning. When he interviewed me for my position, every question he asked me felt probing, no matter how innocent. My hobbies, my family life, he wanted to know it all, as if he didn't know me.

Soon after hiring me, Gant's habit of embarrassing me in front of Martin began. Martin had just been named *Time*'s Man of the Year and, with Gant by his side, received many congratulations. Gant called me over to introduce me to King. To say that I was thrilled would be an understatement. I walked over to them, trying to hide my limp—I wanted Martin's respect, not his pity.

"Martin," Gant said. "This is my new assistant, John Estem."

"A pleasure," Martin said.

Before I could respond, Gant entered the realm of inappropriateness. "You know something, Martin . . . Estem here struggled with polio as a child. Still wears a leg brace because of it. Didn't you have a relative with polio?"

"Yes, a cousin." Even Martin was uncomfortable.

"He's rough around the edges," Gant continued, "but we'll whip him into shape."

"Well, don't whip him too hard, this is an organization of *nonviolent* protest." The two of them laughed and Gant looked right at me.

I wish that photo were in my possession then. Right at the height, the peak of his sycophantic laughter, I would show it to him. Then I'd watch. I'd watch his face contort as he first sees humor in the photo but then makes a quick leap to sheer horror when he realizes that it's his own hand on that man's chest.

But for now, I'll watch him drink his coffee and talk with other staff members, scribble a note, or make a call. I'll stick close . . . a limping shadow. Although, he might grow suspicious as I hang on his every word and movement.

I see Gant talking to Abernathy and Young. I try to listen, hovering around them even though I have no reason to do so. I stand with my hands in my pockets as if I am waiting for Gant to finish. Young stops talking but continues to look at Gant as if silently urging him to do something about his assistant. Gant looks at me and raises his eyebrows. When I don't respond or react, he motions with his eyes for me to exit.

Two days have passed, and my efforts to discredit Gant are appearing to be unfruitful—nothing but tidbits of office gossip. My rendezvous with the agents is fast approaching. Subtlety is not working.

I tell everyone to have a nice night as they leave the office for their homes. *Oh, don't worry about me. I have a lot of work to do. Numbers and such. I'll be working late, burning the midnight oil. See you tomorrow.*

When everyone leaves, I go into Gant's office. Since we are a harmless group of women, preachers, and cripples, he rarely locks his door. At night, his office seems spare and practical, like a cave dwelling. The fluorescence bleeds in from the hallway, casting thin shadows over the space like an opium den. There are pictures all around of Gant with prominent leaders. They are all powerful men, and they truly seem to be friends of his. There are no stiff handshakes for the camera, just arms draped casually around shoulders, a punch or two thrown playfully at each other, and candid shots of a shared laugh at a secret joke.

I've never taken pictures like these. I've always felt like an outsider peering at life from the shadows, and my arrangement with the agents has caused me to realize the permanence of my position. I have chosen a life that will forever render me a nonparticipant observer. The people I encounter will receive the kind of scrutiny reserved for subjects in an anthropological study. I will never truly belong.

Gant, at some point, must have felt this way, but he has played his hand better. A part of me sympathizes with him; it must have been hard, putting up that charade for so long. The man must be an artist of identities, able to peel away, or apply, a persona whenever necessary.

I search for incriminating material—the communist connections, for the good of the country and all that, but I wonder what else Gant is trying to hide, what other shameful secret I might stumble upon. Inside his desk drawer—nothing. Paperwork. Budgets. Nothing that would cause concern. Maybe I'm not cut out for this. Without much effort, Gant is always one step ahead. My only evidence incriminates me, not him.

I sit in Gant's chair and look across his desk at the place where I usually sit. So this is his vantage. I must seem so small to him. I recalled Gant's minor transgressions against me in order to keep from digging up his most hurtful insult. But sitting here brings it back.

We were working hard that night, helping Martin deal with his tax problem. The seriousness of the situation was palpable. Never before had such a burden rested on such a modest bunch of bookkeepers. Everyone's sleeves were rolled up and no one dared wear a tie. Sweat beaded our brows. There was no mindless chatter—only the recitation of numbers and the events that gave them context.

I was diligently adding up some receipts when Gant asked me for Martin's travel expenses.

I remembered vividly, just the day before, scrawling out TRAVEL EXPENSES on a large envelope in bold black ink, then putting the receipts inside and handing it to Gant as he looked at it, smiled, and said, "Good work."

So I was surprised to hear him ask for them. But I answered anyway. "Mr. Gant, I have already given them to you."

He gave the papers and documents around him a superficial glance. "I don't see them, Estem."

"I gave them to you earlier in your office."

He began shuffling papers, not really looking at them, but moving them around for show: a grown-up version of a tantrum. "I don't see them, Estem."

Then everyone stopped working. The adding machines went quiet and the scratch of pencils on ledger paper ceased. All eyes were on Gant and me.

"I gave them to you already. Maybe you misplaced them . . . I don't know what else to tell you, sir." I turned my back to him and continued with my work.

That's when Gant slammed his fist on the table, then stood up, sending his chair to the floor. "Are you calling me a liar, goddamnit? I didn't ask you what you did. I asked you for the receipts. Where are the goddamn receipts?"

Maybe, in retrospect, it would have been better for me to stay silent, but instead I said, "Mr. Gant I've already answered you. I gave them to you yesterday—"

Martin and Abernathy walked in after hearing all the commotion. For a moment, this gave me some comfort. Surely the sight of two preachers would ease the current tensions. But Gant seemed only to be encouraged by a larger audience.

"Estem, quit repeating yourself like some damn minstrel show darkie." He said it with a smile, trying to appear jocular. This seemed to make everyone feel comfortable enough to start laughing. Even Abernathy and Martin got a chuckle out of it. Then Gant started to revel in the approval and laughter of his boss and felt inclined to take it further. "Yessuh, boss," he said giving his best sambo. "I's already gave it to ya'. I's already gave it to ya'," he said again as he *limped* back and forth. Everyone laughed, including Martin and Abernathy. It seemed to go on forever. Then Gant finally tired himself out.

Martin saw that I was the only one not laughing. He walked up to Gant and said, "Hey, take it easy, brother. He's had enough." Then Martin addressed the rest of us. "I want to thank you all for working so hard to keep me out of jail. . . . Now, I want to remind you that I have been to jail before and it don't bother me too much. The last time I was in jail I got some good sleep. I got my own cell. Last time I was in jail, I had a chance to get some writing done—and you know how well that turned out." That received the biggest laugh of all. Martin patted Gant on the shoulder, "Take it easy brother," he said again softly, as he and Abernathy walked out.

People pretended to get back to work as their eyes danced between Gant and me. I kept my back turned to the rest of the room, punching away aimlessly on my adding machine.

"Find those receipts," said Gant. I didn't have to. Later, he found them. He apologized to me, but only in passing and with no audience to witness it. I should have dealt with it then. There was no need for me to be so docile. This is not a man's world; it's a *real* man's world. The men who avoid confrontation don't survive.

Thinking about my cowardice sends me into a rage. I toss papers around his office. I empty out his desk drawers and throw the contents around as well. I kick over his chair, and fall on the floor doing so.

The view from down here is terrible. Fool. Look at this place. I need to get myself under control. I need to develop a new method. I need to clean up this office.

It's too late at night to drive home. I return to my own office and sit at my desk. Cleaning Gant's office left me exhausted. Did I return it to its normal condition? Will he notice? He probably will. I'm too tired to think about it. I may be fired in the morning. Too tired to care.

6

I slept for a few hours at the office before driving home. When I awoke, still in a groggy state, I expected to see Martin lurking around the office. I was somewhat disappointed to learn that he wasn't. It's for the best. Breaking into Gant's office would have been hard to explain.

Now, I only have enough time for a shower and shave before heading right back to work.

When I arrive, Gant wants to see me in his office.

He tells me to shut the door behind me.

I notice a sheet of paper on the floor beside his desk. Did I neglect it? Maybe it's there because of his carelessness, not mine. I want to stop staring at it, but I can't—until he says my name.

"Estem, I wanted to talk with you about that account you closed the other day."

My heart throbs and sinks.

"What about it?" I ask.

"The money that was in it . . ."

There are probably police already waiting outside that door. I look for something to throw at him. Something to stun or daze him long enough to make my escape.

"Money?"

"Yes, Estem. The money that was in the account you closed a few days ago is *needed*."

He knows. He wants to entertain himself by watching me attempt to lie my way out of this situation. If he wants a lie, I'll give him a lie. "Why?" is all I manage to utter.

He rocks back and forth in his chair. Then he smiles.

"Buses. We use that money to buy buses."

"Buses?"

"For the demonstrators, man. We'll have our own transportation. We'll save a *ton* on chartering fees."

"Brilliant," I say.

"Isn't it? Jesus, I just thought of something else—we could loan out the buses to those fools at CORE and the N-double-A-C-P . . . for a modest fee, of course."

"Of course."

"Excuse me, Mr. Gant," Susan, his secretary comes in, and I breathe normally for the first time since I've been in here. "A man claiming to be your cousin is on the line."

The normal haughtiness disappears from Gant's face as he just stares at the phone on his desk. "Thank you, Susan," he says finally. He picks up the receiver, and just the sound of his breathing must have alerted his "cousin" that he is on the line, because he is silent for a while, his eyes blinking and scanning everything in his office except me as he listens. "I understand," is Gant's only contribution to the conversation. He cradles the receiver and tells me to wait in his office as he leaves hastily.

Enough time passes for me to get anxious and consider smoking a cigarette, but I can't light up in here. I take one out, rest it in the corner of my mouth, and go over to Gant's office window, letting the coolness of the unlit menthol soothe me. I poke a finger between the blinds and look outside. It's hot as hell, but there's some serious rain clouds the color of a hot stockpot on their way. I look down at the alley behind the SCLC where a smoke, a sip from a flask, or a dirty joke is often shared. Even from here, I can see the flash of argyle coming off his hurried ankles.

Gant waits a while, but eventually his "cousin" shows up—a middle-aged white man in a wrinkled trench coat. The cousin is prepared for these unpredictable Georgia summers, because the rain comes down in fistfuls. The rain doesn't move the two men. Gant just grabs both lapels, holding them together with his clenched fist.

They talk intently, then the cousin hands Gant a piece of paper—a letter or something—and Gant anxiously tucks it into his jacket to shield it from the elements. The cousin turns to leave, but Gant lingers a moment, just watching him go, as the downpour does a number on him.

Gant walks back into his office, soaking wet. I yank the cigarette from my mouth, crushing it into my pocket.

"So, those funds will be ready for allocation by . . ." He looks nervous. No, more than that—desperate.

"The end of the week . . ." I say, trying to hide my own desperation.

"The day after tomorrow."

"Right. The day after tomorrow."

I get up to leave and return to my office. I need to think.

"Oh, Estem, one more thing. If you're here late, could you make sure that my office door is locked? I think Susan has been in here tidying up. She means well, but I'm a man who enjoys his privacy."

"I understand perfectly, sir," I say as I head back to my own office.

Mathis and Strobe told me to return the money, but I can't, I've already spent too much of it. I'm not sure I would do it even if I could. Mathis said that money was from communist sources. I'm going to put the information in my possession to good use.

I pull out a sheet of paper from my desk, feed it into my typewriter, and type: "Forget about the money. They're on to us."

After work, I drive to Candice's apartment and wait for her to come home. I needed to see her first. Seeing her gives me courage, and what I'm about to do requires barrels of it. I'm not one-sided. I'm more than cunning and ambitious. There's a quixotic nature to my character that I have to protect in these hard days.

My preoccupation with her has affected my behavior. I do this, partly, for her and the life I dream of for the two of us. Chicago may just be a lie I told myself. Thinking of her leaves a mental fog in its wake, changing what I see and grasp.

We grew up together, Candice and I. She lived across the street from us. She defended me when the neighborhood children made fun of my limp. She even brought flowers to the house when the polio first attacked. She was the first Negro I'd known who didn't have a father in the home. I know they say the "fatherless phenomenon" is common among Negroes, but everyone I knew had a father—and wanted to get rid of him.

I remember watching her on a Sunday morning, descending the porch steps at fifteen years old, hair in a very neat, long ponytail, her white church dress failing to hide those emerging curves. On the very last step, she stops and takes in her surroundings. She must know how perfect she is, because when she thinks no one is watching, she strikes a grand pose: with one hand on her hip and the other behind her head, she looks toward the sky and smiles.

At that moment, peeking through the parted curtains of our living room window, I realize I'll love her forever. But I'm no fool. My heart breaks the moment it becomes hers. Who gives a crippled boy flowers, for God's sake? I never had a chance, but she strung me along.

There was a time when I thought there was a chance for us. I wrote her letters from college and she actually wrote me back, appearing to be open to the idea of our love. But when I returned, she grew distant. Perhaps just my being away at school sparked a brief desire in her. Granted, I wasn't too far from home. Morehouse is in Atlanta. I wish I'd known then to avoid women who long for their fathers—they're impossible to please. To them, loving and longing will always be synonymous.

For a time, I avoided her; but throughout that period, I wanted her, and I wanted to hurt her. I wanted to reconstruct myself as an irresistible figure, one who could lure her in and break her heart, break her resolve, and break her down. But then, one night at Count's, I saw her. And to see her is to forgive her. Forgive her for all her faults, her lack of talent and self-awareness. Forgive her for her silly dreams, for her innocence, and for being so painfully beautiful.

Her place is a small bungalow, a box wrapped in aluminum siding. There's a little bush and a patch of grass to make it seem like a home.

A car pulls up, driven by one of Count's men. She gets out and walks barefoot through the grass with her shoes tucked under her arm. The car drives away once she's inside. A balloon of desperation seems to swell in my chest. For some reason, I think she can put me at ease. I wait a while longer before going to her door. I don't want to startle her.

She's still in her makeup when she answers. The soft punch of reefer lurks behind her. An inviting knee peeks through her silk chartreuse robe.

"Johnny? What are you doing here?"

"I came to see you. I needed to see you."

"John . . . not now."

"No. I really came to talk."

"It's late. I don't feel like talking."

I know what follows. I'm all too familiar with it. She begins to close the door, but I stop it with my trembling hand. "I'm in trouble . . . I did it for us."

"Us?"

"I want to be the kind of man you want."

"You're scaring me, John. Just tell me what you did."

We stare into each other's eyes for what seems like a very long while. I'm confused by the moment. I don't know if I'm about to share my dark secret or a kiss. I don't know what my next move will be. She must know what I do not, because she places her hand over my mouth. "Don't. Just don't."

I've said all that I have to say. I leave her house, embarrassed by my dramatic display. Maybe I pushed her too hard, expected too much from her. I came to her and nearly confessed, but she wouldn't let me say anything—maybe on some level, she understood.

I decide to head home and spend the night drinking up a plan.

The next day, I go to Count's before it opens for the evening. I walk in and, at once, I begin to feel uneasy. Pool balls wait silently for a break. There's something eerie about the place without its usual bacchanalia set to music. Like a body with the heart carved out of it, there's an almost gothic stillness.

"I don't fuckin' believe it."

Count's goons are behind me.

"I know this crippled motherfucker didn't have the nerve to come back here after he left his ass kickin' unfinished!"

"I think he did."

"Naw, he ain't got the balls."

One of them grabs my crotch from behind.

"You're right. He don't got the balls!"

I turn around and they slap shoulders and laugh at me. I'm offended, maybe even a bit hurt, but it helps me to remember why I came here, and why I need to get it over with quickly.

"Look," I say. "I'm not looking for a fight."

"Then why the fuck are you here?"

"I'm here to see the Count."

"It's just *Count*, jack. You ain't in Romania."

"I think that's obvious." I see them more distinctly now. They've given up the coordinated outfits from the other night. Maybe it was a special occasion. One is tall and young—only a few years older than me—and with a dangerous amount of muscle. The other is middle-aged with a medium build, but I know from experience that he has a knack for handing out punishment. I'm sure that's why Count keeps him around.

"What you want to see him for?" the older one asks.

"I have a business proposition for him. One that could be very lucrative."

"Lucrative? Motherfucka, you tryin' to set us up? You got them fuckin' cops with you again?" He smiles and seems to enjoy giving me a hard time. Just the good, old-fashioned bullying I'm used to. But the younger one? His hatred is very real.

"I've had enough of this crippled sonofabitch! Fuck the alley, let's kick his ass right here!" says Junior.

"Just calm down," I say. "What will Count say when he discovers you've prevented him from making money?"

"Punch him in his mouth real good, so he'll shut the fuck up!"

Suddenly a voice, like gravel, seems to come from everywhere and nowhere at once. "Cool it, boys. Let him pass." The hoods tense up and spring a leak in their bluster. Count certainly has an effect on people.

Only in mockery, never in actuality, had I studied Count's appearance. His face seems a bundle of contradiction: mouth relaxed, eyes set in a gaze without intimidation or menace, all under the massive bald head of a cyclops. Muscles visible through his shirt, he appears to be both a prizefighter ready to strike and a child eager to shield his favorite toy from the grasp of others.

"You know, I've always pegged you as a strange bastard. That limp. Those square threads. Not to mention that sweet tooth of yours."

"Sweet tooth?" I'm well aware of his reference to Candy, but since he's playing smart, I decide to play dumb.

"Man with a sweet tooth like yours could end up with a mouth full of cavities. But I'm here to take care of you. Consider me your dentist, nigger."

"Well, I can assure you that I'm in no need of dental work, but thanks for the offer."

His office smells like good cigar, and there's a long one spinning smoke from a crystal ashtray on his desk. The desk is large and made of a dark rich wood, most likely mahogany. Its gentle sheen compliments the large leather chair that Count sits in, and the smaller one in which I sit. A small portable bar, gilt handles and mirrored glass, waits in a dim corner behind Count's left shoulder. It's armed with scotch, port, and an assortment of French brandies—the good stuff. Underlining all of this is a large rug that's just loosely exotic instead of specifically oriental.

Something about this place seems deceptively constructed, like a stage setting. I look back at the cigar and notice that the head has not been removed by the merciful handheld guillotine—it's been bitten off.

"Twenty thousand," Count says, as he lifts the cigar from the ashtray.

"I'm sorry?"

"Twenty thousand."

"Twenty thousand *what*?"

"Dollars. Twenty thousand of them."

"Honestly, I'm confused."

"You don't get to be me without knowin' how to read people. That's essentially all that I do. I decipher the things that people want me to know, but don't want to tell me. And you—well, you're an easy read. You're in trouble. A shitload of it. After my boys cleaned up that alley with your ass, you got the nerve to walk back in here like John-fuckin'-Wayne, and without your mysterious white bodyguards. Business proposition? That means you need me to save your ass, and you want to make it worth my while so I don't kill your ass after I save it. Man, that's a whole lotta trouble. About twenty grand worth. Now I could be wrong. Maybe you're here collectin' donations for Dr. King."

He taps off ash, then chomps at his cigar with self-satisfaction. I've held many different feelings toward Count: hatred, envy, even fear. But this new feeling, respect, makes me disgusted with myself. His contempt and pity for me are quite clear, but in his tone, I detect a bit of disappointment, as if he expects more from me. It makes me think of my father and how I look down on him and Count in much the same way. They are both hard, physical men. How they must look down upon me.

I hesitate to tell him my plan, but then I consider the trouble I am in. This is not small-time stuff, no vig for the loan shark, or debt owed to the pusher. I am now a player in the game of political intrigue.

"A man that I work with needs to be taught a lesson."

"Thought you Negroes were nonviolent."

"I don't want him hurt. I don't *need* him hurt. I just need you to break into his home and place this where he can see it." I reveal an envelope from my inside pocket and lay it on the desk.

"Now why can't you do this yourself?"

"Let's just say that I lack the agility."

"Drop it in the mail. I'm not a fuckin' messenger."

"The mail? Presentation is everything. The man comes home and sees this letter waiting for him, nothing damaged, no signs of forced entry—he becomes acutely aware of his vulnerability. He knows that his walls and locked doors can't protect him. He knows that he can be gotten to." I lean back in my chair, feeling as if some spirit had just forced me to speak in tongues. I hope that he can decode what I've said. I'm not sure I'm capable of translating.

He is silent and still, except for the subtle twitching of his eyelids. The twitching stops, and then Count smiles. I speak his language.

I slept well last night. That makes me nervous. I am glad that Count and I came to an understanding, but how easily we reached our rapprochement is unsettling. I've spent a great deal of energy trying to be accepted by Gant and the rest of the SCLC staff—even Martin—with little return on my efforts. Now, I have fallen in with a crime boss with ease, and the agents are waiting for my call.

I feel uneasy as I arrange to meet Mathis and Strobe at their office. When I arrive, the agents don't waste any time introducing me to Bureau efficiency.

"What do you have for us, Mr. Estem?" asks Mathis.

"Well, Gant has a childish scheme to buy buses."

"Buses?"

"Transportation for the marches, he claims."

"Are there any other uses for these buses that he may have revealed to you?"

"Such as?"

Strobe looks at Mathis, but Mathis stays quiet.

"Such as transporting communist agitators around to influence labor disputes," offers Strobe.

Mathis cuts Strobe a look out of the corner of his eye. Even I can see that he has missed the mark.

"No," I say, "nothing like that. The fact is I haven't . . . well, he hasn't purchased the buses yet. He's waiting for me to return the money."

"Which you haven't done," Mathis says.

"No, I haven't."

Strobe and Mathis look at each other.

"What about King?" they ask simultaneously.

"What about him?"

"Communist activity? Any high-profile communists visiting the SCLC?"

"No, of course not."

"What about suspicious behavior?" Mathis asks while crossing his legs. "Behavior that might be seen as . . . unacceptable?"

I feel the sting of embarrassment, as if it were my behavior being questioned.

"No," I say again.

Mathis stays silent while surveying my face. I don't make any attempts to hide my discomfort.

"Listen, John," he says, leaning in to rest his elbows on his thighs. "It's understandable for you to be nervous. It happens a lot when you're first getting started—I'm including myself as well. Primarily, it is important for you not to lose focus. Stay homed in on the task at hand. I've already expressed the confidence we have in you and your importance to us. We need to monitor any activity that can be perceived as anti-American. When we enlisted your help, we did not expect you to become a hindrance of any kind. If Gant needs you to return the money, then return it. If it means getting rid of that car, then so be it. It's too conspicuous anyway. We—Mr. Hoover and the president—are very curious to see what he intends to do with that money."

"We need to know that you're a team player, John," says Strobe.

"Right," Mathis says, moving closer and now standing above me, "a team player. But know this, John," he says squeezing my shoulder a little too tightly, "If you drop the ball, I'll have no problem putting you on the bench."

Feeling defeated after my rendezvous with the agents, I take the long way home. The thought of Gant and the money makes me queasy. I pray that Count works fast and Gant has already resigned in shame. If not, I'll have to suffer through another morning, staring at his smirking face. I drive down Peachtree Street, moving in a straight line past the zigzagging art deco of the picture palaces. Window down, there is no wind. The air is heavy and humid and seems to trap my anxiety in a dense cloud around me. I've had this feeling before, this phantom weight on my chest.

When the polio struck, the doctors feared that the paralysis would spread to my diaphragm and the other muscles required for breathing. Had this happened, my permanent home would have been that despicable contraption called the iron lung. An airtight chamber, designed to push and pull on your chest through alternating pressure, fooling your body into believing that it is breathing on its own, reminding your brain that you cannot escape. That was the first and last time my withered leg seemed like a blessing.

I'm encased in steel, but this Caddy gives me the kind of mobility I've never experienced before. I know it's foolish, but behind this steering wheel, the barriers of class and race seem porous and decayed. At a stoplight I catch my reflection in a department store window. I smile at the idea of myself as a nomadic warrior, armed with a battering ram and attacking the crumbling walls of a citadel that houses the rumored treasures of the American dream.

I've come this far. Further than anyone thought. Smarter than anyone knew. The agents will tighten the screws. So will Count. But I know I'll come out on top. I'm already feeling better.

I pull up to my apartment and notice a large white Buick parked across the street. I squint at the driver's seat, but it's vacant. I get out and place my hand on Black Beauty's hood. I feel the warmth of her engine. I head for my apartment, but I am not alone. I look at my small porch, darkened by the awning above it. Someone is waiting for me.

8

I'm surprised to see Count going solo, and not accompanied by his men. Depending on the news he brings, I may be happy to see him.

"Let's have a talk," he says, motioning to his car waiting across the street.

"I didn't know you worked so fast," I say, once we are inside.

He doesn't respond.

"I'm sorry to say, I don't have your money yet . . . but soon."

Count interlocks his fingers and gives his knuckles a loud crack. "Maybe it's a setup, I say to myself. Maybe I go in there and somebody's waiting for me. Maybe you told this somebody that he shouldn't be so welcoming." He reaches into his jacket pocket and withdraws the envelope intended for Gant. "Maybe there's a finger inside this envelope and it's pointing at me. The way you been eyeing my girl—this would be the perfect chance to get me out of the way. But no, that ain't your style. First you have to make use of your enemies, then you get rid of them. For you it's more fun that way. So forgive me for invading your fucking privacy by taking a peek."

"That's fine, Count. I understand. A man in your position should take precautions. I hope your fears have been abated."

" 'Forget about the money,' " he reads. " 'They're on to us.' " He folds the letter down the middle and looks at me. "I really start thinking now," he says. "Was Little Man putting pressure on somebody and now he's backing off? No, that can't be it. 'Cause then where do I fit? Then I realize, *no*, somebody is putting the screws to *him*. You're trying to convince somebody that the man they answer to wants to call it off. But that's your mistake. You don't really know how their game is played. Whoever they are, this probably ain't their style. You're just pointing the finger at yourself. 'Forget about the money'—man, you been watching too many movies."

He's right, and he may have saved me from embarrassment. What the hell was I thinking? The letter was lacking in so many aspects, but above all, in credibility and authenticity. I have no idea how communists and homosexuals conspire with each other.

"So why don't you tell me what's really going on?" asks Count.

I struggle with the idea of telling him about the money and Gant. I'm not sure what to do, but that lasts only briefly.

"I stole a bit of money from work. Now my queer boss is putting some pressure on me."

"Queer?"

"Yes. Communist too."

"No shit. A queer. How much?"

"Twenty." I've overstated the amount that has me on tilt, but I think I know where Count is headed.

"Goddamn. Either I'm right about you or I'm really fucking wrong."

"They want the money back. They don't know it's me for certain, but they are beginning to look my way."

"They already got the cops involved?"

"Certainly. That's why they were in the alley the other night. They wanted to bring me in for questioning."

"You cooperate? Make a deal? Tell them you'd get the goods on somebody big if they'd look the other way?"

"Of course not. I played dumb."

Count looks out of the window and lets his rough voice leak out. "Exactly, motherfucker—you *played* dumb."

"Look, the money wasn't exactly clean to begin with."

"Okay. Now I see. You needed a dirty hand to give it a wash. What happened to the money?"

"Spent some of it on women . . . at your place . . . so you already have a cut."

"Hey, man, you can keep the guilt trip. Ain't no such thing as free pussy."

"Then there's the car, of course."

"Guess that explains the new Caddy. Hell, even I don't have a Cadillac," he says almost to himself. "What's your story, man? How does an accountant get himself in this kind of shit? You think I'd be doing this if I'd gone to college?"

I don't have an answer for him, so I just look out of the window at the green stucco of my building, still luminous in the night, like the aftermath of a lab experiment gone awry.

"Look, young blood, this type of aggravation is bullshit. Cops and queer bosses. *I'll* give you the money."

"Count, that's very generous of you, but I can't."

"Generous, my dick. You *will* pay me back. With interest. Fifteen points," he says.

"Fifteen points?"

"I know that's strong medicine, but it'll go down easier than you think. We could learn a lot from each other. I'm looking for associates that are more . . ."

"Stimulating," I offer.

"Right. Stimulating. Don't get me wrong—Candy's no knuckle-head, but she ain't exactly gonna cure cancer. Claudel and Otis have to take turns breathing, so that the other can chew gum."

"Claudel and Otis?"

"The gentlemen that roughed your ass up."

So those are their names. I wonder which one is which.

"It's not every day that I get to rub shoulders with an honest-to-God white-collar professional. Now, your collar ain't so white, but it'll do. I'll even let you work some of that money off by doing me some favors." He beams a wild grin at me that sends a chill down my back.

I think Count is finished, so I make an ill-considered move to get out of the car.

"I'm not done with you yet," he says looking at his jeweled pinky, gleaming even in the darkness of the front seat. "There's something I want to show you."

We drive for a while. Eventually, we come to a neighborhood that looks as if it were designed by one of those Xerography machines. All the houses appear to be the same single-story structure, a hodgepodge of brick and aluminum siding.

"Count, what are we doing in Bozley Park?"

"I know what you're thinking—two spooks at night in Bozley Park, that definitely means trouble. But don't get nervous. We won't be long. I just brought you here to paint the picture. Look out the window. Look around you. What do you see?"

Bozley Park consists of ten or fifteen houses. None of these people are wealthy by any means. Blue-collar workers live here: plumbers, welders, janitors who call themselves maintenance managers, and the like—not upper-crust professionals. I see two posts, black and white, sunken into the earth, and fortified with cement. A clear symbol of the barrier between the races. Just one block over—just past those posts—is Bozley *Place.* That's where the Negroes live.

"Now imagine black families living in these houses, with their black children playing in the yard."

"That's ridiculous," I say. "It's still too segregated."

He smiles at that, "Whoever heard of one of Dr. King's men not having any faith? I know all about Bozley Park, and I think it's time they came face to face with integration—and you're gonna help me do it."

Favors, he says. Do I deserve such generosity?

9

Within a few days, Count makes good on his offer. Thanks to him, I've returned the money and kept the Caddy. Now that I'm indebted to him, I can empathize with Candy's situation. He's not shy about giving you exactly what you ask for and being perceived as your savior. It gives the illusion that he is protective of you, that there is something in you worth saving. When his true nature appears, brutal and mercenary, you'll be blinded by the memory of him coming to your rescue.

However, for now, I'll embrace the relief. I enter Gant's office with an unusual jauntiness, as if I've pulled off a job well done.

"Mr. Gant, those funds are now available." I give him a slight deferential bow of the head.

"Good, Estem, good. Forgive me for saying so, but I was beginning to get worried. Especially with that beautiful new Cadillac of yours."

We both laugh.

"How many buses can you get for a Cadillac?" I joke.

Gant smiles. "Five? Ten? I have no idea. I'll probably never know. I'm out of the bus business."

"Sir?"

"Yeah, looks like I got ahead of myself with that bus idea. We're not going ahead with it."

My jaw narrows.

"Guess I made the mistake of thinking above my pay grade. This place has a way of setting you straight. But I'm sure we'll find other uses for the money." He rests his forehead in his hand while massaging the temples. "Estem, how do you feel about your job with us?" he asks without looking at me.

It takes me a moment to respond. I'm too preoccupied with what has happened, and wondering if I could have anticipated it. Gant removes his hand and looks at me, so I give him an answer. "Yes. I'm very happy here, sir."

"Are you sure? Something about you seems so . . . unsatisfied. Are you unsatisfied, Estem?"

"I wouldn't put it that way, exactly."

"You strike me as being ambitious, Estem. Is that fair to say?"

"I guess every man, to a certain degree—"

"It's the ambitious ones that you have to watch. They can be pulled away by so many dark forces. You understand what I mean by dark forces, don't you?"

"I can't say with certainty."

"It's a matter of allegiance, Estem. It's about knowing whose side you're on when everybody appears to be on the same side. I'm sure those knuckleheads at the NAACP and CORE would love to have any of our people."

"Yes, sir, I'm sure they would."

"Estem, I've decided to give you a promotion—make you my right-hand man. Not that you aren't already. But you'll have a new title: assistant financial director. It has a nice ring to it, don't you think?"

I feel a headache coming on.

"You won't be receiving more pay, unfortunately. As you know, we just don't have it in the budget. But you will have greater responsibility in the SCLC. More weight will rest on your shoulders. I'll need you to accompany Martin and me on a trip to LA. Are you game?"

At this point I can only nod.

After work, I head home, already feeling the burden of my new thankless title. I go about the business of removing my brace when I realize I badly need a drink. However, not badly enough to go through the ordeal of putting my brace back on. I hop over to my refrigerator to see what I have: just beer, which I don't like all that much. Staring at the beer, I begin to realize that when I thought I needed a drink, what I really needed was a woman. Not just for the evening, but for an undetermined extended stay. Someone to help me with my brace. Someone to complain to about my promotion in title only. Someone—

My phone rings. It's Mathis.

"John, we shouldn't have to contact you."

"I apologize."

"Meet us in five minutes."

His tone is all-business, and it makes me slightly nervous. I feel that my performance during our first meeting was a failure, and I worry that I will let them down again. I resign myself to the notion that I must not reveal my apprehension and I should always be direct and forthcoming.

I meet them at their office. The somber atmosphere is intimidating.

"What do you have for us?" asks Mathis.

"I've been promoted," I tell him. "I'm thinking about getting a larger apartment."

Strobe takes a step toward me. Mathis raises his hand.

"Congratulations," says Mathis. "It seems the year has been good to you. What do you have for us concerning communists?"

"Nothing at the moment. But once I return from my trip, it's possible that things might pick up."

"Trip?" Mathis asks.

"Martin and I—Gant too—will be taking the message abroad, as they say."

"Where?" asks Strobe. "What hotel will you be staying at? Who else will be there?"

"Gentlemen, once I have all the details I'll relay them to you."

"It's important you get that information to us before you leave," Mathis says. "Let's say by this time tomorrow."

"Why the rush?"

"Who planned this trip?"

"Gant, of course."

"Exactly. He could be using the trip as a cover for some communist rendezvous. If that's happening, we need to know."

"Agent Mathis, I can assure you that I am taking my duties seriously. I understand the severity of the task at hand, and I am approaching it in a systematic and professional way."

"Professional?" Strobe is stone-faced and humorless. He goes over to a file cabinet and reveals a manila folder. He opens it and scans the contents with his finger. "Recently, you were seen in the presence of a Reginald Glover, aka 'Count.' A known peddler of narcotics—and women—within the Negro community. Is that what you call professional?"

The nerve of them, to have the audacity to collect my comings and goings in a file and then read them back to me, as if my life is a performance for their pleasure. I want to feed that folder to him. However, I decide to show some restraint.

"What else do you have in there?" I ask. "Your mother's brassiere size?"

Strobe drops the folder. "You son of a bitch!"

"Strobe!" says Mathis. "Sit down."

He does as instructed. His face, now reddened, is augmented by a wild and savage look in his eye.

"Everyone," Mathis says as he stares down Strobe, "needs to remember what his job is."

He turns to me with a look that practically begs for my forgiveness.

"John, I don't want you to think that we were invading your privacy. We were keeping a watchful eye over you to keep you safe. I apologize for Agent Strobe, but you need to leave here with the understanding that you shall return with results. Understood?"

I look over Mathis's shoulder at Strobe, who's loosening his tie and glaring at me without even a hint of blink. "Answer him, for Christ's sake!"

"Strobe . . . John, do we understand each other?"

"Of course, Agent Mathis. You and I are on the same page."

I leave their office, but I don't drive home. Their disapproving tone makes me want to see my mother—not to be protected but to be comforted. The dynamic has shifted so quickly, and I know that I am responsible. I made it obvious how much I wanted to gain their approval, which was ridiculous. Why would I raise the expectations so high if I knew I would have difficulty delivering? But it is too late; they've seen how eager I have been to comply, and they'll milk it for all it is worth. Right now, the power is in their hands unless I do something to change it.

When I arrive at my parents' house, my father is drinking whiskey in the dark.

"Your mother's asleep."

"I figured as much."

"So what's the special occasion?"

"I can't visit my parents? Say hello?"

"It's in the middle of the goddamn night. You in some kind of trouble?"

It's never just chitchat with him. Conversations are always ruthless interrogations.

"No trouble," I answer. "I've been promoted."

"Promoted?" He slides the whiskey toward me. "Sit down."

I pull a chair up to the table and sit. I roll the bottle in my palm before I take a swig from it. I feel it burn my throat, then my chest, but I don't recoil—I stare deep into the old man's eyes.

"Tell me about this promotion."

"I'm the new assistant financial director."

"Ain't that what you were before?"

"I was the *liaison* to the financial director."

"Uh-huh. You still the bookkeeper though?"

"I'll be an accountant soon, Dad. Not just a bookkeeper. I oversee every penny that goes in and every penny that goes out. I'm good at what I do. I make sure that the money's there. When you see those Negroes on television—the marches, the campaigns, the programs—*I* make sure that it happens."

He looks at me, then smiles.

I feel embarrassed in my excitement.

"When you hear about this promotion?"

"Today."

"You must've known you'd get it. Must've known for sure."

I hate when he does this. "How do you mean, Dad?"

"Well, you've had that brand-new car for a while now. Not that long, but long enough. Yeah, you must've been cocksure of the good fortune headed your way." He sips his whiskey and looks over my shoulder into the shadowy living room. "I'm so old that it feels like I've always been an old man. I forget that I was young. But then I look at you and I start to remember." He leans forward, "You got a woman?"

I look at the whiskey bottle and scratch at its label. "Yes."

"Who?"

I hesitate for a moment, considering whether to withdraw my answer. "Candice," I offer. "You remember her, don't you?"

He smiles, revealing those large yellow teeth. "Naw, you don't got a woman. A woman got you."

I slam the bottle's base hard against the table, like a gavel. I grip it tightly, still holding it upright. I look at him, bracing myself for whatever comes next.

He places his whiskey glass far to his left, preparing a frank path in front of him. "Whatever it is you've got yourself into, you're not cut out for it. You're not made for it, boy. I'm no fool. I know what you want. This country keeps promises to everyone except colored folks. It makes a man desperate. I ain't proud to admit it, but I made a good sum of money running liquor. You don't know what it's like to wake up in the morning and pray for night, 'cause that's the only time a colored man can make some real money without attracting too much attention. It's a hard life. You got to have a stomach of steel to survive it. You can't grow one—you've got to be born with it. You don't have that kind of strength."

I take a large, painful gulp from the bottle to help wash down what he has said.

"And this Candice—you're not the kind of man for that kind of woman. She needs a hard, unforgiving man who can control her like everything else in his world. Your mama was like that. Wild. She was wounded in those days. She drank hard and gambled—could roll some bones like a man. Fought like an alley cat, too. Once cut a woman for looking at her wrong. But when I said enough is enough, she knew I meant it. Yeah. When I look at you, I start to remember. I remember what I was and what you're not." He brings his glass in front of him and tilts it toward his face. He could be sniffing it or looking at his reflection on the whiskey's surface, but he does not drink.

I feel foolish for letting my guard down. He sees a weakness and exploits it; the old habit of an ex-bootlegger. I get up to leave. I stumble a bit; my irritation made the whiskey act fast.

"Take your time," he says, not looking up from his glass.

I make my escape, thankful for the safety of my car. He's hard to tolerate, but I feel grateful to him for simplifying my situation and giving it the commonality of a blues song. *You don't got a woman, but a woman got you!* Truly, he does surprise me: wooing my mother in her less discriminating days. Drinking, gambling, fighting—my mother? I've never met the woman he describes, yet she seems so familiar to me. He saw her potential and reinvented her as he had himself.

He has given me hope to do the same.

As I drive to Candy's, I think about that night Martin and I talked, and I am, for the moment, inclined to grant my father clemency. It seems that all fathers offer their sons trouble and anguish—that must be their duty.

I've grown used to the idea of being alone, and it's easy for me to forget that sometimes people do experience things in the same ways that I do. Although, it is still surprising that it was Martin who reminded me of this.

The clock above his door read one thirty, but we both pretended to ignore it. I wasn't ready for our conversation to end, and he wasn't ready to go home.

"So, John, how often do you attend service?" Martin asked.

"Pretty often," I lied, "but not as much as my mother would like."

He absently scratched his knee. "Whenever I hear that, I am reminded that the majority of His work is done once we leave the place of worship. I'm sure she would understand that."

I nodded, maybe a little too eagerly.

"What about your father? Was he in accounting as well?"

"No, nothing of the sort."

"Oh, for some reason I got the impression that you were involved in the family business—following in the old man's footsteps . . . like me."

"No. My father and I are nothing alike. Our interests couldn't be more different."

He leaned forward, propped his elbow on his knee, and rested his chin on the knuckles of his curled fist. He did not look directly at me, but somewhere off to my right.

"Fathers can be an overwhelming force in a child's life, especially for sons," he said. "The relationship a son has with his father can become frustrating as the child tries to simultaneously please and perform for the parent. I know this firsthand. Imagine the imposing figure of my father—Daddy King, we called him. I desired desperately to free myself from the shadow of his two-hundred-and-twenty-pound frame. Imagine the standard I had to live up to, raised by a man—a sharecropper's son—who yearned for an education and a life that transcended the toil of the fields so passionately that he was brave enough to begin high school as an adult, eighteen years of age, and ultimately earn a degree from Morehouse. Do you see, John? This is where the pressure for excellence originates. He had already left a large footprint in the struggle long before I could have anticipated my own contribution. Even then, I knew a great deal was expected of me. I struggled. I struggled to find the catalyst that would ignite my potential. Then I struggled for the capacity to understand why this potential was given to me and what I was to do with it. But the pressure to succeed never abated. In school, I didn't properly attribute the source material for some papers I had written . . ." He smiles to himself for a moment, "I guess that's a ten-dollar way of saying I plagiarized some papers, and that's just a five-dollar phrase for 'I stole.' But now I can trace it back to a persistent and overwhelming sense of inadequacy. Can you understand such a feeling, John?"

10

From my car, I have been watching her apartment for hours, when a tap on my passenger window startles me.

I lean over to let her in.

"Don't think I'm letting you come in," she says.

"I've got some good news."

Up close, my amorous intentions begin to fade. Her current state does not match the image imprinted in my fantasy. Her hair and makeup are a mess, and I swear I detect Count's odor coming from her. But I continue anyway.

"I've been promoted," I tell her.

"Good, John. That's real good," she says as she lights a cigarette.

I roll down a window for ventilation. Anonymous insects croak in the shadowy heat. "I'm going on a trip with Martin soon. Have you ever been to Los Angeles?"

"What do you think?"

"Would you like to go? I mean, I think I can arrange it."

She looks at me and brings her eyebrows together in disbelief. "What are you trying to do? What point are you trying to prove? That you're just as much a man as he is? Well, you're not, John. He will kill you. If you cross him, he will kill you and never give it another thought."

Cigarette smoke is the only thing of substance between us. I've grown weary of trying to understand her attachment to Count. Maybe the old man is right. Maybe my stomach could use some girding up.

"Is that what you want—an animal that pisses on everything to mark his territory?" I say. "You want to crawl around on all fours like a goddamn animal?"

I must have hit a sore spot. Her shoulders drop. She turns away and looks out the window, but there is nothing out there for her.

"I don't know what I want," she says. "I'm still trying to figure myself out. I thought I wanted to be a singer, but it's kind of hard when no one wants to hear you sing." She faces me again. "I just know that I can't do it by myself. Whatever I want, he can give it to me."

"What'd he give you tonight, huh? A couple of smacks to the face? Did you mouth off? Make eye contact with another man? Or did you not come quickly enough when called?"

"It comes with the territory."

"Don't you want something more for yourself? Maybe he can pull a few strings. But is it worth it? Don't you want to be a better person?"

"Don't judge me—or him. You'd trade places with him in a second." She takes a long drag and blows smoke in my face. "Don't pretend that you don't want anything from me. The difference between you and him is that he can walk away when he doesn't get what he wants. But you're always there. Always will be. Sometimes that makes me hate you. But you just keep on giving. Why can't you be like everyone else and take what you want and go? But that ain't like you. Sometimes I love you. If I had any friends, I'd say you'd be the best one. But sure enough I hate you again, because you remind me I don't deserve it. You remind me that I wouldn't do the same for you."

"If that's how you feel, then give me what I want and I'll never bother you again."

"What do you want?"

"You know what I want."

She gives me a wicked smile and tosses her cigarette out of the window. "If that's what you want, then be man enough to take it. What? You want me to put it on a silver platter for you? If you're waiting for me to choose you, then you're wasting your time, because I don't want you. But here it is." She hikes her dress to midthigh and parts her legs. "Show me what kind of a man you are."

I stare into the dark space between her legs and mutter a desperate incantation to myself, but no magic appears.

"That's what I thought." She pulls down her dress and leaves.

I arrive at Count's, but I don't enter through the front bar. Even at this late hour, it's surging with music. Instead I head for the entrance in the back that faces the alley.

I walk past the crumbling brick, through the shadows that reek of piss and garbage that seems to move as I pass. Then I see it: that door made red by the colored light above it.

I knock on the door in a secret rhythm. Two eyes appear through a narrow slot. The door opens and I enter. The hallway buzzes with moans and screams only vaguely muffled by the thin white walls. At the end of this hallway is a room with the number 21 painted on its door. My girl is waiting inside.

"Fuck or suck?" she asks.

"Fuck," I say so softly I can barely hear it.

She has a young round face, but there is a manufactured innocence in her eyes. She's a big girl; my father would say she's farm-fed. I say she's zaftig. She looks like *her* a little . . . not quite. You have to squint your eyes, let your head fall back, and your mouth hang open, and then they are identical. She is twice *her* size, but that is what I need: two of *her*. I need to be overwhelmed and hide myself in the shadow between her thighs.

"Come on, baby. Come for Mama."

I'm trying, but I'm too self-conscious and aware of my surroundings. My brace seems to squeak with every thrust. I can hear the wet smack of skin against skin, the soft scrape of tongue against tongue. The noise keeps me there and traps me with my anger for Her. It won't let my resentment give way to desire.

I feel a sudden jolt, as if someone had unexpectedly tapped my shoulder. I remove myself from the girl and struggle to get my pants on.

"What's wrong?"

I don't respond.

"You're a real creep! What is your problem?"

I hear a loud thud, wood splintering, and many pounding footsteps.

"*Raid!*" Somebody screams. I hear the policemen shout, "*Freeze!*" and kick in doors.

"I can't be arrested," I tell the girl.

"Me neither. They gonna send me back to my grandmama's house."

"Don't let them find me."

"What the hell you want me to do?"

"*Don't fuckin' move!*" comes from the room next to ours.

"Run out there and distract them."

"Hell, no."

I reach into my pants and pull out some money. "Here."

"Like this?" she asks pointing at her naked body.

I give her more money. "Please."

She jiggles out of the room. "Don't shoot! Don't shoot!"

I gather my clothes and crouch in the corner.

I wait for what seems like a long while, but it's probably just minutes. The chaos seems to subside and I begin to feel safe. Then I hear footsteps. They are faint at first, but grow louder. They echo down the hallway, then pivot and move into the rooms. I cry a little and pray a lot. The footsteps are closer—so close I think I hear the tips of the laces hit the shoes.

The door creaks open slowly. I do not move.

I'm the only Negro in the back of the paddy wagon. Some of the other men seem vaguely familiar, but I'm not concerned with putting names to faces. At the station, I'm photographed and fingerprinted. They corral the white men together in a cell. I have one all to myself.

Dark corners. Only a single lamp outside the cell. My face is crosshatched by the shadows of the bars, adding a gloomy quality to this already hopeless setting.

I'm entitled to a phone call, but I don't use it.

Hours pass. Upon release, I consider fleeing the country.

I hear the jangle of keys. A lanky policeman with a boil on his right upper cheek unlocks the cell door. "Well, boy, it looks like you managed to make friends with the right people. C'mon, now."

The officer escorts me to the station lobby, where he hands me a file. Inside are my mug shot and fingerprints.

Strobe and Mathis are waiting at the front desk.

"He's all yours," the officer says.

11

Mathis and Strobe are silent. I assume that they will drive me home, but as we pass the city limits, my shame and gratitude prevent me from protesting.

"I can't thank you enough," I say to them. "What you've done tonight won't be forgotten."

They do not respond.

The city vanishes in the darkness behind us, yet Mathis and Strobe continue to drive. They drive into the forgotten rural area, past the old barns and fields, past the shacks of tenant farmers still lit by kerosene lamps. The sound of gravel crunching under the tires gives way to the softer thump of a dirt road.

Trees suddenly appear. The twisted branches give mind to the mangled limbs of torture and farm accidents. Vegetation suffocates the trunks. Roots push up through the soil, reaching for air.

We are deep in the Christ-haunted woods of baptisms and lynchings.

"Relax, John," says Mathis.

Finally, we come to a clearing.

"Here," says Strobe.

Darkness is all around us, though briefly interrupted by a light flickering in the distance.

I blink and take in the brilliance of a burning cross.

The sight of a cross on fire should be unsettling to any true Christian. To a Negro it is worse. A unique kind of fear enters your mind, one perfected by the South: that you could die for the most harmless of offenses. You could die just for the crime of living.

This is how it happens, isn't it? Someone becomes too much of a liability and they mysteriously disappear. But that is not how Mathis and Strobe would get rid of me. I can see the headline now: "King's Accountant Murdered by Klan." If I were to disappear, it would be an embarrassment to Hoover and an outrage to Martin. I matter too much. It seems that they brought me here for some type of show—to teach me a lesson. They want to watch me squirm for their amusement.

Strobe opens the car door and pulls me out.

"Well," I say to them, "I see you have a flair for drama, but are these theatrics really necessary?"

"Shut your trap, for God's sake," snaps Strobe.

There is nothing but the cross and darkness. Strobe pulls something from his jacket and presses it to his lips. A birdlike chirp is released. A duplicate sound echoes from the night. We wait, staring into the dark. And then I see it, what I hope is a trick of the mind, a ghostly apparition emerging from the pitch. I stand in disbelief as the white hood and cloak make their way toward us.

He removes the hood and reveals his coal black, sweat-soaked hair. "You boys need to start being on time. Been waiting out here who knows how long." He looks at me, then smiles at Mathis and Strobe. "Would've brought my corn liquor if I knew we was having a party."

"What's the news, Pete?" asks Mathis.

"Might know who killed that salt-and-pepper couple last month, that's what."

"You do or you don't."

"Can't fully recall. Memory's been acting funny since my little girl got sick. Doctor can't tell what's causing it. Bless her heart." He seems to swell under that sheet. He has a large brawny build; not athletic, just the ropy girth resulting from years of physical labor.

"How much?"

"Two hundred might get her through."

Mathis nods at Strobe. He retrieves the bills and hands them to Pete.

An unwelcome smirk comes to my face. Out here in these woods, I am surprised to see someone I think I can relate to.

Pete looks at me, money still in his palm. His close-set eyes narrow. "What is that goddamn monkey looking at?" He puts the hood back on. "You want to look at something, nigger? Look at this."

Strobe snatches the hood and tosses it to the ground. "One more word and you'll watch me piss on it."

Pete attempts to reach for it.

"Leave it," says Strobe.

"Names," says Mathis.

"Frank Billingsley. Sam Cullworth. Brothers—same momma, different daddies. Share a place not too far from here. They been bragging about what they did to the girl while they made the nigger watch."

"And I suppose a man of your stature favors discretion, is that it?" adds Mathis.

"Ain't saying she didn't have it coming. But what them boys did was done *after* she was dead. You got to draw the line somewhere, for Christ's sake."

"Your buddies back there will support a hundred different alibis. What else you got?"

"Took some jewelry off the girl. The nigger had a guitar that Sam won't shut up about. Said it's like the one his daddy taught him on. Sure as hell he's still got it."

A rallying cry echoes in the dark. Pete jerks his head like a dog responding to a whistle. "It's been fun visiting, boys. But I need to get going."Again, he reaches for the hood. "May I?"

Strobe nods.

"You know where to find me if you need me." Pete looks at me one last time. "Be sure to keep that dog on a short leash," he says as he disappears into the woods.

The three of us are silent as we head toward the city. In my mind, Mathis and Strobe have reached their low point. Allowing me to witness their little display of power reveals their true estimation of me. Despite what they have told me, they see me as corrupted and compromised. An unscrupulous man who can be maneuvered and manipulated by his faults, like puppet strings.

I decide to speak up. "Good to see you boys are putting your con-nections to good use. I wish that I could tell Martin what you boys are up to."

"I'm sure you do," Strobe says glaring at me in the rearview mirror.

"I mean that it would put him at ease. Martin's been so troubled about the FBI's lack of protection for us civil rights workers, he'd love to hear that you are going to get those animals."

"Hear that, Mathis?" asks Strobe, "*Martin* would love to hear that we're going to get those animals."

"John," Mathis says, letting out a sigh, "We most certainly do not, and probably never will, give protection to a civil rights worker. The FBI is not the police. We're purely an *investigative* organization. The protection of individual citizens is a matter for local authorities."

He sounds rehearsed, and he knows it.

"So you've obtained information regarding the murder of two inno-cent people," I say, "yet you plan to do nothing with it?"

"I can't believe this son of a bitch is developing a conscience," Strobe says.

"We'll give the information to the sheriff once we've followed up on everything."

"You and I both know these redneck sheriffs won't make an effort," I say. "It's your job to ensure that justice—"

"I've had enough of this degenerate. Put the bastard out here and let him walk home."

"Strobe, enough. John, our job is to *know*. Period. Now, you need to focus on *your* job and that is helping us do ours. We brought you out here to show you that we can be trusted—to remove any doubt about whose side we are on. We are on your side, John. When you act in the manner you have, it gives us the impression that you take our relationship for granted—that you don't trust us . . . and that we can't trust you. You must stay focused, John. If you fail, we all fail. You will be an embarrassment to the FBI, to King—to everyone. Don't you see it? We have people planted inside an organization that is the sworn enemy of the Negro people. We're working to destroy them from the inside out. Yet you continue to treat our arrangement with a disrespect that puzzles me. The barbarians are at the gates,

John. Saboteurs, both foreign and domestic, are threatening America. You have to capture, for good, any part of you that wants to flee, and suppress it. Your responsibilities to your people and to this country are too great."

Mathis tosses an envelope to me in the backseat.

I see his eyes in the rearview mirror, surveying me to assess the effect of his words. I don't have to look in the envelope. I can tell by its weight that there's cash inside.

"Get the information," says Mathis. "The next time we meet, you'd better be a goddamn encyclopedia."

As we approach the lights of the city, we pass a billboard displaying our town's new civil-minded slogan: "Welcome to Atlanta, the City Too Busy to Hate."

12

Heat rises from the pavement, blurring everything behind it. Slowly, they begin to materialize: marchers, headed down a road that bisects a seemingly limitless field. I stand in the middle of their procession, watching them as they pass. They are mostly young and Negro, but there are others as well: college-age white boys with their shaggy beards and shades, nuns and white women of various ages, from those with the legs of their denim rolled up to their calves, to those in loose free-flowing paisley housedresses. A young man missing his right leg hurries past me on crutches. My eyes follow him in disbelief, and then I see Martin up ahead in his preacher-blue suit. "Martin!" I call out to him. I hurry to catch up, but I cannot keep pace. Again, I call to him, "Martin! Wait!" This time he stops, as does everyone else.

"Come on," he says. "Come on and join us up front."

It takes some time for me to reach him, but when I do, an angry mob appears and begins to throw rocks at us.

"Well," he says. "You coming or not?"

Before I can answer him, shots ring out. Only his shoulders twitch, subtly. The shots repeat in rapid succession. I do not move.

Martin motions the crowd to move forward.

I am left alone.

But the gunfire continues.

I can't tell where it's coming from. I crouch and then lie down on the ground. The gunfire doesn't stop, and now an incessant ringing accompanies it—over and over and over.

My phone wakes me. Reluctantly, I reach for the receiver.

"Hello?"

"Is your LA offer still good?"

Am I still dreaming? If so, how would I answer this in a dream? "Yes."

"Good, then I'm coming with you." Her voice doesn't sound apologetic; she assumes I have already forgiven her.

I head to the office, but it takes a while for me to get there. I'm bouncing around between excitement and incredulity. My cynicism had spread like a cancer; now I find myself smiling when I think of Candy and all the possibilities. Her call saved me from a nightmare; how can I not view it as a good omen?

The door to Gant's office is open. He sits at his desk while looking at the contents of a large black folder and casually nibbling the end of a pencil. As I look closer, I see that he's staring at something far away from whatever is in that folder.

I tap on the door to get his attention.

He looks up but doesn't say anything. It's as if he needs a few moments to recognize me.

"Yes," he says finally. "What is it, Estem?"

"Sir, I had a question regarding our trip to Los Angeles."

"Go ahead."

"I was wondering if anyone would be bringing their wives?"

"Why do you ask? You're not married, are you?" He smiles wryly. "Have you been keeping a secret wife? Why, Estem, I don't know you at all."

I manage a smile. I speak through a stifled laugh to show that I am a good sport. "No, but I was hoping to invite a friend."

"*Invite?* Estem, this isn't a cotillion we're going to." He seems genuinely irritated as he closes the folder.

"Yes, sir, I'm aware of that, which is why I'm asking."

He stands, placing both palms on his desk. "Martin rarely sees his wife. The same can be said for Young and Abernathy. I'm quite sure they would love to bring their wives along, but these are the sacrifices they made for the movement. It displays solidarity and commitment if we attempt to make the same sacrifices."

"Of course." I want to explain the importance of female companionship while abroad, but I don't think a queer would truly understand.

He sits back down. His chair is on a swivel, and he slowly turns
his back to me. "But then again," he adds, "these trips can be trying,
and a certain amount of downtime is required." He turns the chair
to face me again, but he reopens the folder and puts the pencil back
between his teeth, letting it rest on his lip as if it were a long wooden
cigarette. He removes it before deciding to speak again. "So no one can
stop you from *making* friends once we are there. Discretion is the key,
Estem. It is always the key. Remember that next time."

"Understood, sir." I don't push the issue further. He's given me
enough room to maneuver. I'll need to get a ticket on another airline
and a separate room. Not the romantic getaway I imagined, but it will
have to do.

"Here," he says lifting a piece of paper off his desk.

I walk over to take it. It's the itinerary for the LA trip. His eyes
begin to drift to that place he was visiting when I first walked in. I
leave him to his thoughts; that's where he needs to be right now. I am
not a mind reader, but I am an accountant; I know the look of calcula-
tion when I see it.

Later, I contact Mathis to give him the details. I call him from a
phone booth that I would often use to call Candy. Most of the time I
couldn't do it from my apartment. Looking around my modest means
would rob me of the confidence that is necessary when a man talks to
a woman. It's across the street from a pawnshop with abandoned symbols of desperation glittering in its windows. However, the modeling
school next to it attracted most of my attention. Seeing those girls—
not all of them pretty—saunter after their dreams with perfect posture
gave me a much-needed boost of courage. Even before I went into the
bank that day, I called her. I wanted to hear her voice one last time,
just in case things went horribly wrong.

"Los Angeles. Ambassador Hotel," I tell Mathis when he answers.
"What room?"

"I don't know yet, but we will have the entire sixth floor."

He thanks me, but I hang up in his face.

———

Five days pass, and I haven't heard from her since the wake-up call. I start packing for the trip to LA. Although the flight leaves in a few hours, I pack mainly to keep myself busy and to keep the disappointment from setting in.

A knock at my door interrupts the exciting task of mating my socks.

She has never been inside my apartment before, so I am understandably nervous. I take a moment to catalog the image of her in my doorway. Her wide-brimmed hat is white and tilted at an angle so that only one of her almond-shaped eyes is visible. Her pastel blue dress is sleeveless and shows off her small sloping shoulders. It flares at the knee. Her gloves are short, white, and leather. She holds a suitcase. The suitcase is not leather—maybe pigskin. It's an unusual cloudy rust color, like iodine mixed with milk.

I stand there holding the door open, not saying anything, just taking her in, savoring that contrast of blue and white against her brown skin—a rich and luminous brown, like brandy resting above a warmer's flame.

"Well, aren't you gonna invite me in?" she asks, growing tired of my staring.

"I'm sorry. Come on in. Put your bag down anywhere," I say.

She enters my place and I tell her to have a seat before I remember that the only options are my bed and a wicker chair that loves to give splinters.

She chooses to stand.

I begin to close the door behind her when I hear a voice far too rough to be Candy's.

"Where are your manners, little man? Ain't you gonna invite me in too?"

I look at the empty space of doorway that Candy once occupied. It is no longer empty and we are no longer alone. Count has arrived.

I don't respond. I just stand there feeling my throat tighten as the realization suffocates me. He doesn't say anything either—he just gives a sly smile with only a hint of teeth. He watches my face, waiting for acceptance and capitulation to coalesce in my eyes.

When he finally sees what he's been waiting for, he walks in without my prompting. His linen suit is eggshell white with ash gray pinstripes. The shoes are yellow and reptilian. He seems better attired for a night of roulette in Batista's Havana than a Southern summer day. He looks around my place. The yellow stone of his pinky ring flickers as he rubs his chin with genuine pity.

I turn to Candy, but she looks away defiantly.

He goes over to the table where my phonograph rests. The copy of Candy's dance single is still lying next to it. He picks up the record and strokes Candy's image with his index finger. He looks at me and begins to fan himself with it.

"So you're the one," he says. "Should've known." He looks over at Candy standing in the small space between my bed and the dresser. It's the farthest away from Count and me that she can get without actually leaving.

He throws the record at me like a Frisbee. I catch it and place it on my nightstand, surprising myself with my careful display.

"Little man, things got pretty crazy the other night, huh."

"How do you mean?"

"Oh, come on now. My place gets raided and *you* get pinched. But here you are, lookin' sharp, well rested, breathin' free man's air. But it's funny how there ain't no word of it anywhere. Not in the paper, on TV, nothin'."

"Why would there be? I'm no one special." The sides of my tongue burn after saying that.

"Look at you. You about to fall on the floor after saying that shit. Anytime one of you Martin Luther cats gets arrested, it makes the paper. Speeding tickets, loitering, lookin' funny, walkin' too goddamn slow—it makes the paper. Now one of you Negroes gets arrested in a cathouse, and nobody says shit."

"I don't see your point. I just made bond like everyone else, before someone got wind of it."

"Made bond, huh? Why do I get the feeling there ain't gonna be no court date? You know something, my place has never been raided—never. Too many respectable white men come to my place for a good time. Me and these peckerwood cops got an understanding. So, it's strange that the first time I get raided you're there. And here you are, breathin' free man's air. For a world that's hard as hell on niggers, your black ass sure does get rescued a lot."

"I don't know about that. I guess I'm just lucky."

Count grins. "Good. I'm glad to hear that." He walks over to my window and parts the curtain. Briefly, he takes in the wonderful view of the stairs that lead to the second floor. "Time for me to call in that favor."

"Sure thing," I say while crossing my arms. "What do you need?"

He lets the curtain close and turns back to me. "There's this fighter I used to sponsor. Pulled the nigger out of the gutter, and now he done forgot where his loyalties lie."

"A boxer?"

"Yeah. Got a fight lined up with Boca, but the Eye-talians got to him. Motherfucker's gonna take a dive. Uh-huh. But he don't know that I know, you see?"

"Not quite."

"*Not quite.* Man, you really need to stop talking like that. People'll start thinking you're queer. I need you to convince him not to take that dive."

"You need me for that? Why can't your boys take care of it?"

"When did you become a fuckin' reporter? If they see my boys, then they see *me*. I can't be seen talking to Lester before a fight. It'll draw too much attention."

"That's where I come in . . ."

"Exactly. An upstanding, professional, college-educated Negro like you adds a little bit of polish to my outfit. He'll know that I don't have to use no muscle to get what I want. I can use reason to get him to see how doin' things my way works out in his favor. Tell him it's time to stop being a coward. It's time to be a man. A real man. He's making me look bad. I didn't help his ass just for him to be some organ grinder's monkey. You think all the time and money I poured into him was done just for him to take *dives*? If he's ready to be a real man, then all is forgiven. You give him this to show him I'm serious." He withdraws a bulging envelope from his inside pocket and hands it to me.

"How do I go about such a thing? Where do I go to talk to him?"

"He trains at a place called Uncle Ray's Boxing Club. People know it. You won't have a problem."

"What if he doesn't take the money? How do you know these Italians aren't offering him something better?"

All the humor has left his face. His eyes flash, not with anger but with contempt and disappointment.

"I'm offering him the chance to be a man again. What can be better than that?"

I immediately feel ashamed and I don't know why. "If he does take the money, he'll be worthless to everybody—except you."

He looks at the wicker chair and considers it, but thinks again. "Listen, little man, things happen. I understand. If for some reason you can't get him to do the right thing—"

"Place a bet on this Boca . . ."

"No, goddamnit! You come back with my money. All of it."

I look at Candy, but she's not ready to make eye contact. She's still holding her suitcase with one hand while the other holds her wrist for support.

"Count, can I ask you a question?" I take a moment to stop looking at her and turn to him.

"Go ahead," he says.

"Why does she need the suitcase?"

"Why don't you ask her? She's right over there. Can't miss her in this place."

"I think I should be asking you. You're the man with the answers."

A dull thud comes from Candy's corner. She's no longer holding the suitcase. "Goddamnit. I can speak for myself," she says without any hint of anger or insult, which makes the comment all the more effective. "I have my suitcase because I'll need clothes while I'm in LA . . . making sure that things go the way they are supposed to and helping you if you need it."

Count nods and smiles. "Good job, baby," he says. "Tough, ain't she? Little man, I think she makes a lot of sense, don't you?"

She stares at me, but it's strange how easily I look away.

13

I arrive at the airport and look up at the sky-blue panes covering the terminal's façade. They remind me of tiles shimmering at the bottom of a pool. In LA, swimming pools must be as common as sunshine. Just past the entrance, a stylized mobile hangs from the ceiling: a modern-art interpretation of a phoenix rising from the ashes. Since I'm too busy looking up, I bump into a man walking by. "Hey, watch it, buddy!" He wears a sign that reads: FLIGHT ENGINEERS ON STRIKE! 14 ACCIDENTS—83 KILLED BY STRIKEBREAKERS!

After reading his sign, I apologize. I know how it feels to be taken for granted. I shouldn't care if she makes it or not, but I look for her. We took separate cabs. I don't want to have to explain her to Gant. I see lovers holding hands, trotting to the planes that would carry them to some romantic destination. Is this better than spending the weekend alone? In my mind, I do a strange dance between self-congratulation for being wise to her charade and self-flagellation for allowing myself to fall for it. I should despise her, but I can't help but think that joining me in LA means something more than she is letting on. Maybe Count is the one being fooled. Maybe she's breaking it to him at this moment, which is why she's so late.

I stand there looking at the arched awnings above the terminal windows. Long U-shaped shadows work their way inside. A few cabs pull up to the curb, but they all carry strangers.

As I watch cars and people pass, someone grabs my shoulder from behind.

"Estem, are you ready?"

I look at Gant's face and decide that no matter what happens with Candy, I must spend the weekend with someone prettier than he is. "Yes, sir, I'm always ready." As I turn to follow him, I hear the click-clack of high heels. All of her assets are bouncing in a divine hurry. A lack of punctuality is among her many faults.

There are two men at the front of the plane, one holding a microphone, the other a Bolex camera. They are interviewing Martin as he tries to talk above the loud whirring engines. Gant sits in front of me, talking with Abernathy. It seems important. I probably should do my best to listen and relay whatever I overhear back to Mathis and Strobe, but my mind is elsewhere. I think about that hotel room and Candy waiting on those crisp white sheets. Entrapping her in my fantasy is empowering. What would she be wearing if I had things my way? A corset? Garters and stockings? Maybe nothing but a string of pearls. After I've had my fill, still sweaty from racing across every inch of her body, I'd slip into a robe with the hotel insignia on the breast. Poor girl wouldn't know what hit her.

Even though Count seems to be in control, I'd be a fool not to take advantage of the opportunity that lies in front of me. Candy and I have never been alone without some obstruction. Through every long night in that city there has been *him*. He is that city. She knows that as well. We have both been sent away to run his errands, but she must have breathed a sigh of relief—as I have—just to be free of him, if only temporarily.

A burst of laughter wakes me from my daydream.

"Like Estem," Gant says.

This is followed by more laughter.

Yeah, he does seem like the type!

Again, there is more laughter at my expense. Like a fool, I join in.

We arrive at the hotel later than expected. There was trouble getting through the swarm of reporters who wanted to interview Martin after we landed. When my coworkers are out of earshot, I ask the clerk if Candice has checked in. It's hard for me to contain my excitement when he says yes.

My plan to make a beeline toward Candice is interrupted by Gant's instructions to meet him and the others in Martin's room.

Members of the West Coast chapter of the SCLC are here also. The rest of the SCLC sycophants are laughing at Gant's vain attempt to be humorous, but only after the appearance of Martin's approving grin. He gets competitive around Martin, because he knows the man has a savage wit. I see it as juvenile envy. Martin must see it this way as well, but with his legs crossed, left hand on his ankle, and a cigarette dangling elegantly in his right, he seems unaffected by it. The suits surround him, as Martin assigns nicknames that are both double entendres and biblical in nature. Robinson is Noah, because he likes his women in pairs. Ferguson is Moses because he'll part a sea to reach any woman's Promised Land. Martin is about to bestow me with a nickname when Gant steps in front of me and interrupts.

"Martin, share with us a loving memory of our fallen president," Gant says, smiling.

He seems reluctant at first, but the rest of the group egg him on by cheering and stomping their feet. Martin smiles back and nods. He then proceeds to tell a story about President Kennedy.

"An unnamed senator routinely disturbed the president while he was in the Oval Office. Every morning, the senator would come to see the president, stating adamantly that he had a question to ask of him. But the president would refuse to see him. One morning when the senator came, the first lady was in the Oval Office as well. The president, having grown exasperated, told the first lady to see the senator, and to say yes to whatever he asked. The president said he would hide behind the door and listen while she spoke with him. She agreed."

I want to stop Martin, but I don't. I know Mathis and Strobe are listening, from where, I do not know. The lampshade, behind the mirror, Martin's lighter? It's unclear. But it is clear how Gant laid the trap, and how readily Martin stepped into it.

"*Do you have a vagina?*' the senator asks the first lady. '*Yes, of course,*' is her reply. '*Good,*' says the senator. '*Then will you please tell the president to stop fucking my wife!*'"

The men laugh through the thick wall of smoke and slap each other on their backs. I imagine Mathis and Strobe in their cramped quarters straining to do the same.

I try to slip out of the room unnoticed when Gant reminds me of tonight's soirée.

The plan is to invite her to the event. She has always dreamed of being a celebrity but has never seen any in person. I will change all that. Tonight, I will introduce her to a new world, a different kind of prestige and glamour than she has ever known. Here, among the soldiers of the most important struggle since the Second World War, I have access. Even Count cannot offer her this. I see now that that must be the defining distinction between the two of us. I can't compete with him in the game the he has created. I've been foolish, trying to match his every move. I must focus on the talents that are unique to me. She will love my invitation, not because of my generosity but because it immediately elevates her out of the juke joints and away from the humiliation of being a gangster's mistress. She will feel grateful and indebted to me. She will no doubt try to think of ways to repay me. Unfortunately, I'll have to tell her to remain clothed.

14

I thought about going to one of those boutiques they have out here, getting a dress and surprising her with it, but there was no need. She must have anticipated that I would ask her to accompany me tonight, because she answers the door to her hotel room already wearing a flattering party dress. It's black with a deep neckline and a knee-length skirt. "I'd tell you how good you look," I say, "but you're probably sick of hearing that." She smiles and takes my arm as we head down to the party.

The room is a large, square space. I imagine conventions for insurance salesmen and the authorized dealers of General Motors have been held in this room. The patrons are well dressed, talkative, and influential. Celebrities, politicians, the Adam Chance-Burtons, the Katherine Archer-Fields, and other three-named WASPs bless us with their fame, prominence, and, hopefully, wealth. Gant seems to be holding his breath in anticipation of their generosity.

Candy and I stand silently in the swarm of chatter around us. The conversation ranges from the conflict in Vietnam and the role of religion in a postracial society to that loudmouth Cassius Clay teaching Sonny Liston a lesson.

Martin is on the other side of the room, standing close to the wall while he talks to two other men. I see Candy smiling to herself.

"What is it?" I ask her.

"It's nothing. I just thought he would be . . . taller. But his smile makes up for it."

We are practically the same height, I think to myself, straightening my posture. I'm not sure if she knows, but she has managed to divert

Martin's attention away from the men. He notices that she has noticed him.

I nod at Martin, and he nods back approvingly.

"Is that Harry Belafonte with him?" asks Candice.

I look closer at the men with Martin, and yes, it is Belafonte. Gant always claimed to have many Hollywood contacts. How bloated his ego must be at this moment.

"Oh, sweet Jesus, is that Sidney Poitier?" Candy asks in a breathy whisper.

Yes. Looking at his suit makes me feel like I need a new tailor, but then I look at Candy and I can tell that she loves all of this.

I feel awkward and conspicuous standing here empty-handed, so I tell her that I'll go and grab some drinks. I make my way through the crowd, get to the bar, order two club sodas with a lime twist, and head back to where we once stood. I'm about fifteen people away from her when I see her talking to Martin—and everyone else sees it too, including Poitier and Belafonte. I wonder how those movie star egos are holding up. They probably made a silent wager between the two of them: who will she approach first, the dark knight or the island prince? But they've been outdone by the portly preacher. A silver tongue gets them every time. Martin does most of the talking, and she nods with genuine sincerity and interest in whatever he's saying. I stand there gawking, splashing a bit of club soda on my sleeve as my elbow is bumped by a reckless navigator of the crowd. I should feel jealous, but I don't. I know what's going on and I don't want to interrupt it. Part of me enjoys what's happening here. I've seen her dominated and controlled, never charmed and finessed. It's validating, knowing that he wants something that I have.

I approach them with the drinks. I don't say anything, I just hand Candice her glass and smile at Martin.

He doesn't smile back.

"Well, it was nice meeting you, Candice," Martin says, glancing at me under an arched eyebrow, "but I have to go and mingle with some other people."

"The pleasure was all mine, Dr. King." Candy says as he begins to walk away.

Something about that makes him stop and look back at her over his shoulder before walking away again.

She winks at me and gives me a playful poke in my side. Here she is, standing only a few feet from people of fame and notoriety, and I brought her here. I made this happen. It makes me smile again, but I mistakenly aim it at Gant. He takes this as an invitation and begins to make his way over to us.

I look over Candice with a critical eye. Is her dress appropriate? Makeup just right? Did her hot comb melt away the coarseness of her hair to an acceptable degree? She passes my impromptu test just as Gant arrives.

"My God, Estem. You do make friends quickly." He eyes Candice up and down, examining the contours of her face and cleavage. In his mind, that is what real men do. It's very convincing. How many leading men did he observe to get that look just right? It's sad that he feels he has to maintain such a shameful façade.

"Yes, I do," I respond. "It must be my amiable personality."

He looks at me, pauses for a moment, and then laughs. "No, I don't think that's it." He turns to Candice, and in an admittedly elegant gesture, he offers her his hand. "Aaron," he says, "And now it's your turn."

"Candy." She seems instantly comfortable in his presence.

"Of course it is," he says with a wide grin. "Tell me, Estem. Where did you find this enchanting creature?"

"Oh, we grew up together," Candice quickly answers.

"So you didn't meet at the hotel?"

"No. We're old friends," she says.

"Old friends?" he laughs.

"What? We don't seem like old friends?" she asks.

"No, it's just that—forgive me, but yours strikes me as the kind of friendship that was forged recently, one expected to last *temporarily*. You know what I mean, Estem?" he asks without turning to me.

"Well, sir. No, I can't say that I do." I feel a sudden need to adjust my tie.

"I know what he means," her top lip disappears completely. "He's saying that I look like a whore for hire. You may think you're talking above my head, but I know when I'm being called a whore."

"Oh, I'm sure you do."

A confused and defeated expression conquers her face. Then her eyebrows rise, indicating a sudden realization. "You know, I've seen this before," she says. "Back in school, when the other girls would pick on the new girl for having nice dresses or being too pretty. It was just plain jealousy that made them so mean. But we're grown now. Let's put the petty schoolyard stuff behind us. We *girls* have got to stick together."

"Candice, please," I say.

Gant smiles. "I see I've overstayed my welcome. I apologize if I've offended you. I hope the rest of your evening is pleasant." He grabs my shoulder, still smiling, and leans in, "Discretion, Estem. Discretion. Remember that." I have to hand it to him; he was never frazzled. He seemed completely unaffected by Candy's comment. Calm under fire. I never would have guessed that.

He leaves us and disappears into the crowd.

"Candice, that man is my boss."

"How could you sit there and let him talk to me like that?"

"How could I defend you when you practically called the man a sissy to his face?"

"I said that *after* he called me a whore. I had to protect myself. Sorry, but I'm not used to doing that when there's a man around."

"Don't stand there and act like a goddamn saint. Maybe you're upset because he saw something you see in yourself."

"So now you're calling me a whore too? Oh, excuse me, you're saying I *know* I'm a whore. To hell with this."

As she leaves, I know that I should apologize, but I feel like this is a test. She's angry with me for letting someone else see into our secret world. She's disappointed because I let myself appear to be a coward in front of Gant. That is not the kind of man she wants. I watch her head for the hotel bar. I choose not to follow her. I decide to let the liquor do the hard work for me.

I pass time by walking through the crowd, stopping to hover over the fading remnants of conversations. I look at my watch. She's been at the bar for at least an hour. Enough time to make her forgetful and forgiving.

I leave the event, certain that no one will notice my absence, and head for the hotel's bar.

She is not there. I look around but all I see are a few men, a piano player who should've given up a long time ago, and women pretending to be guests—working girls well past their prime, who should've given up long time ago, too.

I figure she must have gone to her room, so I head there.

I knock on her hotel room door.

"What do you want?"

A bottle of Night Train has made a final stop at her nightstand. She's good and wasted. No wonder she wasn't down there—she's brought the bar to her room.

"Can I come in?" I ask.

She puts her arm up to block the doorway. "Depends on what kind of news you've got."

"I told the son of a bitch to go to hell, and if he ever talked to you like that again, I'd do my best to kill him." I push my index finger against the crease of her arm to move it downward and out of my way.

She knows that I'm lying, but she smiles anyway, showing that she appreciates the effort. She wears only a terry cloth robe. It's carelessly tied, which gives me the impression that she was completely naked only moments before I arrived. Even though the most scintillating parts of her are covered, I can only think of the fading occasion of her bare body.

Men take what they want from her, she once told me. She thought she was with a real man tonight, but I disappointed her. I tell her to take off her robe. She attempts to speak, but I kiss her before she can utter a word.

I guide her to the bed and she offers no resistance. I undo her robe, and even before I've touched her skin, I can feel the heat of her. Every part of her is there and mine for the taking. This makes me nervous, intimidated. Before I realize it, my heart is thumping and I'm breathing hard. She sprawls out at the edge of the bed, and I just place my head on her stomach, feeling the rise and fall of her breathing, like the supple movement of water. I smell her. The mingling of sweat, alcohol, and perfume soothes me. I think I have the courage to move forward.

We are in the throes of passion when I realize that she's just going through the motions and, in a sense, so am I. For some reason, I can only think of the look on my father's face when the doctors told him that there was a strong possibility that the polio would take away my ability to function sexually. He looked as though he had lost a child. I was no longer his son; I was something other: a shadowy reminder of the man his boy would never become. Thoughts such as these, to put it bluntly, have a dick-curdling effect.

What is wrong with me? I have come this far. Her naked body next to mine should be inspiration enough. She also feels this. She sees the trouble I'm having, but she makes no attempt to arouse me. She only looks away, like she's at a horror movie and waiting for the scary scene to end. I do try to save myself from embarrassment: sneaking my hand to my genitals, pretending the touch is hers.

I try to enter her, but no luck.

I'm tired of struggling with myself.

"I'm sorry," I say as I get dressed and take my useless prick back to my room.

I feel overcome by hopelessness. I've just embarrassed myself in front of my only friend. I need to talk to someone. Someone who understands me. I pick up the phone and start dialing. As the line starts to ring, I feel embarrassed and exposed by the number I've summoned. I hang up before anyone answers.

I sit at the edge of the bed and light a cigarette. I trap the smoke somewhere between my throat and chest as I lean back into the pillows. The phone rings. I let out a cough before I rise to answer it.

"What is it, John?" As usual, he's all business.

"Hello, Mathis," I say.

"Hello, John. What's our boy up to?"

There is a long silence between us. The air rustles on the other end of the line. I look at my watch; it's one in the morning back there. Does he sleep in that office?

"Are you married, Mathis?" I manage to ask.

"Excuse me?"

"Married. Do you have a wife, any children?"

"Now isn't the time . . ."

"So there will be a time? A time when this is all said and done, after the winners and losers are designated? Maybe then the two of us could sit down and have a drink?"

"John, I really don't see that happening."

"So we retreat to our respective corners?"

"Could it be any other way?"

"You tell me. What side are you on?"

"I'm on the side that serves the best interests of the country."

"What side is that?"

"The side of order. Stability."

"I see. And fighting for what you deserve—for what is yours by *birth* isn't—" I can't find the words to continue. There is another long silence.

"Yes, John. I'm married."

I apologize for calling so late and hang up.

It's strange how bad habits are the hardest to break at night. Before I realize it, I've dressed myself and made my way downstairs to the front of the hotel. I don't snap out of it until I see that my Cadillac is not here. If I were back at home, this would be one of those moments that ends at Count's.

The doorman tips his cap at a guest as the bellboy approaches him and offers to finish his shift. It's late. I doubt that he'll be tipped much. I watch the two men for a moment, and then I realize that I've run out of smokes. I head to the corner store across the street. They don't have my brand, so I grab a pack I've never seen back home. There's a palm tree under the cellophane, but at least they're menthol.

As I leave the store, I see Gant walk out of the hotel. In all areas of performance, I've been coming up short. I should be watching Gant more closely, putting him at ease, making him feel comfortable so he'll drop his guard and make a mistake. But Candy has distracted me. This may be my chance to make up for lost time. I decide to follow him, but following him on foot won't do. He's too fast. I'm too obvious.

He doesn't spot me. I make my way back into the store and its jaundiced lights. I watch him through the store window. He seems to be in a trance, drawing him into the darkness of downtown. He's not sightseeing. He appears to know exactly where he's headed.

When he's a good distance up the street, I step out and hail a taxi. "Follow that man," I tell the driver, pointing at the solitary figure on the sidewalk. I inform him to keep his distance and drive at a modest speed to prevent us from being spotted.

He walks for a long while. The driver becomes impatient. "How much longer do I have to follow this guy? You can do that sort of thing yourself in this part of town."

"Not much longer," I say. Where is he going? Mathis and Strobe want the goods on him. He could be meeting with his communist counterpart, but other than what the agents have told me, I've seen no evidence of such a connection.

Headlights and neon signs reflect in the sheen of the black pavement. Gant continues to walk, until the atmosphere and surrounding environment begin to take a subtle turn. Swank hotels and banks change into rooms for let, pawnshops, and tattoo parlors with blackened windows. He walks by a young white man leaning against a brick wall in front of Rocky's Pool Hall and Billiards, with his leg bent behind him for support. He wears a leather pilot's jacket that comes to his waist and a fedora that shields his eyes. Gant stops, turns around, and motions with his head toward a nearby alley. I can't confirm from the car if the man is Russian or not, but he could be.

They head into the alley together.

I pay the driver and get out. I then ease to the edge of the wall and peek into the alley. It goes deep into the darkness behind the buildings and then veers to the left. I don't see Gant or the man, so I carefully enter. As I approach the corner wall, two young men scramble out, startling me. They pay me no attention and walk away in opposite directions once they hit the sidewalk.

I take a moment to collect myself, and then I look around the corner. Gant talks to the man, as he reaches into his pocket and looks around to see if anyone is watching. They are backlit by a lamp above a receiving dock at the end of the alley. Their frames cast long shadows that seem to stretch to the street. Gant offers something to the man.

Again, he surveys the area. This time I duck. What has Gant given him? What have they exchanged?

When I look again, I see that no sensitive information or material threatening national security has been exchanged. The man is on his knees in front of Gant. Gant tosses his head back in apparent ecstasy. Gant may be many things, but he is no communist.

Upon leaving the alley, I feel as if I've stepped into another world—one that is strange and off-kilter. I had not noticed before, but they are everywhere: men in clinging T-shirts and snug denim, or leather jackets, or simple plaid. They wait silently, like urban scare-crows, under streetlamps and in darkened doorways. The night is their domain, a snare they've mastered—it must be, because other men, on foot and in passing cars, slow for them as if caught in the net of their vigilant gaze.

I know that urge that sends you wandering into the night, I know it all too well. But for men like me, there are safe havens, places of refuge. Not so for Gant. That photograph, shown to me by the agents, said it all: no place is safe. Someone is always watching. I've tried to hate him, I've tried to believe the worst about him, but the sad episode I just witnessed only evokes deep sympathy for the man. It's disturbing to see someone of his stature relegated to being sucked off in a piss-soaked alley. I feel, for the first time, he's been dealt a worse hand than mine—and I need to walk it off.

I need to reassert my manhood after what I just saw. The walk did me some good, and I feel like I can give it one more try with Candy. But when I knock on her hotel room door, she is merciful and does not answer.

I'm still a ball of unspent energy, and my room can do nothing to contain it, so I head back downstairs.

The bellboy is a young Negro of about twenty. He thinks his uniform gives him an air of sophistication, but I detect in his eye the lessons of the street.

" 'Night, sir," he says looking straight ahead.

I walk over to him. "Where can a man go for a good time?"

"Most colored guests go to Lacy's Lounge."

I need to make him feel more comfortable. "C'mon, Jack. You know that ain't the kinda good time I'm talkin' 'bout."

He doesn't smile. "Oh, I know exactly what you're talkin' about, and you can get *that* at Lacy's Lounge."

I'm not up for the challenge. I walk past him to smoke a cigarette under the awning.

"Hey, man, where you get that limp?" he asks. "Was you in the war or somethin'?"

"Something like that."

"Korea?"

"Not exactly."

I can see him mulling over whether or not to ridicule or pity me.

"Okay, dig this," he takes off his hat and looks over his shoulders. "I can get you another girl, but I can't get you the same rate I gave your friends."

"Friends?"

"Yeah, man. A couple of them cats you checked in with wanted some trim. Them girls was friends of mine working without a pimp. This chick I'mma get for you got a pimp, so she cost more. But she's worth it, man. Believe me. Foreign or somethin'."

It must have been some men from the local chapter. Everyone else is too recognizable, and Gant is out of the question. "What did they look like?" I ask.

"The girls or the two fellas?"

"Forget it. How much?"

"Fifty."

"Fifty?"

"Fifty, and I'll send her right to your room."

"Foreign or something" is an appropriate description of her. Who knows in what arbitrary category Europeans would place her. Her face is round and framed by hair that's a wild collection of corkscrews. She has the fullest lips I've ever seen on a white woman. Her accent is thick and breathy. German, I think. She smiles, but there is a cold detachment in her eyes that I, strangely, find comforting. She undresses without prompting.

Her whole body is trapped in crisscrossing net—a fishnet bodysuit. I've captured a mermaid.

She says she is glad that I'm Negro. She likes Negroes. Negroes have a hidden power. Especially me. She can tell. She says I have a strength that people refuse to see.

My erection presses against my thigh, and I feel the same relief that I felt when I was a teenager and discovered that the doctors were wrong.

15

The next morning I arrive at Uncle Ray's Boxing Club, the gym where the boxer trains. I look around, trying to find him. Men spar, work the heavy bag, and jump rope. They all seem very fit but not in the shape one would expect of someone competing in a heavyweight fight. Then I see him: a man so big and black that he must have been extracted directly from the source of all Negroes and all men.

"Lester Smalls?" I ask over the thud of fist against leather.

He raises an eyebrow in response, never taking his eyes off the rhythm of his pummeling.

"May I have a moment of your time?"

The trainer holding the bag motions for Lester to stop, then walks over to me.

"What the fuck can I do for you?" He's an old black man of about sixty, wiry, and with hair like rounded cigarette ash.

"I'd like to have a word with Lester."

"Lester is in the middle of training. He don't have no words."

"It's important. It concerns his health outside of the ring."

"What? Who the hell sent you?"

"I am a friend of Count's."

He laughs. "Man, you probably the first person in history to say that. Count don't have no friends, just people he ain't killed yet. Now get the hell outta here. Me and my boy got training to do."

"Why are you training so hard if Lester's going to lose?"

"The hell you say?"

"You're right. I'm not Count's friend, but I guess you could say I work for him."

"You? Is the motherfucker cutting corners?"

I feel like it's time to cut to the chase with this simpleton.

"He knows about the dive," I tell him.

The trainer looks around the gym for a response.

"Man, are you crazy? You can't be saying that word in a joint like this. You trying to get us killed?"

"Not at all. I'm trying to help."

Lester looks concerned and makes his way toward us.

"What's the problem, Mike?" He mumbles.

"Nothing, Les. Man says Count knows about the dive."

"That's not good, huh?"

"No, Lester," says Mike. "That's not good."

"However," I say, "Count doesn't want you to lose . . . at least not on purpose."

"If my boy don't go for a swim, them 'talians will see to it he don't come up for air. That's why we left the South, to get out from under small-time hoods like Count. Man, this is Los Angeles! This is close to big time. Yeah, I know it ain't the best start, but you want us to throw it away by getting killed?"

"Look, I don't know your history with Count, but at least with him, your record stays clean. If Lester takes a dive, that's all he'll ever be good for. No matter what they've promised you, there are no title shots after this. With Count—"

"I never felt right about takin' a dive anyway," says Lester, jumping in. "I know I can take Boca. Why can't I just show everybody what I can do?"

"Wait a minute," Mike says. "Lester, you need to think about this. Remember what it was like when we was with Count."

"I remember."

"You remember how he took everything from us? Everything you fought for?"

"I can handle it this time."

"What about Etta? You remember that?"

Lester throws a punch at the bag so quick and loud it could have been mistaken for a gunshot. "Damnit, I said I remember!"

He moves past me, barely grazing my shoulder but knocking me off balance nonetheless. Mike places a stabilizing hand on my arm, then grips it tightly.

"What kind of shit you tryin' to pull?" asks Mike. "You know as well as I do, Count only means him harm. Count only means everybody harm."

The old man's got a grip too strong for his age. It's unreal. "Let go of my arm," I tell him.

"You puttin' some dangerous ideas in his head. Is Count gonna offer some protection if Lester changes his mind? Huh?"

"Look, I just came here to relay a message. Whatever you and Lester decide is up to you. Now, let go of my goddamn arm."

He lets go and I take a step back. I can still feel the phantom pressure of his fingers on my biceps. We lock eyes for a moment, sizing each other up. I weigh my chances of taking him out. They don't look so good. "I've said all I needed to," I tell him. "I'll see you at the fight."

I walk for a long while. It takes some time for the deadbeats and derelicts to fade away and a decent supply of cabs to appear. It seems like you can walk forever in this city and still be nowhere.

I finally hail a cab and hop in the back. I put my hand to my face, trying to wipe away the sweat and frustration of my encounter with the boxer and his trainer. I couldn't care less what Lester decides to do. He's buzzard meat either way. I feel something poke me in the chest. I look at the inside pocket of my jacket and discover the nuisance: a well-fattened envelope. Things got so heated back there I forgot to give Lester the courtesy of hearing Count's counteroffer. Why would Lester listen to me? After I left, I'm sure Mike convinced him to go through with their original plans. It would be a shame to let such an opportunity pass me by. I hold the envelope in my hand, weighing my options.

"Hey." The driver cocks his head toward me without turning around. "Where you going, man?" He has a Spanish accent. Rosary beads hang from his rearview mirror.

I put the envelope back inside my jacket. "Where would one go to find a bookmaker?"

"*Que? Los bookies?* You wanna make a bet, man?"

"That's right."

He looks out the window at passing traffic and then looks at me through the rearview mirror. "Look, I don't speak English so good. You know?"

I know his game, so I retrieve some money from the envelope. "Among other things," I say handing him the money, "Benjamin Franklin was a pretty good translator. You know?"

When I get back to the hotel, Gant informs me that Martin isn't feeling well and that our meetings have been canceled for the day. This gives me some free time, so I decide to see how Candy would like to spend it. But when I knock on her door, she does not answer.

16

I'm glad I stayed in my room tonight. Just cigarettes and a bottle of Thunderbird—hobo's lemonade. I need some time alone to convince myself that I am not mad about Candy's disappearance. I have a mind to go over to her room and break the door down to see if she's still breathing.

Who am I kidding?

That sinister guesswork is only a salve for my ego. She's probably out there trying to become a star. Isn't that how it happens? Country girl with neon ambitions comes to Hollywood, and a handsome movie star dazzles her with celluloid promises. Probably having cocktails right now with Belafonte—no, Poitier—she likes them stony and mysterious.

Yeah, Atlanta ain't Hollywood, and I brought her here.

I hear a deep resonant voice out in the hall. It sounds familiar. I make my way over to the door, open it, and peer out. All I see is a girl walking away. I can't see her face, but I can tell, just by that walk, that she is beautiful. She seems to be wearing a wig—too blond and stiff to be real. She holds her high heels with two fingers hooked inside, and her stockings are now a sheer scarf draped across her neck. My door creaks and catches her attention, but I close it before she sees me.

The hallway air makes me realize the smoke is piling up. I need to air out the room. The window opens to reveal a fire escape and the back of a building that's painted completely black; everything, including the windows, is coated with black paint.

It's a familiar setting. I've seen it in the movies. The weary hero retreats to a fire escape like this one to smoke, to think, and to retrieve wisdom. Always at night, he hovers above the city on an iron cloud, contemplating the chaos and cruelty down below.

I want to go out there, so I put a chair close to the window and put my bad leg out first, followed by my good leg, using it to pull my behind over the sill. I reach out to the railing and pull myself up. Exhausted with my efforts, I reach for my cigarettes—but I left the damned things inside.

I stare at that black wall, its black windows, and take in a lungful of hot air. This is definitely the desert. None of this should be here. But my excesses seem at home in LA—maybe too much.

I look around at the other fire escapes below and above me. I look to my left and then I see him, two escapes away. Of course, we would have the same idea. How long has he been out here? Did he watch me struggle? I try to wave at him casually, but I'm sure it looks exaggerated as I try to maintain my balance with one hand.

Martin waves back and then points at me. "You'd better pray," he calls over to me.

Guilt travels at light speed in the night. His preachy command makes me feel ashamed. I don't like his accusatory tone, so I act like I didn't hear him.

"You'd better pray there isn't a fire," he says louder, and follows with a laugh.

I wonder what the hell he's laughing at, but then I look down and realize I'm just wearing my boxer shorts.

The next night I put on my good suit and head downstairs. Lester's big fight begins in half an hour.

I hail a cab and get in, but someone grabs the door as I begin to close it.

"Move over," Candy says.

I do as instructed and Candy slides in next to me.

"You saw the boxer already, didn't you?"

"I left early. Where the hell have you been? I tried to find you."

"You're trying to do this without me." She doesn't look at me, but at the back of the driver's head. "That's not a good idea. You might need my help."

Her fiery red dress reveals the other night's many missed opportunities.

"Candy, I'm sorry about—"

"Let's just not bring it up. Let's promise ourselves we'll do our best to forget it."

Saying that will make it impossible for me to forget, and she knows it.

"Cosgrove Hall," I tell the driver.

It's hazy and dark inside the venue. A massive cloud of smoke hovers above the crowd. The glowing embers of cigarettes and cigars shine through it, like stars in a distant galaxy. But in this dress, Candy is the brightest star of all. As we head to our seats, the eyes of a few people dance between the two of us in disbelief. Some men are even bold enough to whistle. Others offer me a congratulatory nod.

The bell rings, sounding the beginning of the first round. Boca comes out swinging, but Lester is incredibly nimble for his size. He dodges Boca's right jab and left hook as if this were a choreographed dance intended to make Boca look slow and inaccurate.

Lester counters with a combination that angers Boca. He returns the favor with an uppercut and pummels Lester's body, but even in this flurry, Lester is unfazed. It's like watching someone fighting with an oak tree.

Lester stuns him with an onslaught of punches that nearly sends Boca between the ropes and into the audience.

Candy does not turn away from the punishment Lester administers. She looks on with an interest for the violence you don't see from most women.

Lester toys with him, feigning with his right shoulder and then throwing a jab with his left. It is obvious that Lester has him, but then Lester throws a wide, telegraphed punch, a hook so slow it's practically traveling by stagecoach. Boca ducks and responds with an uppercut that sends Lester to the canvas.

The promise of money starts to whisper in my ear, but Lester has other plans for me.

He doesn't like it down there. He's not used to it. As the referee starts the count, Lester's poor excuse of a mind starts to change. I can see the wheels turning in his head from here.

The crowd shouts for Lester to get up.

Even though she doesn't say it, Candy mouths those same words.

On the count of eight, the mountain posing as a man makes it to his feet. The only thing restricting my panic is that I only bet five hundred dollars, and not the entire two thousand of Count's money. That cab driver gave me a momentary distaste for greed.

Boca is in trouble. Lester punishes Boca's body until he backs him into a corner. He goes to work on Boca's head until blood covers his face. I feel sorry for him—Lester, not Boca—Boca has the ref to save him; I'm not so sure who can save Lester.

Boca stumbles around the ring like a drunken uncle at a wedding. But Lester's not done with him yet. He plays with Boca, slapping him between his giant paws like a lion prolonging the killing of its prey.

Lester pushes Boca into the ropes. As Boca struggles to make it back to center ring, Lester looks at three men sitting ringside. They do not look happy.

Boca's got heart. He agreed to an arrangement, and the bloody mess standing in front of Lester wants to keep his end of it.

Again, Lester looks at the men at ringside. He looks back at Boca but doesn't move. Boca summons up whatever residue of strength he has left and throws a wild haymaker at Lester's head. He puts his weight into it, all 245 pounds of him. Even I could sidestep a shot like that, but Lester waits for it.

Candy's eyes are wide. She covers her mouth.

He hits the canvas unconvincingly. He might as well be crawling into bed. The booing starts.

Boca collapses into the ropes. The only thing keeping him up is that his left arm is hooked around the top rope, but just like the rest of Boca, that left arm is tired too. When it finally gives up, Boca joins Lester on the canvas. The throwing starts: trash, bottles, even old shoes. The referee doesn't even consider counting anyone out and leaves the ring.

Candy and I make our way through the angry crowd and head toward the area that holds the fighters' dressing rooms. LESTER SMALLS is written in black crayon on a piece of wax paper taped to the door. No one answers when I knock, so I walk in and Candy follows. The crowd's anger is still audible inside the room, which is more like a lifesize scrapbook than anything else. Old yellowing posters of small-time boxers and their forgotten fights line the walls: Baby-faced bantamweight Panama Al Brown versus Battling Battalino; and Mickey Rimera versus Percy Clark in the bout that left poor Mickey paralyzed.

Lester and Mike walk in and close the door on the crowd. Lester takes a seat quietly in a corner. Candy eyes his muscles, massive and glazed with sweat. Mike paces while shaking his head. I think of the money I lost trusting this fool.

Lester looks down at his gloves and touches them together. "What am I gonna do?" he finally says.

"I don't know, Lester," I say, "but I'm sure I'll think of something."

Mike stops pacing. "What the fuck you mean, you don't know? You got us into this mess." He moves toward me. "I outta knock your ass out."

I stand firm and look at him over the rims of my glasses. "How did *I* get you into this mess?"

Mike's face is an inch from mine. I can smell the blood and sweat on him. He looks threatening at first, but then his brow relaxes into a concerned expression. "You can't tell Lester too many things at once," he says. "He gets confused."

I look over at Lester. Candy carefully dabs at his face and body with a towel.

"It took me a week to get him to understand that he was to fight hard but still end up losing," Mike says. "He would just look at me and say, 'If I fight hard, how can I lose?'"

I nod at what Mike has told me. Then I look at Candy and Lester again. She unlaces his gloves. Then she picks up a pair of scissors and begins cutting away the tape that covers his large hands. Every now and then, their eyes meet, and Lester looks at her as if she were the only person in the room. Mike is wrong—Lester is not as dumb as he seems.

The door opens and two large men enter, wearing menace as if it were aftershave. A small elderly man follows. He wears a dark double-breasted suit that's well tailored but a little old-fashioned. Large dark sunglasses cover most of his face from brow to cheek. The lenses seem thick enough to double as airplane windows.

"Lester, you disappoint me," the old man says. "Are you Sicilian?"

"What? No, sir. I'm from Georgia, born and raised."

"Lester, you are like the man who stole food from my family back in Sicily. I killed the man who took food from my family." He looks over at Mike, who isn't acting so tough anymore. "Mikey, what's the problem? Didn't you tell me you had everything straightened out with him? You said that. He didn't look so good out there, Mike. *We* didn't look too good neither. He made me look like a fool, and you look like a liar. A liar." He looks at me, then at Candy. "Who's Sammy Davis and Dorothy Dandridge over here?"

Mike is becoming dangerously nervous. He only wrings his hands while looking at his feet.

The old man walks over to me. "Do I know you?"

"No, sir," I say. "We're just Lester's family . . . cousins from back home."

"Cousins, huh?" He lifts up his glasses and looks me over with an eye that's cloudy and scarred from glaucoma or from seeing the worst humanity has to offer. "Is it you? You behind this?"

"I don't know what you mean. We just came to see my cousin fight."

He leans in even closer to me and then inhales deeply through his nose. He brings his glasses back down. "No. It ain't you. Not you." He walks over to Candy, smiling. "Now this little dish here could cause a lotta trouble. Tell me, sweetheart, are you trouble or are you a blessing?"

Candy doesn't know how to respond, but then she decides to turn on the charm. "It depends of what kind of mood my man is in when you ask him."

He laughs. His men laugh. Candy laughs with them.

"You've got a big hearty laugh," she says, pressing her luck. "It's nice and kind. You seem like you know how to be a good friend." She strokes the lapel of his jacket. "So do I."

The unnamed Italian looks at his associates. He smiles, appearing flattered and genuinely tempted. Suddenly, with unexpected speed for someone his age, he grabs Candy by the face. "If I wanted it, sweetheart, I'd take it. You don't get to offer. Now get your nigger hands off my coat."

Lester rises. "You came here for me. I'm right here. Let her be."

"Easy, Lester," one of the large men says as both of them reach under their coats.

"Wait a minute," Mike says, finally gaining the courage to speak. "We did what you told us. He didn't win, okay. Goddamnit, he didn't win."

"Enough!" the old man shouts, pointing his finger at Mike. "You had your chance to talk, Mike. All you had to do was get Lester on board. You screwed up. If I hear another sound from you, I swear to Christ I'll cut out your tongue." His wide lenses are dark mirrors reflecting the entire scene. He turns those big glasses of his on Lester. "Lester, I don't want to see you no more, okay? No more," he says shaking his finger back and forth in front of Lester's face. "LA ain't for you. You understand me? If I ever see you again I'll have your black ass skinned and turned into a punching bag."

Lester grits his teeth, probably thinking of the hundred different ways he could hurt this old man before his men even drew their guns. He thinks better of it and nods instead.

"Good boy," the old man says. "Good boy."

As he goes to leave, he takes one last look at Candy. In a startling shift of demeanor, he says, "Sorry about my hostility, sweetheart, but it comes with the territory. Thank you anyway for the offer. You make an old man feel young again." He reaches toward her face, without aggression, but she recoils. His hand hovers for a moment and then he gently pats her face.

He heads for the door, and his two men let him pass. They walk out still facing us, with their backs to the door.

Candy lets out a pained sigh of relief and starts to cry. I move to comfort her, but Lester has already pulled her close to his chest. He strokes her tenderly with his large, rough hands. The whole thing seems false and comically incongruous to me. I think of King Kong, and a young Fay Wray sitting in his hairy palm.

18

They scrapped the fight like it never happened. They call it a mutual forfeit—nobody wins. Mike wished Lester all the luck in the world, but he insisted they had to part ways. Mike didn't feel it was safe for him to leave from the exit like everyone else, so he squeezed himself through a small window, and just like that, the man who had been like a father to Lester was gone.

I take the long ride back to the hotel alone. Candy's off with Lester, I guess, to make sure he gets home safely. What a difference a few nights can make. I came to LA with the intention of offering Lester a lesson in manhood, but he's shown me a thing or two. Maybe I shouldn't be too hard on myself. Lester is a gladiator. His talent is punishment and survival. In ancient Rome, a woman like Candy would have been his reward. Maybe his time has come around again. That's easy to picture, but where do I fit in?

I spend most of the next day in my hotel room. I don't bother to see if she's in hers. I'm unprepared for the answer, and I am definitely not prepared to deal with Gant right now.

The phone rings a few times, but I don't answer. Instead, I stare at my closed curtains and wait for the day to finish its striptease and shed itself of light.

I throw on some clothes and head to the hotel bar. There's a band preparing for its set. The party girl at the end of the bar does her best to show that she's not interested. It's fine—I'm not in the mood for much other than drinking.

The bartender serves me my gimlet, and I'm already regretting my choice: all bitters and no lime.

"I would ask you to order me one too, but you don't seem to be enjoying yourself."

I am too busy stirring my drink to notice that Candy has found me.

"Can I sit?" she asks.

"Do as you like," I respond.

She starts to talk, carefully making no mention of Lester and the night before. Our conversation is mundane at best, empty prattle to fill the void. It's tolerable. This I can stand, but the way she looks at me has changed. The wavering affection was always there—I could see it—but now she gives me a look of indifference, marked by a high degree of permanence. I fear we have reached the end of our game. There are no surprises to hope for.

She keeps talking. The liquor's starting to sink in, and in my head, I start working on an apology for not being able to fuck her good and proper. As I start to speak, the hotel band begins a mediocre version of "Lover Come Back to Me," and then Lester arrives in a tight, short-sleeved shirt that makes all the men question whether they've successfully completed puberty.

"Mr. Estem?" asks Lester, his thick neck fighting to be free of its collar.

"Lester, please call me John," I say, still looking into my drink. "After all we've been through together, I think we're on a first-name basis."

He leans in close to me and whispers over my shoulder, " 'Bout that money . . . remember?"

He has my full attention now. I never mentioned the money to him; I'd forgotten. Yet he knows. Would Candy bring it up during pillow talk?

"Lester, the fight was declared invalid. Nothing came of it," I tell him.

I look at Candice to corroborate, but she remains silent. Lester's presence has cornered her attention. She gives him *that* look: the look of longing. The look I've offered her countless times.

I turn back to Lester, and he's reciprocating. They are having a moment. A moment so big the room strains to confine it and Lester's frame. Once again, I am on the outside.

"Lester, let me talk to you in private." He follows me to an area just outside the bar, where the hotel lobby ends in a small set of steps.

"John," he says, "is everything gonna be okay?"

I feel compelled to be brutally honest with him. "For your own sake, Lester, get out of LA. At least for a while."

"Where I'm gonna head to? I don't know too many people."

I dislike him more with every simple word. "Go to a bus station. Look for someone with a friendly face. Ask him where he's from, and buy a ticket that takes you there. You'll get to know people."

The sad truth of what I'm saying starts to seep in. He looks at people as they pass, hoping they might offer an alternative.

"I know you're right," he says, looking down at the carpeted floor and its endless sea of fleur-de-lis.

"Of course I am. You can ask Candy—she'll tell you the same thing."

"I always took my advice from Mike. It's strange not havin' him here."

Even with all of his strength, outside of the ring, he's powerless. I would have never imagined that I could feel sorry for someone like him. I reach into my wallet and pull out a few hundreds. I put the money into his hand, big and weathered, like an old gravestone.

"Just take it and go," I tell him.

He looks at what I've given him. "Thank you, sir. Thank you. That's mighty kind of you. But I don't know when I'm gonna be able to pay you back."

"Don't worry about it, Lester. Just be sure to stay out of trouble."

He slowly lifts his head and stares at me. His eyes are surprisingly sharp and lucid for a boxer. "That lady, Candice . . . she yours?"

His glare has the effect of a polygraph.

"No," I answer quickly.

"So it won't bother you none if . . ."

His sudden honorable display irritates me, and I decide to tell him so.

"Don't you think you should have asked me that *before* you spent the night with her?"

"I didn't spend the night with her, Mr. Estem." He looks genuinely surprised. "I mean I ain't gonna pretend I didn't try—but she didn't feel like she was ready. I didn't want to ruin what could happen with us. Plus she said she had to get back to the hotel for somethin'."

I'm not sure what to make of what he's said, but it doesn't really matter; it's pointless for me to be angry. "It's not me you have to worry about, Lester. It's Count."

"Yeah, I figured that. I remember seein' her a couple of times when I was back in Atlanta."

He looks over my shoulder and watches Candy as she delicately strokes the stem of a martini glass. "Guess I'll be seein' ya. Thanks again, Mr. Estem." He makes his way back into the bar to view her technique up close.

"Yeah, Lester," I say to myself. "See you."

I replay the recent events in my head, trying to understand where things went so horribly wrong. But this isn't a matter for the mind, now, is it? This is about instincts, a twang in the gut, this is about flesh, about blood . . . and that mysterious, untrustworthy thing that makes it flow.

Bitterness, resentment, and envy have arrived. Yes, they are here in full force, warming my eye sockets and throbbing at my temples. But part of me, the small part that has grown weary of abuse, is grateful to Lester for freeing me from the routine that Candice and I have prolonged. Our little seesaw game is no longer fun. Lester has added his weight to the other end.

Lester and Candice slow-dancing. Scotch on the rocks. My fourth cigarette. Gant's unwanted hand on my shoulder.

"Elusive creatures, aren't they?" Gant says, while adjusting his pocket square.

"What's that?" I ask.

"Women," he says, nodding toward the misshapen four-legged mammal that is Lestercandice.

"Yes. I guess they are."

"You know the problem with women?" he asks.

I smile into my drink. I'm genuinely interested in hearing his observations on the fairer sex. "No, but please tell me."

He gives me an eager smile. "The problem with women is that when a man gets a lot of women, he's fooled. He fools himself into believing that he's successful. The reason is . . ." He takes a long and deliberate sip from his drink.

"The reason?" I ask.

"The reason is that women, like money, are elusive. For most men, there are never enough women, and there is *never* enough money."

"Is that really a problem with women—or a problem with men?"

"Women *are* the problem with men."

For the first time, Gant makes sense to me.

"Remember why we came here, John. Some of us have forgotten. We came here for the money, not for the women. Keep your priorities in order and you'll be fine."

Thankfully, he leaves.

Regretfully, Lester stays.

I've grown tired of watching Candice and Lester while nursing my drink, so I ask the bartender to send a bottle of scotch up to my room. He nods and looks at me sympathetically. He's watched me watch them: the way I would stir my drink with my finger, wait for the ice cubes to stop circling the glass, then take a sip while watching them over its rim. He's seen it all. He hands me a bottle. Macallan. "Take it," he says. "This one's on the house."

The good stuff; that's what the bartender gave me. I'm tilted, but I only feel tipsy, in a sophisticated sort of way. I lie on my bed and stare at the ceiling while thoughts drift languidly through my mind.

19

There's no sign of Candy when I check out of the hotel. As we head to the airport, I have that nagging feeling that I've left something behind. I'm leaving a mess in Los Angeles, but it won't have a problem finding its way to Atlanta. There's no hope for anything between Candy and me, but I feel obligated to Count. I think he'll notice a few things missing. I was flush when I got on that plane to LA, but now I'm coming back minus two grand and one gorgeous girl.

I walk past the throng of reporters tossing questions at Martin and Abernathy and crawl into the plane that waits on the noisy tarmac. Soon, the deafening churn of plane engines forces me to retreat into myself. Before long, my thoughts are all I hear. What will I do about Count? When will the patience of Mathis and Strobe finally be exhausted? And where the hell is Candy?

I don't remember much of the landing or the ride home. It's as if the plane landed in front of my apartment and let me out at my doorstep. I look around my place. It seems even smaller than when I left. I notice Candy's record still on my nightstand. She doesn't seem to fit in here any longer. I need to redecorate.

I haven't had the chance to unpack my suitcase when the phone rings. Mathis tells me to meet him at the office on Peachtree in half an hour. I'm tired. There wasn't much rest in LA. "I really don't have much to report," I tell him. "Nothing happened out there, Mathis."

There's a long silence on his end. "Are you finished?" asks Mathis.

I offer nothing from my end.

"Good," he says. "Half an hour."

———

I meet the agents at their office and begin the business of lowering their expectations. "I hate to disappoint you, but Gant did not put on his Red shirt while we were in Los Angeles. I didn't see any behavior that could be interpreted as dangerous, or a threat to the stability of our nation, or however you boys like to put it."

Mathis sits reverse in a chair while Strobe stands. He points to a chair a few feet from his, and I sit down. Neither agent seems very talkative, but they stare at me with indifference. I know they're expecting more. I feel guilty about that. My obligation to them is just one more on a long list I have yet to fulfill. Before I know it, I'm offering up every detail—*almost* every detail—of my trip.

"Some members from the LA chapter of the SCLC were there. I'd never met them before. Ferguson and Robinson were their names if I remember correctly." The agents don't reveal any interest, so I move on. "There were a few celebrities there, many wealthy people . . ." Mathis taps Strobe on the knee and motions him toward a large reel-to-reel tape machine in the corner. My eyes follow Strobe and I keep talking. "The fundraising was successful. I estimate we brought in close to fifty thousand."

Mathis holds up his hand for me to stop. "We know all that," he says.

"Of course," I say.

"All set," says Strobe from the tape machine.

"Did you happen to notice any other type of behavior?" Mathis asks me.

"Such as?"

"Behavior that was . . . improper."

"From Gant? Listen, don't ask to me recite those kind of details. You know what kind of man he is. Haven't you boys had enough fun with those photos?"

Mathis smiles dryly. "Not just Gant. What about the others? Abernathy? Young? What about King?"

He's toying with me, testing my loyalty. For him to ask that question shows that he already knows the answer.

"Martin?"

"What can you tell us about his . . . sexual appetite? Does he share your proclivities?"

I'm taken aback by his directness. I never thought I'd ever hear the phrase "sexual appetite" uttered from that rigid slit he calls a mouth.

"I'm not sure I know how to answer that question."

"Just answer it," Strobe belts from the other side of the room as he pours himself some coffee.

Mathis stands and walks over to the tape machine that Strobe has set up.

"Listen to this," Strobe whispers to me. Mathis flips a switch and the reels start a slow spin.

Over the tape's hiss, I hear what sounds like Martin's voice, telling someone how good they make him feel, and to take what they deserve. After this, a female voice offers him encouragement, followed by a second woman who joins in as well.

I feel ashamed finding comfort in knowing that he struggles as I do. A leader of men and a follower of urges, but Martin is above the puritan and the scoundrel. Mathis should know as well as I do that great men deserve a reprieve.

I look down at my clasped hands. "Stop it," I say so softly it gets lost among the whispers of the tape. The recording continues and with each intimacy played, I feel increasingly exposed.

I look Mathis in the eye. "Turn it off," I tell him.

Strobe receives a look from Mathis and stops the machine. "That's from a hotel room in Florida last month. It's hard stuff to listen to, I know," says Strobe. "But you're missing the good part, John. At one point, he's really giving it to her and he screams, 'I'm not a nigger tonight!' Amazing. Those were white girls on that tape," he says with a laugh.

"Okay, Strobe," says Mathis.

"White girls," Strobe says again, looking at me, daring me to challenge his disgust.

"Enough," Mathis demands.

Strobe holds up his hands in concession.

"Listen," says Mathis turning his focus back to me. "We are

redirecting our attention solely to King's behavior—his personal behavior. We think he is beginning to act carelessly. This is a problem for a public figure, possibly a problem for the country. While he's supposedly marching for the freedom of the Negro people, he's held captive by his own libidinous nature."

I give Mathis an expressionless look to show that I am not persuaded. "Okay," I tell him, "you have your tape. What does this have to do with me?"

"You can relate to him, can't you?" Strobe interjects. "Don't you have the same weaknesses in common?"

I let out an exasperated sigh.

"Think about it, John," Mathis says. "Women are the source of many problems for men. What if someone uses a woman to manipulate King? Someone who means us harm. Someone like . . ."

"Someone like communists," I offer.

"Yes," he says nodding, "like communists."

There is a moment when nothing is exchanged between the three of us except looks and the occasional blink.

"Since your duties have changed somewhat," says Mathis, "we'll be willing to increase your stipend by two hundred dollars." Mathis goes over to a file cabinet and opens the top drawer.

"Wait," says Strobe. "I want to give it to him." Strobe withdraws an envelope from the drawer and walks over to me. "Here," he says, "take the money."

I want to tell him where to put that money, but then I remember that most of that money is Count's money. I take the money from him and stand to leave.

"'Atta boy," Strobe says as I walk out.

I get in my car and toss the envelope in the passenger's seat. I need that money, but I haven't decided if Mathis and Strobe will get much in return. I'm in no position to judge Martin, nor would I. Preachers and women of loose morals tend to have an affinity for each other, and Martin is no exception. I hate to admit it, but Strobe had a point when he referred to the "weaknesses" that Martin and I share. Ever since our late-night discussion, I felt a connection with him. It's pleasing to know that someone else has seen it as well.

Martin and I had run out of things to talk about that night. It was past 2:00 a.m. by then, and I'm sure the novelty of chatting with the help had worn off. The conversation had grown stale, as it so often does among men. When that happens, the only thing left to discuss is women. But there would be no macho banter. His mood had already retreated to a dark place.

I looked at his face. Guilt and shame had resurfaced. He appeared as troubled as he had a few hours before.

"A wife can either make or break a husband," he said, but not to me. I was just one of the many shadows in that room. "Part of me acknowledges that I allow myself to indulge in my weaknesses because of her strength—when I am weak, I have her strength to fall back on. When I am falling, she is standing. She understands sacrifice. She understands the importance of the struggle and that all of its participants—those involved directly and indirectly—must accept a higher level of discomfort and disappointment than they would normally. She has to anticipate a high degree of sadness and pain—and accept it." His thumb absently traced the bottom of his wedding ring. He smiled to himself for a moment and then let out a sound that combined a sigh with a laugh. "I knew things had gotten out of hand when President Kennedy called me out to the Rose Garden, presumably to discuss my suspected association with communists. However, the conversation quickly shifted from socialism to sex. He asked me about rumors regarding my sexual habits and could I confirm or deny them. The irony that my interrogator was John F. Kennedy was not lost on me. So I said, 'Mr. President, I'll be happy to answer that, but first, promise me that you'll address the rumors I've heard regarding your sexual habits. Can you confirm or deny them?'"

He laughed, so I laughed too. I felt embarrassed when he suddenly became serious again.

"It's sad that that was the last time I saw him alive. I've often viewed sex as an escape from the pressures of the world, especially the movement. I am by no means a perfect man. I have looked at the gifts that God has granted me and spat!" His eyes became wide, bright, and lit with a prophetic fire that could have belonged to John Brown or John the Baptist. "Do you see, brother? There is a dark beast that hides in us all. No one is exempt—no one. The beast is strong . . . but he is a *fool*. And I have embraced the struggle to suppress it. I have made a conscious effort to accept the challenge when he surfaces, and wrestle him to the ground as Jacob did with the angel."

A startled look seized his face, as if he didn't expect to see me sitting across from him. Without saying anything, he stood up and put on his jacket and hat. I stood up as well. Both of us seemed to be avoiding eye contact. He walked ahead of me and hit the light switch. His office went dark, but the light was on in the hallway, so I could still see him in silhouette.

He turned his head just enough to line up his chin and shoulder. "Most people let the beast in them run amok, John. And they merely shrug their shoulders at the damage left in its wake. America has let that beast run wild. I may not be morally perfect, but we are on the right side of morality. We need to remind America of its moral obligation to accept the struggle within itself. It's not one fight, but many fights that need to be fought. It's America's duty to live up to its promise, in practice and principle, and to accept that challenge whenever it is presented."

I nodded, but he did not see me.

20

My nights have been restless and without event. I still have no idea what has become of Candice or Lester. I've been avoiding Count, and he hasn't sought me out. That makes me nervous. I decide to talk to him in person before my absence makes me look guiltier than I am.

I arrive there early, before they open for the night. Before walking in, I center myself, take a deep breath, and let my eyelids droop slow and heavy. I run my hand over the bulge coming from my breast pocket. I hope it isn't too noticeable. I've brought protection just in case Count gets out of hand. Maybe I can reason with him and appeal to an aspect of his nature that is not atrophied and hardened.

I feel there is something amiss when Count's men let me enter without difficulty or hostility—the closest thing to hospitality for them. I smile, but no one smiles back. Count's henchmen, Claudel and Otis, have taken a defensive stance. Count, seated at one of his tables, simply leans back in his chair. Then I see Lester. He acknowledges me with a nod and then turns back to the task that I have interrupted.

"Like I was sayin'," Lester says to Count, "you need to leave Candy alone. She's mine now."

"Listen to this shit." Count looks at me and laughs. "She ain't yours. The reason you have her is because *we* let you borrow her, motherfucker." Count winks at me. "Ain't that right, little man?"

I'm scared—no, embarrassed—for Lester. He has no influence outside of the ring. Count may have inferred that we are on the same team, but he's the master of a sport in which he's the only player.

"Me and him don't like you comin' in here all ungrateful and whatnot. Especially when your big dumb ass is only alive 'cause I allow it."

"She's with me now 'cause she wants to be mine. But she's afraid you'll stand in her way. She wants to open up her heart to me, but she's sacred of what you'd do to her."

"Goddamn, this dumb bastard is a riot. Did you practice this shit? Did you stare at your stupid face in the mirror, cryin' and snivelin', 'She want to be with me but she scared.'" Count laughs, then moves his hand from under the table, revealing a pistol that's been aimed at Lester this whole time. "You damn right she's scared. But she ain't scared of what I'm gonna do—she scared of what she gonna do without *me*. How she gonna take care of herself? You? A washed-up boxer? I feed her. I clothe her. I take care of her like she's my child. You just babysitting, nigger."

Lester takes a moment to weigh the logic of what Count has said.

Claudel and Otis seem as if they are ready to make a move, but Lester gives them a brief look that promises a lifetime of pain. Lester tries the same look on Count, but he does not seem intimidated. More like hungry and aroused.

"You and me already been through somethin' like this before," Count says. "It didn't work with Etta and it ain't gonna work now. You know how this ends, Lester—with a win for me and you kissin' the canvas."

"You just stay away from Candy. Just let her be." Lester turns suddenly to me. He startles me, and I step back, putting too much weight on my bad leg. I almost fall, but he grabs my collar—for menace or support, I cannot tell.

"Mr. Estem. Keep him away from her. I know you care for her, even though she don't want you like she want me. There's still a place in her heart for you." He grabs my shoulders, straightening me up. "I really am sorry 'bout all this," he whispers. He gives Count one more threatening look and walks out.

Claudel and Otis relax their shoulders in relief.

Count places his pistol on the table and stares at me.

I lean against the bar, still littered with beer bottles, shot glasses, and dirty ashtrays. "Well," I say smiling, "at least Lester didn't take a dive . . . not exactly. I tried to talk some sense into the man before he threw away his life by crossing you, but he's hard to get through to, as you can see. I thought you should hear it from me before you heard it somewhere else."

Count sits quietly with his index fingers and thumbs forming a triangle. His men look at each other and smile.

"Just thought you should know," I say again.

"You thought *I* should know?"

For some reason, I nod a little too eagerly.

"There isn't a thought in that peanut head of yours that I don't allow to be there."

"Tell 'em, Count!" shouts Claudel or Otis, I can't tell which.

Count stands up and begins to unbutton his shirt. "When I give you a list of chores, you'd better check 'em off like a good little boy."

Again from the goons, "Yeah, like a good little boy."

"Look at my back." He removes his shirt and shows me a patchwork of scars across his shoulder blades. "A white man did this to me when I was a boy. Caught me tryin' to steal chickens to feed my family. I still thank him for it, though. Changed my life. 'Cause that's when I learned to stop tryin' to make it in his world—I learned I have to make my own. You are in my world now. I'm a *hunter*, and boy, you are scarin' the game away. You know what that means? You takin' food out of my mouth! You causin' me to starve. And starvin' . . . that's a *slow* death. Is that what you want? You want me to die a slow death?" He folds his shirt neatly on the table. He then grabs his pistol and cocks it at my temple. "Is that what you want? For me to die slow? 'Cause I don't wish that on you. I want you to die quick as hell."

"Count, I apologize. I apologize." He takes the gun away from my temple and pushes me with his free hand. Hard. My back hits the floor.

"Who do you think you're talkin' to?"

He answers his own question with a kick to my ribs.

"If you did somethin', you damn sure did it for yourself."

A heel in my abdomen.

"I take you in, try to show you the ropes. I lent you my girl and she comes back loaned out to somebody else!"

I roll over. The contents of my breast pocket put pressure on my chest. I remember what I've brought for him in case something like this might happen. I turn over, yielding something that should quell all this violence.

"I still have your money," I groan, holding up the swollen envelope the agents had given me.

Count slaps the envelope out of my hand. Bills scatter everywhere like falling leaves. "It's all my money," he says as he steps on the hand that had held the envelope.

I receive a stomp to my braced leg. It's not from Count, which I would have accepted, but from one of his minions, which I cannot accept.

"Get up," Count tells me.

I think about that night in the alley while I struggle to my feet. I made a promise to myself after that first encounter: given the opportunity, I will hit back—and hit harder.

"Are you Otis?" I ask the one who kicked me.

"Nah, I'm Claudel, faggot."

I grab a beer bottle off the bar and I swing it across Claudel's head. That first swing causes a dull thud like a slab of meat hitting a butcher's block. Claudel is dazed and stumbles back. The second swing causes the bottle to crack. He falls to his knees. The bottle breaks in half on the third swing, forming sharp, jagged edges. I continue to swing. Swings four through ten slice his face; lacerations drool blood.

Otis points his pistol at me, but Count fires a warning shot with his own gun.

"Let it be, Otis," says Count.

My foe lies defeated. I stop when the blood comes. Claudel writhes on the floor and holds out a pleading hand, while the other tries to stop his face from bleeding. I'm in a mind-numbing haze of exhilaration. Never have I felt *this*. An overwhelming feeling of contentment brings me to tears.

Count comes to me, embraces me, and kisses me on my forehead.

"Welcome home, little brother. Welcome home."

I sit at the bar with Count and sip whiskey to stiffen my leg and loosen the knots kicked into my stomach.

The rag Claudel holds to his face is already soaked with blood.

"That ain't right," Otis whispers to Count, "sittin' there havin' drinks with the man after what he just did to Claudel."

"I don't need you to tell me what's right, Otis. Now go take Claudel to have his faced looked at."

"Come on, Claudel." Otis guides him out by the arm. Claudel mumbles something to me, but it sounds wet and muffled through his rag.

"Tell me why I shouldn't kill her," Count says to me.

I think for a moment, placing myself in Count's shoes. It's hard to come up with a defense of her life, let alone Lester's. Even though she owes me nothing, part of me wants to see her pay. Still, there's another part that wants to save her.

"That's not the way, Count. That's not the way to teach her a lesson. Let her live. She'll see that life is not much without you. Lester's ruined his boxing career. No fighting for him—watch him suffer. It won't be long until she comes to her senses. She'll think of the world you created for her and she'll feel like a fool for leaving it. Let her live, and she'll come back to you."

Count tosses back his bourbon so fast and easy that I don't even see him swallow. He slams down the glass and covers it with his palm. He looks at me—into me, past my eyes, and directly at the part of me that, until now, I was convinced remained hidden. "Remind me," he says, "to never get on your bad side."

It felt good to send Claudel to the hospital, and I slept well last night. But it's morning, and the thrill has already gone. I've often wished for the courage to stand up to my tormentors and respond with the same level of violence that they use to threaten me. But what have I really done to rid my life of monsters? Mathis and Count have asked me to do terrible things, and I've offered little protest. They know I will comply. Their trust is the biggest indictment of my character.

I head to the office and learn the news. Last night, I cut a man's face open and Martin has been nominated for the Nobel Peace Prize. But Martin's executive staff doesn't seem as jubilant as one might expect. In fact, they don't seem jubilant at all; they look frantic, distant, and downright scared.

Gant walks by without acknowledging me. His eyes are large and troubled, as if he's escaping some unseen atrocity.

I look back at the secretaries up front. They all seem to be fine, getting an early start on the day's gossip. As I head to my office, Abernathy and Young exit the conference room with the same look of fear expressed by Gant.

The door to Gant's office is open. I look in. He stands behind his desk rubbing his temples and brow with one hand.

"Mr. Gant, is there something wrong?" I ask.

He stops the rubbing and looks at me. "No, Estem. Everything's fine. Close the door, please."

"Sure thing."

"Wait a second. . . . Estem, come in here and have a seat."

I do as instructed, closing the door behind me.

"The only reason I'm telling you this," he says, "is that I don't want to be alone in my horror."

Immediately, I feel uncomfortable, but I nod, urging him to continue.

"Martin received a letter this morning. The letter was sent anonymously but it spoke in detail of his personal life—transgressions in his personal life." He looks pained. He sighs and sits in his chair. "The letter said all these details about his personal life will be made public if he doesn't kill himself within thirty days."

He looks at me to share in his distress, but all I can manage is an expression of even-keeled solemnity. That letter may have been sent anonymously, but one monster can identify the work of another.

A grave mood dominates the office for the rest of the day. My knowledge of the tape, and now the letter, makes the hours pass in a torturously slow manner. My coworkers don't know how close they are to the author of that letter, just one degree of separation. There was a time when such an act of dissemblance would have been satisfying, but now I feel guilty. Maybe there is still hope for me.

I need a cigarette. I don't want to smoke with the rest of the staff and listen to them talk about Martin, so I step out back behind the building.

I pull out a menthol, but I smell smoke before I've even struck a match.

"Don't look so down, John," Martin says, exhaling smoke and tapping off ash. He has managed to stay positive, even if it is for our benefit and not his own. "You look as if you've just left my funeral. It's not just me," he says smiling. "All of us are in danger."

I stare at him blankly.

"They think we all look alike, brother, so we're all in trouble."

We both laugh.

"You're especially in trouble, since we're the same height. They might confuse us. But don't worry, John. When your end comes, I'll be sure to preach at your funeral."

The thought of that fills me with both honor and fear. He seems so comfortable talking about death. I don't have that kind of courage. I wouldn't know how that feels. "Thank you," I say, managing to smile.

"Would you care to hear a preview?"

"Of course."

He takes a wide stance, adds a solemn weight to his eyes, and lifts his head slightly as if regarding an imaginary congregation. "John Estem was a fine young man," he says in that exaggerated preacher's drawl, "but he thought that all the women in the city should like him. He had to be sharp every hour of the day. He bought sharp suits and wore them as pajamas, just in case he met a fine woman in his dreams."

Again, we both laugh. Maybe he laughs a bit harder than I do this time. It has been a while since our conversation that night. He must have felt that he shared too much, because he has been especially indifferent toward me since then. I'm probably partly to blame. I do have an intensity that can be off-putting. He probably sees how I look at him with the strained objectivity of a psychoanalyst: the look of someone who knows too much about you—much more than you'd like—but doesn't want it to show.

"Congrats on the Nobel," I say, trying to make sure my thoughts maintain a positive tone. "Is pride a sin in this instance?"

"Thank you, but please note that I haven't won anything yet."

"But still, just the idea of being nominated . . ."

"Man gives awards, John. God gives rewards. The eyes of the world were on us before, but from now on they will be wearing their spectacles." He pauses as if taking a moment to contemplate what he has said.

Even while trying to give him the deference he deserves, I can't keep from thinking of that tape and how we are so much alike. We are reckless in similar ways, and we are both headed for a dangerous end.

"How is that lady friend of yours?" he asks. "What was her name?"

He's been thinking of her.

"Candice. She's fine."

"How serious are the two of you? Are there any plans?"

I consider lying to him, but I don't see the point and I don't have the desire.

"We're not serious at all. We're just old friends."

"I see." He must sense something from me that troubles him, because he quickly becomes somber. "You have a nice evening, John," he says without a smile.

"You do the same, Martin."

He stamps out his cigarette and heads back into the office.

I'm not ready to go inside, so I light up again.

22

It's night, and my routine is broken. Until sunrise, it's just my robe and whiskey. Normally, I would be at Count's, admiring Candice or spending money on her stand-ins, but Lester has her locked away, and the agents have me paranoid that I may be performing in front of an unwanted audience.

It's as if I'd heard myself on that tape. Like Martin, I foolishly believed that my shameful indulgences were out of reach, unseen, that their lifespan was extremely short, that they died in the shadows almost as soon as I had given them life. But these agents have the power of resurrection and omniscience. They are moving closer and closer to becoming deities. Martin is a man of God, but he is just a man.

As I take a sip of my drink, I hear a car horn outside. I tighten the belt of my robe and peer out of the window. It's Lester, standing in front of a shiny yellow taxicab.

I open the door. "What is it, Lester? Please don't tell me you've taken a cab here and don't have the money to pay him."

"No, Mr. Estem. Not at all. This here is my cab. Got me a job driving it. Sorry to pop up on you like this. Candy told me where you live."

I let out a sigh that smells of scotch.

"I just want to tell you in person that I'mma pay you back every penny. That's why I got this here job. Also, I want to apologize, man to man, for what happened with Candy and all. Me and her is real close. She tells me everything, and she told me how love-struck you was for her. I know how it is to love a woman who don't love you back. She told me how you don't have any friends and how few people got respect for you. But I'm here to tell you that you got me as a friend now. And I respect you. Anything you need, you just holler. Me and you is friends now. Okay?"

I don't believe him. This is a man who laid many traps in the ring, tricking his opponents with false intentions. Maybe I'm being overly suspicious, but not without reason. I've seen this look and heard these words before. The smile and false declarations of friendship: I know what lies behind them. It's strange, but I sense intimidation behind his kindness.

I look at his small driver's cap with a head like granite underneath. Muscles bulging through his shirt, he has the shoulders of a statue. The sight of this man saddens me: a physical specimen gone to waste. An athlete with promise, but through the bad luck of unfortunate associations, his potential has been squandered. I force a smile when I think of his earnest effort to take care of Candy. Maybe this is the kind of man she needs—someone who would sacrifice and embarrass himself for her. He is not an aggressive negotiator. He does not threaten you with violence, but he wins you over with his honest simplicity. Is this what being a muscle-bound child brings you? I should want him out of the picture, but his guilt about stealing Candy is endearing . . . although I must admit I feel compelled to use him to my advantage.

It has been a few days since I've seen the agents and they played their tape of Martin. I have not contacted them. When my phone rings, I don't even answer it.

I haven't been to Count's either. Just work and dry nights. I don't want to see Claudel's scarred face. Part of me is ashamed of my savage actions; the other is afraid I might gloat.

There's a knock at my door. My heartbeat surges. I have changed for the worst. Curiosity doesn't enter my mind, because I already know it's the promise of danger that has come calling. Without hesitation, I go to receive it.

Claudel stares at me. Silent. His forehead and cheeks feature three long wounds that look like pairs of pink lips stitched together.

I look at him, readying myself for whatever he has to offer.

"Cut me up pretty bad, huh," he says.

"Looks that way," I say.

His eyes narrow and his fingers curl into fists.

I am not afraid.

"Count wants to see you," Claudel says. "He's waitin' in the car."

I close the door on Claudel, and then put on some pants and shoes. Count's car is across the street from my apartment. He sits in the backseat. When I approach the car, Count opens the door. "Get in," he says.

I do as instructed.

He motions for Claudel to wait outside, then gives me a knowing smile. "Don't worry about Claudel. A face like that is good for business. Felt like you needed to hide in your hole, right?"

"I just needed some time to myself," I answer.

"Yeah, things ain't never really the same after the first time you bring a man close to his death. But just like most of the hard things in life, you learn to accept it."

I pray that day never comes.

"I want you to know something. Even though your behavior has been real shitty lately, I forgive you."

"You want me to apologize again?"

"Did I say that? Just shut up and listen. Even though your little fuckups have been costin' me money, I've decided to cut you some slack. Candy and Lester? I'll give you a pass on that too. You've really pissed me off, but I realize I've been thinkin' small. Now I'm startin' to see the bigger picture. Do you know what that bigger picture is?"

"Please, indulge me."

"That little goody-two-shoes preacher you work for has been makin' a real name for himself." He flashes a wide death trap grin.

"Yes, Martin is becoming very popular."

"Yes, Martin is. I bet a lot of money comes across his fingers."

"Money? That's ridiculous."

"Ridiculous, huh? Speeches, books, TV appearances, and you tellin' me he's not rakin' it in?"

I can already see the target on Martin's back. But am I fast enough to push him out of the way? "Yes, his fees are high, but that all goes back into the movement."

"The movement?"

"That's right. He takes just enough to live on. The rest goes toward the operating costs of the SCLC."

"So he puts most of the money back into this organization?" he asks under an arched eyebrow.

"That's right. He has nothing."

"But the organization, this . . . SCLC has all the money?"

"Yes, but . . ."

"So the SCLC is really bein' carried on King's shoulders. If something was to happen to him—I mean if for some reason he wasn't so popular no more, then . . ."

"What are you saying, Count?"

"I'm saying it's in the SCLC's interest that he stays popular."

"He will."

"No doubt. But what if somebody had some info on the preacher— some info that he didn't want made public. SCLC might want to pay to keep that kind of info under wraps."

He might as well be sniffing the air. He smells blood.

"Well, it's a good thing there isn't any information like that out there."

We stare at each other while he gauges the weight of my lie.

"C'mon, man what's he into? Boys? Girls?"

"The SCLC wouldn't pay a dime out of pride."

"Considerin' the generous contribution I've already made, it's a good thing I've got a man on the inside to convince them otherwise."

"Count, I think you're going about this all wrong. What about that field trip to Bozley Park? If I recall, you were the optimist that night."

"I don't need you to remind me of my plans. I didn't forget about Bozley Park. This has everything to do with that. Look, this is my way of hedging bets. Call it my integration tax. You see, that preacher of yours, he wants a nigger-free world, one where colored folks can do whatever white folks can do. I lose money in that world. I make money when the white man keeps his foot on the black man's neck. Negroes come to see me to forget what's out there. They come to me. Some white man been giving you a hard time while you been driving him around all day? You come to me for a drink, maybe a game of craps.

You want a woman—maybe a white girl, a taste of forbidden fruit? You come see me. I get it for you 'cause you can't get it out there. I'm God in this world. Niggers need me and I need niggers."

I feel as if I've emerged from a basement illuminated with a thousand lightbulbs. When did the world become such a dark place? How could I have guessed that the interests of the Count and the FBI would someday be aligned?

I look at him, maybe with too much pity. "Count, I think you're wrong. Martin is not a threat to you, at least not in the way you think. Negroes don't go to your place to feel like white men—we go there to feel like men."

Through the window, Count watches Claudel pace in front of the car. "I think we're saying the same thing," he says.

"Maybe, but I'm not interested in having any man's foot on my neck. Surely, you can understand that."

He lets out a loud deep laugh, almost theatrical, operatic.

"You don't owe him nothing," he says. "What, you think you and him is friends? You think you're some type of civil rights leader? You're not with them—you're with me. Me and you are the same. That's your problem, little man, you don't realize you're one of us. You still got yourself caught up in some bourgeois Negro dream. You want to be an accountant, a respectable member of the Negro community. Nice car. Nice house. You dream of a day when you can walk down the same side of the street as a white man and he'll tip his hat at you as if you were the same as him. That shit won't happen. There ain't no place out there for you as some Negro professional. You bourgeois Negroes still believe in some fantasy of a black paradise, where all the businesses and the banks are Negro, and the money is Negro too. That's a dream. All the assets of all the Negro banks combined can't match a country bank in Kansas. Look around you. Open your eyes. You throw cocktail parties, society parties, and debutante balls, and you speak proper English, hoping that a white man will look at you one day and say, 'You know what? These darkies ain't so bad.' It won't happen. Stop believing in fantasies. There's only one Negro business, and that's vice. I'm talking dope, liquor, gambling, and pussy. That's big business, little man. That's how a nigger makes some real money in a white man's world. That's how you get your pockets stuffed. Real money, not this fake shit you motherfuckers chase. Meanwhile, I'm over here making real money, providing real services. My customers come to me with confidence. They can relax, because they know I'll be here night after night. When they put down their money for a good time, they're investing in their sanity. I don't know what you Negroes believe in, but it's a fucking dream. I don't mean to be so hard on you, little man. I understand your motivations. Even though we have different approaches, we want the same things. I'm just trying to show you the right way to do it. You've got to think realistically."

"Thank you for your candor, Count. Maybe you're right. You've given me a lot to think about. But I need a chance to work it over."

"Take your time." He gives me a look that tells me I'm dismissed, and I get out of the car. Claudel takes a step toward me, but I keep walking.

The last few days have overwhelmed me with a feeling of aimlessness and confusion. Mathis and Count have asked me to choose sides, but wasn't it they who offered me prosperity and inclusion? Hasn't my choice always been clear?

23

When I arrive at work the next day, everyone is already heading home. They're closing the office for the day. This time, no one tries to pretend everything is all right.

Gant tells me what's wrong and places a consoling hand on my shoulder. He must think my exasperated look is directed toward him, because he walks away without saying another word. Martin didn't even show up today, and with good reason.

I get in my car and drive. I drive for a while. I don't know where I'm headed, until the buildings start to look familiar and I realize I'm approaching the agents' office.

I sit in my car for a moment, just staring at the building and the windows that reflect the action on the street but reveal none of what's going on inside.

What will I do once I'm up there? Give orders? Demand answers? I don't know. I decide to surprise myself.

I make my way up the stairs slowly, one step at a time, gripping the railing so tightly that my forearm starts to tremble. But I am not in a rush. The old man says I don't have enough steel in my spine. I want to take my time and give my anger a chance to harden. I start to sweat as I drag my dead leg and all its metal up those steps.

I'm still sweating, but not tired, by the time I reach the second floor. I wait for a moment outside the door of the agents' office, to give myself a chance to regain my composure. I can see their silhouettes lurking behind the beveled glass. I reach for the doorknob, but quickly withdraw my hand. Their blurred frames have stopped moving. They seem to be looking at me from the other side. It's as if they see something equally dark and misshapen as well.

I open the door without further hesitation.

They look at me without a flinch or tell of surprise.

Mathis sits with his legs crossed, while Strobe stands and stares with his hands tucked under his armpits.

"Well, if it isn't our man in the dark," Mathis says, rolling a pencil between his fingers. "I hate to say it, but after all the money you've received it's good to see you sweat."

"How could you do such a thing?" I ask Mathis, not blinking.

He stares back at me, eyes surveying my face. "I don't know what you're talking about." He smirks a bit.

"The tape," I say. "How could you send that tape to his wife, for God's sake? Don't you have any decency?"

Strobe laughs. "You're asking *him* if he has any decency?"

I swallow and push my glasses up higher on my nose.

"Listen, John," he says. "I was just doing my job."

"Just doing your job? That's funny, because I remember a certain night in the backseat of your car when you told me that an agent's job is purely investigative. How the hell is this investigative?"

"Okay, you just watch your tone. You be careful right now . . . be very careful." Mathis stands. I've always thought of Strobe as the muscle, but now I'm not so sure. The menace in his voice is real and can't be ignored.

"Just tell me what's going on here. You told me I would be helping to protect the country from *communism*. You wanted me to see if *communism* was infiltrating the SCLC. What the hell does this have to do with communism?"

"Get off of your soapbox, John. You know exactly what this is about. The United States government has the FBI, the CIA, and the goddamn army. Do you think we really need a crippled Negro to stop communism? This is about your ego. The agenda has changed. Deal with it."

"The agenda has changed to what?"

"If I decide to tell you, I will tell you. At the moment, I don't feel like now is the right time. You need to understand that you will continue to do as I say, when I say, and as long as I see fit. You have no other choice. I work for J. Edgar Hoover, he works for the president, and you work for me."

I almost feel sorry for the man. I work for him? He has no idea what line he's crossed. I turn to walk out, replaying the events in my head. I ask Mathis why he is doing this, but the truth is, I already know. I had hoped I was indulging in some macabre misjudgment, but I am not. The FBI wants to destroy King, and Mathis wants to use me to do it.

Strobe walks over to me feigning innocence. "I know this is hard to accept, John, but you must accept it. You and I both know that your beloved reverend is a reprobate. You know that, don't you?" Strobe places a hand on each of my shoulders. "One of the other agents interviewed a Vegas prostitute—a regular and reliable source. She says she spent the evening with King once, and he got pretty forceful—downright violent—with her. 'He hurt me so bad I'll never see him again.' Those were her words. It seems Mr. Nonviolence likes it rough."

I shrug my shoulders to get his hands off me. Strobe smirks, then turns to Mathis and asks, "Can I play him the one from LA?"

Mathis, now seated, gently strokes his chin and nods.

The tape clicks to a stop. I try my best to appear unaffected by it, but I am troubled. For some reason, this recording of Martin has begun to haunt me. Already my mind has chosen to replay it.

"Say something, dammit," shouts Strobe. "Is that enough for you?"

"Look at the two of you," I say. "I've never seen you so . . . invigorated. You seem outraged, but you're enjoying this. Is there some sort of FBI commendation for distinguished Peeping Tom?"

"You heard that tape. You heard it," says Mathis. "That's the man who wants to be the moral conscience of the Negro and dictate America's moral obligations. You heard that tape. That man is a danger to himself, and with his power and influence, he's a danger to the country. So the mission has changed from assessing perceived influences to administering immediate intervention. Can you take your dick out of a hooker's snatch long enough to grasp that? Now look,

John. None of us are saints. And despite Hoover's desire to appear so, neither is he. But you have to give the man some credit. He has restraint. And, despite whatever his dark desires are, and we all have them, he keeps his in check. He's dedicated himself to the American people—that comes at a price. I think it is in the best interest of the country that King knows that he's being watched, not just his public persona, but his true self. It has been seen, witnessed, and documented, and he needs to know that."

His true self has been seen. I mull this statement over.

"John, no one's forcing you to do anything. It's important that you understand that. Since we've met, you've been allowed to make your own choices. Now I am asking you to make another one. If King engages in any reckless activity, will you tell us? You can say no, but you should remember our financial arrangement. Once you leave our protective bosom, it'll be cold out there. And you know that among Negroes there's no warm places for a—what's that expression? An Uncle Tom."

"You have your tapes. You've sent your letter. What do you need me for?"

"I'm not sure what letter you're talking about, but the FBI can't go around recording citizens engaged in private acts and then make the tapes public," says Strobe. "It's beneath us."

"Personal accounts are more convincing. Are you with us, John?"

Be smart. Bluster and indignation won't work on them. It never has. I need to stay put until I can think of a better move.

"Yes," I say. "I'm with you."

For a moment that seems to satisfy Mathis, but his attention shifts to the door and the mysterious figure lurking on the other side of it. No one moves. Whoever it is we can hear him breathing. The doorknob turns, producing a clinking sound that makes its handler stop and try it again. This time, the door opens slowly.

Mathis jumps up and turns over his chair in the process. Strobe reaches for his gun. The old man, a Negro holding a mop in a bucket, is silent and still.

I give the agents a pitiful look, and the old man a comforting pat on the shoulder. "You should get that lock fixed," I say as I walk out.

24

The room is smoky and appointed with dark wood and leather. A cone of light shines down on us through the nicotine cloud. Martin puts his arm around my shoulder, bringing me closer to him. "Thank you," he says, patting my chest with his free hand.

There is an audience—all of them men, and all of them in gray suits, but their faces are blurred like fogged glass.

I put my arm around him to complete the embrace, but when I bring back my hand, I am holding a letter opener with blood on the blade. I look at the weapon, then at him. His look of horror mirrors my own.

I open my mouth to apologize, but my voice does not follow; the only sound I make is a loud mechanical shriek.

My phone rings. I yawn and roll over to answer it. My mother greets me with a long empty sigh followed by silence.

"What's wrong, Mama?"

"Talked to Mrs. DePlush the other day. You remember her, don't you? You went to school with her daughter. Hope I didn't wake you. Thought you might still be up, being a night owl and all."

"Mama . . ."

"He ain't come home yet."

I look at my clock—damn near two in the morning.

"Don't worry about it, Mama. Go back to sleep. I'll go get him."

I get dressed and then start the long drive out to Mike's bar. I hate that he's gotten me out of bed for this, but there is a certain pride I feel in coming to my father's rescue—running out into the vast and deep uncertainty that lies hidden in the night, saving him from drowning—saving him from himself.

I walk into Mike's and look around at the desperate, lonely souls, a bunch of buzzing barflies that have lost their way inside a maze of wonder, temptation, and danger and have forgotten how to get back outside. They are all white, except for the one Negro sitting at the bar by himself.

Mike comes from around the bar and stops me at the door. "Look, I don't want any trouble. We already got one in here and that's enough. Not everybody is as . . . progressive as I am."

I look away from Mike's big broad shoulders and barrel chest and into his eyes so that he can see my face. "It's me, Mike."

"Oh. Hey, John," he says. "Sorry about that. He's at the bar."

Mike's an ex-con who used to work for my father's landscaping business. When he got out of jail for manslaughter, my father was the only one who would hire him. Eventually, Mike was able to save enough to open a pawnshop, grease some palms, and open this bar. He was always grateful to my father for giving him a job that didn't require him to degrade himself completely. Mike repaid him by letting him come into his bar, even before segregation had begun to weaken. But that situation lets me know just how much of an unjust world this is: a white ex-con can buy a business and a bar and condescend to my father by letting him come in here and drink himself to death.

I go over and take the stool next to my father's. The man on the other side of me is already sloppy-drunk. He finishes off his drink with a hard swallow and slurs, "Who keeps leavin' that door open? All these goddamn flies keep comin' in here."

Mike grabs a mug, holds it under the spout, and wrenches open the tap. He turns to the irritated man and slams down the mug so hard it sends a small wave of beer onto the counter and into his lap. "This one's on the house," says Mike. "Drink up."

The drunk gently brushes off his lap, picks up the drink, and before tilting it toward his lips, says, "Mike, you always are the gentleman."

My father nurses his drink and only acknowledges my presence with a grunt. I already know why he's here. I never remember the date, but I remember that look—and his face is the only calendar I need. It's his birthday. Fred's birthday. My dead brother's birthday.

"C'mon, Dad. It's getting late, and you've had too much to drive home by yourself."

"Car won't start. That's why I'm still here."

"Dad, how long are you gonna drive that Edsel? Why don't you let me get you a new car?"

He looks at me. "I don't need you to get me shit, man. It's an okay car. Just ugly as hell."

He slams his drink down after taking a gulp that makes him wince. He grabs both elbows and leans forward, emitting something like a sigh and a gasp.

He loved the son that came before me, before he met my mother, made with a woman he was never married to. Fred suffered a head injury—he jumped from a tire swing at the edge of a creek and dove head-first into the shallow water. He met with the rocky bottom a lot sooner than he expected. But according to my father, the delirious boy walked two miles—dazed and bloody—just to die at home. My father no doubt loved him. I've never seen pictures of him, but I'm sure he must have been a strong and handsome boy. Dad's spitting image.

He stands and grabs my shoulder, then my neck—firmly, in that way that fathers do to their sons. That act that says I love you and I'm proud of you in more ways than I can show or say, so I'm just going to do this simple gesture.

But then I realize he is just trying to steady himself after too much drink. His legs don't have any steadiness to them yet.

"Give me a few more minutes, son," he says as he sits back down and knocks on the bar for another dose. "I'm not ready yet."

I decide to smoke outside until the old man is ready to leave. Across the street, the neon sign in front of Lucky's diner catches my attention. It glows lucently over the large encompassing window that makes the place look like an enormous aquarium. Inside, the patrons are hovering over their lukewarm coffees, their collection of cigarette butts and greasy plates under jaundiced fluorescence. No one seems to be bothering anybody. Everybody maintains their invisibility, lonely souls only aware of themselves. It seems like a place I'd be comfortable in. For a moment, I think about going in. Lucky's has been desegregated recently, but I don't see any Negroes inside and I've seen enough trailblazing for one evening.

But then I see Mathis sitting inside, and this sends a shock through me that deadens my good leg. With a folded newspaper and cigarette hanging precariously from his lip, he leans back and lets out a puff of smoke. I quickly retreat into the alley between Mike's and a trade school. Shielded by the backstreet darkness, I watch for a long while, amazed that our worlds have collided in this way. And it's here that I become aware of his vulnerability.

My head becomes hollow. All sound disappears, except the question: If they are watching us, who is watching them? Just by asking that question—epiphany isn't strong enough—suddenly in the darkness, a gilded path presents itself before me.

Something like half an hour passes. Mathis gets into a black Ford when he leaves the diner and drives onto Luckie Street. The old man can occupy himself with another drink. I'll pick him up later.

I get into my Caddy and follow him, just to see how far I can take it, but he makes a turn onto Jones, then Northside, and he disappears into the darkness. I've already lost him, but everything is bright and clear in my mind.

25

These are hard times, and they seem to be calling for a far more aggressive approach than the one that Martin has been offering. There is a man up north who uses just a letter, a symbol, *X*, for his surname. He tells us to shake the enduring ties to our former masters and rid ourselves of our slave names. I think of my own name: Estem. My great-great-grandfather was a slave owned by a Spanish-Frenchman named Esteban-Margeaux. When slavery finally ended, my grandfather couldn't even read or spell the name his old master had given him. *Esteban-Margeaux.* All he could write was E-S-T-E, followed by an M.

Estem.

Even in my name, I bear the exclusive brand of the Negro—cursed by society with woeful limitations, but blessed by nature with an uncanny knack for reinvention.

I give the agents a call, but not from my usual place; I'm much closer this time. I tell them that I won't be making it to our rendezvous, that something's come up, and then I wait in front of their office building for a very long time, until the streets empty and the sky becomes dark. I see both of them. I could put the tail on Strobe, but he is just an ornamental pillar. Mathis is the keystone; weaken him and the whole thing comes tumbling down.

Again, I follow him up to the intersection a few blocks away. I suspect the beginning of a pattern: Left off Peachtree, right on Sixth, straight on Spring. I commit it to memory and keep my distance. I don't want to get too close.

The trail leads to a large square box, adorned for no functional reason with dead gray concrete columns. Mathis's car drives toward the darkness under the building—some sort of underground parking lot.

I wait again for a while. Many cars leave, but not one of them belongs to Mathis.

A few days later, I finally meet up with the agents. I offer them some bullshit story about how Martin's personal behavior is causing concern at the SCLC, and there is talk about having Abernathy replace him. All the while, I think about how to get to Mathis. I thought the story would be some sort of peace offering and that the sensational aspects would smooth things over for missing our meeting. But Mathis just sits across from me, his legs crossed and an unlit cigarette crammed in the corner of his mouth, and taps a matchbook from the Quiet Time Motel rapidly against the desk. There's a sleeping hillbilly on the cover, and I watch his head bounce up and down.

I finish my story. Mathis's unlit cigarette makes me hungry for my own. I reach into my pockets for my lighter.

"Don't," Mathis says.

I withdraw my hands, then cross my arms.

"This is the information we waited days for? Listen," says Mathis, "when we make an appointment, you keep it. If you can't make it, it'd better be life or death."

I look at him more closely. I've never seen him this irritable. His eyes are bloodshot, he needs a shave, and his shirt looks like it has been working overtime. All this irritability and nervous tapping must be due to all those late nights at Lucky's diner and their ulcer-inspiring coffee. Or is it something else?

"Mathis, I apologize. It won't happen again."

He stands. "You're goddamn right it won't happen again!"

"Take it easy," says Strobe.

"You people just don't get it! You think you can just press a

goddamn button and we come running. You think we're just government machines and we don't have lives of our own?"

"Mathis . . ." Strobe says.

I sit quietly, taking a peculiar interest in this breakdown.

"Is that it, dammit? You don't think we're people too? We've got
lives—children, bills, taxes, mortgages—just like the rest of you." He
gets about an inch from my face. "And all I ask is that you have the
decency to keep a goddamn appointment when you make one!"

"Dick," Strobe says, placing a hand on Mathis's shoulder.
"Enough."

I wipe the heat of Mathis's breath off my face as I stand.

"I think we're done here," Strobe says.

I don't say anything. I just close the door behind me.

Mathis was practically on the verge of hysteria. A man in that state
needs to be watched. It's almost comical listening to him go on about
mortgages and property taxes—his membership dues in suburban
conformity—to show he's like the rest of us. What kind of desperation
would prompt that kind of frantic outburst? I need to find out, and he
may have given me a way to go about it.

26

I meet her again in front of the county assessor's office where she works as a clerk. She's still skinny, but she's added a few pounds, I hadn't noticed that, and I can tell she is not married even before I see her bare ring finger. Pearls, white gloves, shoulder shawl—she's dressed like a woman expecting a man to call on her, like she's ready for a date.

Samantha DePlush. Her mother is friends with my mother. A preacher's daughter, smart as a whip. She went to Spelman, the all-girl college next to Morehouse, and was in a co-ed accounting class with me. We Morehouse boys used to pray for classes that would allow us to penetrate that fortress of steel and brick and stone, so we could catch a glimpse of those golden-brown treasures that waited inside. She had a thing for me back then. Well, more than a thing really, but I was too busy pining over Candy to even notice or act on it. It's not that she was unattractive. She had a nice enough face, but her body was a little too boyish, not curvy like I like them—like most Southern men like them. The weight of her desperation seemed to add to her thinness, flattening out the roundness of her breasts and hips.

I got her phone number from my mother—who was more than happy to retrieve it from Samantha's mother, despite the possibility of being embarrassed about her delinquent property taxes. She seemed excited enough to hear from me, so we scheduled a time for me to meet her outside of her work.

I get out and open the door for her.

"Ooh, nice car, John," she says once I'm inside.

"Thank you."

"I was surprised to hear from you, but I'm glad you called."

"After I saw you that day, I've been thinking about you."

"You've been thinking about me?"

"Yeah, I'm in a bit of a bind and I need your help."

Her eyes drift dejectedly out the window. "Of course. You need some help and you thought of me."

"No, Sam, this isn't like cribbing your notes in accounting class. It's not like that at all. I'm working for Martin Luther King—"

Her eyes light up. "Really?"

"Don't act like you didn't know. We've got the same kind of mother."

She laughs. "Okay, I knew. Go ahead."

"This man wrote us a bad check and I neglected to collect on it in time. The money has already been spent, creating a deficit in the books—"

"Right . . ."

"The address he gave me is a dead one. He either moved or never lived there."

"That's terrible. What do you want me to do?"

"Well, I was hoping you could get me a current address."

"John, this is my job. That's illegal. There's no way I could do that. How could you ask me to do something so . . . so *unethical*?"

"I know, Sam, I know. I'm in a lot of trouble here . . ."

"Well . . . what's in it for me?" she asks, looking first at her folded hands, then directly into my eyes. I'm not sure what to offer her—my time or the fattened envelope inside my glove compartment.

"All you have to do is tell me what you want, Sam. What is it that you want?"

She answers my question with a dive toward my mouth. A hard lustful kiss, more breath, mouth, and tongue than actual kiss. Something must have changed in me over the years. I feel myself responding to her.

"Is there some place we can go?" she asks.

We drive back to my apartment with the awkward silence dragging time, despite the shortcuts I pursue.

———

The experience was far more pleasant than I anticipated. She did most of the work—not like she was merely servicing me, but more like I was her plaything and she did with me as she willed.

I open my eyes after a brief postcoital slumber and she looks at me triumphantly. I feel myself growing smitten in that moment.

Fluttering those long eyelashes and parting those lips, still tinted with a passion-smeared shade of ruby red, she says, "I gotta go," and jumps out of bed and starts getting dressed.

I sit up and pull the sheets to my chest. She puts on her undergarments with her back turned to me.

"Give me the name of the guy you're trying to find," she says, "and I'll call you from the office when I do."

"It's Dick Mathis," I say to her back, waiting for her to turn around and give me some recognition. "Try 'Richard.'"

Now dressed, she faces me. "When I have it, I'll contact you. Don't worry about driving me. I'll find a cab or a bus—or I'll walk or something."

"You want to get some dinner some time—my treat to say thank you?"

She keeps her eyes on me, but I can tell she would rather look away. "John, I want to apologize to you."

"Apologize about what?"

"Well, back in school, with the way people chattered about you. Sometimes that place was so much like high school, with people making their snide comments all the time."

"I'm confused. What does that have to do with me?"

"I just want you to know that I am a good Christian woman. I normally don't condone that sort of thing, but sometimes the peer pressure is just too great and we do things we don't want to do to fit in. I always felt guilty for not defending you, but now I see that I should have told you, maybe it would have given you a chance to change . . ."

"Are you saying that you and other people were talking about me behind my back?"

She adjusts her shawl in response.

"Well, what sort of things did they say about me?"

"You know . . . just the usual obnoxious sort of things."

"Such as?"

"Well, the obvious—look, I'd rather not get into it. I just wanted to apologize."

"No, it's okay. I'm a big boy. I can take it. The obvious stuff, like what?"

"John, please, you're making me uncomfortable. I just wanted to say I'm sorry. That's all."

"I see. So people were making fun of my brace and limp, is that it? People were making fun of me for surviving a childhood horror. I'm walking around with the battle scars to prove it, and people were making fun of me? And you're joining in on it?"

Her posture stiffens at that moment. "Actually, no, John, that's not what I meant."

"Well, what did you mean?"

"It was your tendency to put on airs, to seem above it all. Your strange sense of superiority—arrogance, I think is accurate . . ."

"Okay, thank you."

"Your naked cynicism and obvious disdain for other people."

"Okay, Samantha, enough. I get the picture. Apology accepted."

"Thank you, John. You have a good night."

"Wait, Sam. You're right, maybe I could've benefited from spending more time with you, but why can't we start now? You never answered my question about dinner."

"You're sweet," she says. "But after I do this for you, don't ever contact me again."

160

21

I had trouble sleeping that night—the newly christened air still lingered with her, and my distracted mind toyed with the cultivation of a new priority: ruining Mathis or winning her over? But my window was cracked, and by morning the night breeze had aired out the room.

Samantha provided two possible addresses, but the sign in the window proclaiming *Jesus Saves Niggers Too* quickly narrowed it down.

His home is a modest one-story in the Devonmoore district. The house could use a good paint job, and the yard is patchy with yellowing grass. Hearing that last tape of Martin put me in an extended daze. My actions were foggy, but now I see that I was propelled by an unconscious determination. As I watch his home, waiting for Mathis to surface, I am not completely sure how it is that I am sitting here.

"How long's this gonna take?" Lester asks me.

I turn my attention away from the street and look at Lester in the driver's seat. "I'm not sure. But don't worry—I'll give you a day's fare for this."

"Why do you keep havin' me follow this guy, Mr. Estem? He owe you money or somethin'?"

The first night was a bust. Lester instinctively slowed for every person waving on a corner, and we lost him.

"That's right, Lester. He owes me money. Well, not me exactly—he wrote a number of bad checks to the SCLC, and since I keep the books, I intend to collect." As I finish lying, Mathis comes out and gets into his black Ford.

My Cadillac may be too easy to spot after so many failed pursuits, so I've paid Lester in advance for his exclusive services, making him my driver, essentially. I know he's attempted to extend his hand in friendship, but I have to admit it feels good relegating him to being my chauffeur. I used his need for money to put him in his place. Now I know how Count feels.

For the first few days, Mathis is consistent. Only work and home. However, today he takes a different route, and I sense he's not heading back to the office. I fear that he knows we're following him. I tell Lester to ease up—give him more room, set a rhythm for our strange dance. He may discover us. For a moment, I consider turning back, but then I embrace the consequences, and they do not frighten me. If he knows, to hell with him. If not, to hell with him anyway.

Finally, he turns onto a street with little traffic. We give him some room, and he pulls into a motel parking lot. I tell Lester to park in front of the union hall across the street from the Quiet Time Motel. The hillbilly on their large flickering neon sign slumbers identically to the cover of the souvenir matchbooks. The rooms are designed bungalow style—individual apartments, about twenty-five of them, slathered with stucco. A manager's office with a cold hard fluorescent light bleeding out the barred window sits up front.

I scan the parking lot, looking at the cars—the off-duty cabs of Lester's competitors, an assortment of clunkers, a rusted pickup with a tin Confederate flag anchored to the bumper with wire, and right next to that is Mathis's black Ford. I watch him in the rearview mirror, as he runs a comb through his hair, perfecting the deep groove of his right-sided part. He looks down and to his right, presumably at his glove compartment, then rubs both cheeks with both hands, as if he were applying aftershave. He gets out of the car and goes over to one of the bungalows and knocks. The door opens slowly. He enters, but I can't see who was waiting for him. All the other bungalows are dark. Blurred televised images flicker behind the gauzy curtain.

"What are we doing here, Mr. Estem?" asks Lester.

"Watching. Gathering information. We're trying to find information about a man who has been very dishonest and deceptive, a man who wants to collect the secrets of others but doesn't want to share his own. So, Lester, we have to seek what he wants to hide. We must find the answers for ourselves."

"And this man—does he work at this motel?"

I look at his dim pupils.

"We're going to find secrets about him in this motel?" he asks.

"Maybe, Lester. Maybe . . ."

A good deal of time passes, but I am still watching. I need to know who opened that door for Mathis, so I feel compelled to be patient. Lester, on the other hand, is growing anxious and feels the need to talk.

"All this waitin' around reminds me of when me and the boys would case a joint before we robbed it," says Lester. "Man, I was terrible. I was taken in by an uncle after my daddy—or at least the man I thought was my daddy—found out that I didn't belong to him. He made my mama choose. 'Him or me,' he said. She loved that man. So my mama put me out when I was fourteen. But I got a real bad temper, always have. So when that man that I used to call Daddy got in my face, I beat him so bad he reached out his hand and asked my mama for help. They sent me to live with my uncle, but he was too old to handle me. I get real angry sometimes. I know it, but I just can't help it. I'm better now, but at that age, I was a handful. I used to run with this gang—the Royal Peacocks. We used to get into some real trouble, especially me. I found out I loved to break into places, just for the challenge. I got this strange talent for knowin' how locks work. I broke into this funeral home once, because I noticed they didn't have no heavy-duty locks. I wasn't plannin' to steal nothin'. It was just for the challenge. But a night watchman found me. He started screamin' he's gonna send me to jail, and this and that, so I beat him senseless before I knew it. I guess I found out I was good for that too. My uncle got me out and put me with Mike. He taught me about boxin' . . . about life . . . about everything. I owe him everything."

A police siren kills the quiet of the street and, thankfully, Lester's soliloquy. The bungalow door opens. Confident, relaxed, and not at all ashamed of what has gone on in that room, Mathis walks out. Behind him is a young girl.

28

That's not his daughter, and that's not his wife. I'd say she's no more than seventeen, and that may be a generous estimate. It's jarring to see Mathis giving in to his desires. I've always pictured him as an asexual automaton. But here he is, quite the opposite, romping behind the shed like some teenaged peckerwood. Who is this girl that has Mathis acting on his carnal impulses? From what I can tell, she is beautiful. For a moment, I am proud of myself and pleased with my sleuthing, but only for a moment. I hoped to find something on Mathis that would bring the sort of embarrassment he wished on Martin, but this is the South; seventeen-year-old girls get screwed by middle-aged men all the time. I'm not sure what kind of leverage this will give me, but I'm sure his wife will provide a clue.

Mathis drives his Lolita to a street corner in Bozley Park, then lets her out. Lester and I continue to follow him.

The smile on Mathis's face is gone once he approaches the door. He looks behind him. At first, I fear that he senses he's been followed, but now I realize he is deciding whether or not to escape with that little girl and head for Mexico. He turns around and enters reluctantly.

A few minutes pass; then muffled shouting makes its way outside of the house. Then it stops. Lester and I continue to wait and watch. I'm not sure what answers this will provide, but then I see her. A woman—I assume Mrs. Mathis—walks out wearing a form-fitting blue dress, but she doesn't get into Mathis's car. She looks up and down the street and then directly at us.

She heads toward the cab, and I tell Lester to stay calm even though I'm already visibly nervous.

"Are you waiting for someone?" she asks me.

"No," I say. "Just dropping someone off."

She's already in the backseat before I can say anything else. "Good. Then you can take me to the Blue Stripe. It seems my husband has misplaced the car keys. I'll pay you extra to wait for me."

Lester looks at me in silence, but I give him an encouraging nod. He sucks his teeth, sighs, and then starts the cab.

Her resemblance to Mathis's young girl is striking. She could easily be her mother—or an older version of her. I guess when Mathis meets her for those secret rendezvous his Ford doubles as a time machine. Although Mrs. Mathis is attractive, she has a world-weary countenance—I suspect weathered by disappointment or liquor or both. My quest began with wanting to know more about Mathis. I had no idea I'd stumble upon the most revealing aspect of a man: the women in his life. Now I find myself asking a very dangerous question: how can a Negro get close to a married white woman . . . without being killed?

As requested, we stop at the Blue Stripe, a watering hole for the well-heeled. A man can get a woman anywhere, but here a woman can get a man. Lonely upper-crust housewives can have their pick from a bounty of desirable men. A good portion of them are gigolos, the sly and foxy type, with small mustaches and well-oiled hair, a little gray at the temples. Most important, it's one of the few places in the South where a woman can drink by herself and not be judged. I've heard talk of their velvet ropes, vibrantly colored drinks, and tinted-light atmosphere, but I've never experienced it firsthand since I'm the wrong hue. Negroes are not allowed in there—that's fine. I don't want it to be too easy. After all, this is Mathis's wife, and it wouldn't be worth it if I didn't have to employ some guile.

I'm glad we drove her here. Mrs. Mathis needed a driver. There's something about the valet, and I don't like the looks of him. I can sense that working here has made him cynical, and he would have handed down some judgment if he were to approach the car and see Mrs. Mathis behind the steering wheel and an unmanned passenger's seat. It's better that she has avoided all of that.

Lester and I wait for Mrs. Mathis to reappear.

A few hours later, she walks out drunk. When she reaches the cab, I start the show.

I adopt a deferential tone to my voice. "How was your evening, ma'am?"

She looks around droopy-eyed and then climbs in back. "No luck tonight, boys. I guess they could smell the vengeance and desperation. Just take me back home."

"Devonmoore Hills, wasn't it, ma'am?" I ask.

"That's right." She leans back in the seat, then quickly sits up again. "Wait a second," she says. "Why are there two of you?" It's strange how liquor can blur a thousand details while bringing one into vivid clarity.

"Oh, he's my boss, ma'am," Lester says. "I'm new on the job and he's supervisin' me." He smiles, but his eyes narrow.

That seems to satisfy her, and she relaxes again.

We drive past Duncan and Claymoore streets, the intersection where they killed that colored boy for whistling at a white girl. I watch Mrs. Mathis in the rearview mirror. She was drunk when we picked her up, and she still is, but now she tries to appear sober as she struggles to apply her lipstick during this bumpy drive. She has just finished the bottom lip, and a bit of her chin, when our eyes meet in the mirror. I quickly look at Lester. He keeps his eyes on the road and hums a Negro spiritual, "Mmm . . . that cross was heavy . . ."

"Why are men such bastards?" asks Mrs. Mathis.

We don't respond. She must be talking to herself.

"Did you hear me? I'm talking to you. Why are men such bastards?"

I have to bite my tongue. I want to tell her that women are a constant disappointment to men, and that any pleasure or gratification received is fleeting and momentary.

"Sorry, ma'am," I say. "I don't know why that is."

"You give them everything and they just take more."

"Yes, ma'am. I know a lot of men like that."

"I'm sure you do. Are colored men that way?"

"Which way is that, ma'am? Are we bastards? Well, I reckon a good portion of us was born out of wedlock, but I don't have a particular number, percentagewise."

Her eyes turn into amused little slits. "Are you having a go at me?"

"Ma'am?"

She laughs. "You know exactly what I mean. You can quit the Stepin Fetchit–Amos 'n' Andy routine. I know when I'm in the presence of a halfwit. Save the act." I can see her smirk in the mirror. Her ability to see through our ruse impresses me.

As we continue to drive, Mrs. Mathis stares out the window, smiling and blinking lazily at passing streetlights. With a grin and a sigh, she welcomes the wave of alcohol that has washed over her as she gets comfortable in her seat.

Lester wants her out of his cab and all of this over. He's had enough, I can tell. He tightens his grip on the steering wheel and starts driving too fast.

"Slow down," I tell him with a stern whisper.

"Listen, you boys need to slow down. Don't do anything reckless— my husband is a G-man. Do you know what a G-man is?"

I assume she's asking me. "Do you mean a federal agent ma'am?"

She leans forward. "'You mean a federal agent, ma'am.' You see, I knew your Amos 'n' Andy act was horseshit. Which one of you is Amos? Which one is Andy?"

"What she mean by that?" Lester queries. "My name is Lester." I cringe as he gives his real name.

"Oh, I guess he's both," she says, falling back in her seat. "Yes, my husband is a G-man. You know, it's funny. I used to think it was exciting being married to one of those heroes they always show in the movies or television shows. But I'll be the first to tell you it may be exciting for the men, but it sure as hell is no fun for the wives. You see, G-men are never really married to you—they're married to J. Edgar Hoover, and the wives are just glorified mistresses. Nothing comes before the Bureau. Why is it so hot down here? Can you answer me that? So hot . . . and balmy. I have to be honest with you—I do resent you people. When I say you people, I'm not sure if I mean Negroes or

Southerners in general. You just can't seem to get it together down here. Every time some colored person tries to sit at some 'whites only' counter, I hate him a little bit—because that means one more day that I have to spend down here. All because a Negro tried to force progress on someone who doesn't want it. And when a redneck sheriff stops a little colored girl from going to school, I hate him too—that means another damn day. Do you know what a homosexual is? Of course you do. Hoover is one, you know. A homosexual. So I guess it's quite appropriate that all of his men are married to him. Most people know it, too. But most people know how to keep their mouths shut. There were rumors that he attended parties in dresses. He told me that much, my husband did. I guess he shouldn't have. Hoover wanted to get some dirt—no, wanted to *ruin* whoever said such things about him. I guess my husband didn't do a good enough job. Suddenly, he's reassigned to the South. And it's not the glint and glitter of Manhattan anymore. It's backwoods preachers, redneck sheriffs, and protesting Negroes. It takes a toll on the marriage. I know we're not making it. I know we're breaking down. I miss that life, that city life. I could wear a pretty dress and it didn't get sweated up by the heat. Not like down here. We were alive in that city. One thing's for sure—the South is killing us. Listen to me going on like a Tennessee Williams play."

"I know what you mean," I find myself saying.

"I've thought about ending it all," she says, while smiling. I hope she isn't serious. Negroes and a white woman with a death wish are a bad mix. "Do you know what I mean by that? Taking my own life just to escape this godforsaken place. But who would notice down here? There's so much violence. But I'd probably take some pills or slit my wrists or something. What can I tell you? I'm from Manhattan—I have a flair for drama. Then I think about my poor husband—not that he'd miss me, mind you. I'm sure he'd find relief in it on some level, but I wouldn't do that to him. After spending this much time married to an agent, I know they'd think he killed me. They always look to the husband first when the wife ends up dead. I'm not sure I hate him enough to put him through that. What do you think?"

"About what, exactly?" I ask.

"No, not you, the other one. What do you think?"

"I don't think nobody should be killing themselves," says Lester. "It just ain't right. It seems God didn't put us on this earth to make it easy. Seems he put us here to fight . . . to fight for what we want. If you want it bad enough you got to fight."

"You make a lot of sense," she says. "What's your name again?"

"Lester, ma'am."

"Yes, Lester, you make a lot of sense. You must fight. But the problem is, I'm tired of fighting—or have I ever fought? Maybe I'm scared of fighting. But you do make a lot of sense."

Yes, he does, I think to myself. He makes a great deal of sense for someone with so little of it.

"Now, my husband," she continues, "he knows about fighting. Right now, he is fighting for his life—fighting for his youth. Even though I know he's out here representing J. Edgar Hoover, I can't help but feel he's also trying to replace me. He's out there right now looking for my replacement."

We finally arrive at the Mathis home. "Thanks for the ride, boys," she says with a slight slur. "This was a whole lot easier than driving."

"Yes, ma'am," Lester says. We nod our heads and drive off. I sit low in my seat as Mathis comes out to question his wife.

Lester looks weary. I can tell that he has had enough of me, but I am not through with him yet.

I look out of the window, projecting imaginary scenes of their relationship against the black night. The Mathises' bond is a puzzle. I should be congratulating myself, but I am not. She spoke to perfect strangers about her husband without prompting. Suddenly, I feel incomplete, lonely. Is there anyone in my life that would have me be the topic of discussion? I look at Lester. Do he and Candy have that kind of bond? I lack that kind of connection, but then I think better of it and I start to laugh. Mathis and Strobe. I'm sure the agents have had many discussions about me.

Lester looks at me while I laugh. "I don't know what's goin' on here," he says, "but I know that man don't owe you no money."

29

A few days later, I made a visit to the pawnshop that's next to the modeling school and across from my phone booth. I was looking for the essential tool for my new hobby. Everything was covered with a thin veil of dust—television sets, radios, jukeboxes, record players, even military uniforms, all of it dusty—and I wondered how the pawnbroker stayed in business buying all this junk from people. I thought it must be the jewelry that moves, but then I looked at his glass display case, lit from the bottom with a ghostly pale light. Yes, everything was dusty, except those guns inside; they were shiny, almost brand-new. His biggest sellers, he confessed.

In a dull chrome graveyard of forgotten appliances, I came across something that looked like an antique cigarette lighter, but upon further inspection, I realized it was a miniature camera called a Minox. I removed the slim case, reveled at the small dials for adjusting aperture and speed, and spied the pawnbroker through the tiny viewer. He started with some yarn about two government types coming into the shop and selling old surveillance equipment because they needed to make room for the new stuff. I confess that my mind did wander to my boys coming in with their fedoras tipped at a concealing angle, but then I thought better of it; the pawnbroker had just developed an elaborate sales pitch. There was also a standard camera and an assortment of professional lenses. It seemed an aspiring photographer had hit hard times. The pawnbroker offered me a deal so sweet that I didn't consider pressing my luck.

Then Lester and I continue with the business of following Mathis.

Although it takes a few days until he sees her again, when he does, I am ready with my new camera as they leave the motel room.

As Mathis allows his precious cargo to rest in the passenger seat, I press the button and the camera's shutter gives an audible affirmation. It agrees with me and says yes to everything I decide to document, even the most innocent interactions between Mathis and his girl. But I am patient. And when the young girl makes a bold move, to Mathis's obvious displeasure, and kisses him in broad daylight, my camera is ready.

I'm not sure if I've seen enough. Do I have all I need? I feel a certain amount of relief, pride even, that I've mastered the brand of voyeurism that compels Mathis and Strobe.

We follow him, and when he drops the girl off near Bozley Park, I tell Lester to stay put. I want to know more about the girl—where she lives, what her family and friends are like, what attracts her to Mathis.

I get my camera ready for more pictures. "Okay, Lester. Almost ready. I'll make it quick," I tell him, but a policeman has tapped his baton on Lester's window.

"What you boys doin' out here?" asks the officer, a middle-aged man with a hard, swollen red face.

I am too nervous to speak. I look at Lester, but he is already formulating an excuse.

"Oh, nothing,' boss," says Lester. "We just had a call for a cab, and we just waitin' is all."

"Call, huh?"

"Yessuh."

"Who's your friend there? And what's with the monkey suit?"

"Oh, that's my supavisuh, is all."

"Supervisor. . . . What house you say you waitin' on?"

"That one over yonder," says Lester pointing to small white house on the corner.

"So if I go over there, somebody's gonna say they called a cab?"

"Yessuh."

He looks at Lester hard. Even though he's outside, his glare mimics the harsh light of the interrogation room. The officer looks at me again. "What's with the camera?" he asks.

I don't say anything and neither does Lester.

The officer looks where Mathis and the girl were, but Mathis has driven off, and the girl is already gone. He looks back at Lester. "Why don't you boys get out of the car," he says.

Lester doesn't move, and neither do I.

"I said out!"

A strange look comes over Lester's face. He's not as scared as I am, but it's a look that I can only describe as focused desperation. Lester mumbles something that sounds like it would be offensive if it were said clearly.

It must hit the mark, because the officer responds with, "What'd you say, nigger?"

Lester mumbles again.

"Speak up, boy!" He places his head inside the cab, a few inches from Lester's face, not enough time to avoid Lester's right fist.

The officer's chin hits the door as he slides out and begins his nap on the sidewalk. Calmly, Lester starts the car and drives away.

30

I have blackened out my windows. Only blood-red light fills my apartment, but soon I will see them in vivid detail. The baptism has begun. A small wave washes over them. I remove them from their chemical bath and let them dry. The halide does its magic, and slowly, like conjured spirits, Mathis and the girl appear in my home. The solution stings my nose a little, but I expected that. I bought a book on photography development to guide me through this. I can't have too many eyes on these photos, only the ones I intend.

I have decided to send Mrs. Mathis a bit of entertainment that will double as informational material. Photographs. Shaky, mind you, not quite as crisp as the photos taken by the good fellows at the FBI. I've never been formally trained. Since Mathis has sent recordings of Martin to Coretta, I think, as Martin's friend, I am entitled to employ the same line of attack on Mrs. Mathis. Let's see what kind of man he is. I try to think of this as less like revenge and more like a social experiment. When Mrs. Mathis views that incriminating material, how will he react? Will he cower, or will he be man enough to embrace his actions and his feelings?

I catch myself after thinking that way. I know what I'm doing is risky. I might as well begin chiseling my own name into a gravestone. I offer bluster, but I am afraid. But the fear doesn't dilute my desire to seek a twisted sort of justice.

Right on cue, Mathis calls me after I have developed the pictures. He wants me to meet him. He doesn't tell me why. The fear seeps in quickly; my bravado evaporates. I've gotten too close to him too fast. Has he spotted me? Have I blown my cover? I look around my place, and think of Lester and the cab, all the foolish mistakes I made trying to tail Mathis. I look at the pictures I developed—I see them less as trophies and more as evidence implicating me. I almost panic, consider hiding all of this or getting rid of it. But then I think better of it. This is something else, nothing to do with what I've seen of Mathis. If he knew what I've done, if he knew what I know, he wouldn't call first: he'd come silently and without warning.

When I arrive at the agents' office, I'm greeted by a confusing smell: cinnamon, lavender, tobacco . . . and fried chicken. The smell triggers my adventurous spirit—though I've never been, this is what I imagine Cuba to smell like. Mathis, with his sleeves rolled up and napkin tucked into his collar, dives into a golden thigh. He gives me a greasy smile.

"Sit down," he says.

I sit across from him while moving my eyes between him and the chicken.

"Dig in," he insists, pointing to a white box beginning to darken from oil.

I look at the box and that confident rooster in boots and spurs. It's from the Pick Rick. I've never eaten there because its owner refuses to serve Negroes. He even threatened a black man with an axe handle when he tried to eat there.

"I figured you've never had it, considering the owner's . . . beliefs. But I just had to share this with you. This is damn good chicken."

I eye him steadily, considering what kind of self-righteous stand I can make over fried chicken. But I remember that I am an FBI informant and the damage has been done. So I grab a piece and take a bite, and—segregation be damned—it's good.

Mathis cleans his bone, wipes his mouth and hands, then takes a drag off one of those cigarettes, sending a cloud of perfumed smoke in my direction.

"What are you smoking?" I ask him.

"Smell great, don't they? Try one."

I eagerly do as I'm told. There's no writing on the package, only a gold griffin embossed in a signet that could have been used in the Middle Ages.

"Got them off a guy we turned when I was back in New York. A Russian grifter who specialized in forgeries of all kinds—art, checks, antiques. All of his work had this distinct smell. He was addicted to them. Smoked them all the time. I can see why."

So here we are, cigarettes, chicken, and fake civility.

"What's going on, Mathis? Do you want to trade high school football stories? Sorry, I don't have any."

"It's a peace offering, John."

"Go on . . ."

"I want to apologize for how I acted the other day. I was out of line and should have handled the situation differently. I want to make amends for it."

"I see. Well, this is a very kind gesture, and I appreciate all of it. But let's be honest. We don't have the kind of relationship where apologies are necessary—from either of us."

"I felt misunderstood and disrespected. I didn't handle it properly. Then I realized that we just had a communication problem."

"Again, that isn't the nature of our relationship, Mathis." I take another languid draw from the cigarette. "From what I remember, you said you wanted it that way."

"Well," he says, getting comfortable in his chair, "things change."

"Yes, they do."

We sit in silence, the smoke becoming a third being in the room, and then Mathis says, "I've been meaning to ask you something ever since I met you. Why'd you do it?"

Again, that panic and fear that he knows something kicks in like a built-in reflex. "Why did I do what?"

"Why did you take the money?"

When I try to remember the lie I told myself, only the truth comes to mind. The girl, Gant, power, respect, because I could. But then I remember. "I thought our services were needed in Chicago, but they felt otherwise. We had the money—more than enough. I figured I could get something started up there myself since we had a surplus and all."

"But you didn't go to Chicago . . ."

"Are you asking me or telling me?"

"You've never been to Chicago."

"So?"

"So it's bullshit."

"Of course it is, so what? I can say that since we're friends now."

"I'm just trying to have a conversation with you. Man to man."

I don't know if it's Mathis's interrogation, my full stomach, or these damn cigarettes, but suddenly I feel honest. "I was tired of being the joke that everyone's in on. I was tired of feeling insignificant and powerless. I mean this is America, and the quickest way to remedy those feelings is to get your hands on some money. But that's my job, isn't it? My hands are on money all day, but the effect never seemed to wear off on me. So there it was, and I took it, because I could, and no one would ever expect I was capable of it."

I'm embarrassed by my impassioned confession, so I try to change the subject. "Where's Strobe at?"

"Just me and you today."

I take another draw from my cigarette—it's down to a nub. I want another, but I'm afraid of what I'd have to concede in order to get one. Now that our bond's been fortified, what type of devil's bargain would it be? I grind out the butt in the ashtray, freeing a small dying cloud that carries a new note of ginger and tea.

"Are we done here?"

"Sure."

"Thanks, Mathis," I say over my shoulder as I leave the office.

"Don't mention it," I hear once I'm down the hall.

31

I'm still thinking of those damned cigarettes when Count calls me after I get home. I don't like being jerked around and made to jump at his every beck and call. But what can I do about it, especially in this situation? There's no turning the tables on Count. Trying to find the dirt on him is a pointless exercise—he's covered in it.

Now here I am, still at Count's, sitting at the bar hunched over my bourbon, while the music of the wailing bluesman behind me taps at my shoulder like a persistent stranger. I look at the door to Count's office. I'm still not sure what went on in there, but I am certain that he's reveling in it.

I just know that I breezed past Claudel and Otis and entered Count's office.

"I just want to let you know we're going ahead with it," Count said.

"With what?"

Count tossed me a letter across his desk:

WE KNOW WHAT YOU'RE UP TO. WE KNOW ABOUT ALL THE WOMEN AND THE HOTELS AND ALL THE SNEAKING AROUND. WE HAVE PROOF AND WE'RE GOING TO EM-BARRASS YOU. UNLESS YOU GIVE US $10,000 TO MAKE US GO AWAY.

WE KNOW ABOUT THE QUEER WORKING FOR YOU. WE'LL SAY YOU'RE SCREWING THE QUEER. WE'LL TELL EVERYBODY. UNLESS YOU GIVE US THE MONEY.

What disturbed me the most about it was not its crudeness, in all aspects, but the obvious sense of entitlement that was conveyed in so few lines. It might as well have ended with "Can you blame us?"

So, it looks like I will have to protect Martin from Count as well. FBI agents are hard enough, but a gangster?

"He won't pay you, Count," I said.

"That's where you come in, little man—to see that he does. Besides, I don't know how careful you read, but this letter ain't for the preacher."

"It's not?"

"Nah. It's for that boss of yours—the queer one you told me about. I figure we get the letter directly to him and you can persuade *him* to pay up."

"What if it doesn't work?"

"I expect you to do your best. Haven't I been good to you? Just once, I want to see you do right by me."

I was sick of his presence, but I decided to see if the bartender had the right medicine, and after my fourth dose, I can say that the tincture he's peddling works just as good as my mama's chicken soup. But nothing changes the fact that I'm Count's errand boy, no matter how many agents I follow or scandalous pictures I take. Nothing.

"How much they get you for?"

I hear him say it but I'm not sure he's talking to me, so I ignore him and take another trip to my whiskey glass.

"How much they hit you for?" This time I look at him—an old man, older than my father even, in a baggy dark brown suit that once fitted him properly when he was a younger, more muscular man. His wide silk tie has a gold tiepin, dead center, which winks at me in the darkness. I look at the old man's wrinkled face under his porkpie hat; his eyes tell me that tonight he's young again.

"Excuse me?" I respond to his previous question.

"How much they charge you?" His voice is a delighted liquor-soaked rasp.

"For the drink?"

"Nah, man. You don't remember me, do you?"

I try my best to place him. A volunteer with Martin? Friend of my father's? Nothing.

"Yeah, man," he says. "I saw you a few days ago with those white men at that insurance office."

I can hear my heart thumping its own loud rhythm over the howling blues.

"Were you lookin' for a job there or somethin'?" he asks in response to my blank stare. "Even that day, I felt I recognized you, but I just couldn't place where I'd seen you before. But then, I see you tonight, and that's when it sank in. Here, man, let me buy you a drink. Tonight's pay day and I'm here to spend money." He motions for the bartender to repeat our remedy and fills the once empty stool that stood between us. "You work for those white men?"

"Something like that."

"How much does a job like that pay?"

That's when it dawns on me—he's the janitor who stumbled into the agents' office with his bucket and mop and was introduced to their anxious pistols. This man has access to the building, and no one knows how he comes or goes or even cares. He can slip in and out like a shadow. At this moment, he's the most powerful man I know.

I tell him the drinks are on me and, after a while, he loosens up, telling me stories and lies about women and war, and the weight of being a black man in a white man's world. I indulge him through eight songs before I decide to see how well the old man can dance.

"How much money you make in a year?" I ask him.

"What kind of fuckin' question is that?" he draws his arm back, drink still in hand, and spills some of it on the bar.

"Just making conversation. How much would you say? Give or take . . ."

"I ain't never made more than two grand in one year outta all my years," he confesses to his tumbler before gulping it down.

"I want to give you three thousand dollars."

His stare is cold stone. He didn't get this old by being a fool. The money sounds sweet to him, I can tell, but he's wise enough to resist his initial temptation.

"What the fuck for, man?"

"I need to get into that building. Those white men you saw me with have some information I have to get my hands on."

"You want to pay me to get the information?"

"No. I want to pay you to switch places."

"The hell you mean?"

"I want to see what it's like to be a janitor for a night. You got the keys to the building, don't you?"

"Of course, man."

"Good. You can just take the night off and let me borrow them. Maybe a couple of months off. "

"Man, if somethin' happens in there and I'm gone, they gonna look at me 'cause I got the keys."

"That's why you'll make copies. Tell your boss that you're going on vacation. Leave the master keys with him, and give me the copies."

He lets the idea soak in his drink before looking at me from the corner of his eye. "Those white men must really got somethin' on you. . . . What's stoppin' me from tellin' them your little plan and seein' if they offer some kinda reward?"

I feel cornered—but it lasts only for a moment. "You can do that if you want to," I say, smiling into my drink, "but you know better than me what kind of offices are in that building. Just because those glass doors say 'Dentist' and 'Insurance' doesn't guarantee that your teeth or your life are in good hands."

We sit shoulder to shoulder in silence for a while, as the bluesman on stage and the crowd both grow weary. Finally, he takes a gulp of his drink that makes him wince, then signals to the bartender for a refill. He turns to me and extends his hand. "No need for names," he says as we shake. "I'll just tell you when and where."

A few days later, I met the janitor in the Buttermilk Bottom, the tenement slum at the edge of the city. Was it so named ironically—buttermilk for cornbread or hotcakes is a luxury they seldom see—or was it the sour smell in the air, the foulness coming from the piles of refuse and puddles of waste? The dirt path, the wooden hovels crowded with desperate souls and their vacant yet calculating eyes transported me to the days of bondage. From the metal of my brace, I heard the rattling chains of the slave block; from the leather straps, I felt the master's whip.

When the janitor saw me, he descended a wooden porch and led me to a place where we could make our exchange. The approval his presence granted was enough for those lost spirits that watched me—the stranger or savior, the mark or prey—and they retreated slowly into their dark dwellings like feral animals.

He gave me the keys as promised, and my money followed. It was more than a year's salary for him. He's probably long gone by now. He didn't even look like he'd make it another six months.

I'm just glad to be away from that slum, and anxious to see if these keys work. It's late enough—no lights or signs of movement are visible in the agents' or the other offices. I make my way behind the building to the door that guards the stairwell. I turn the key and think *Open, sesame* as the bolt abandons the plate. Up the stairs, slowly, dark and silent, I only hear my brace and my breathing. As I approach the agents' office, I see that someone has installed a shiny new lock on their door. None of the janitor's keys work. If I had any real courage, I'd go to him and shake him up a bit, tell him to give me my money back; but I have no desire to ever return to the Bottom. I'm gratefully rid of that place. I've made it this far . . . I just need to come up with a new plan.

32

Lester did a good job saving our hides from that Bozley Park cop, but I'm not done with him yet. He may not want to see me, but more of my money means more of his time.

"Second floor," I tell Lester once we are inside.

Lester bounds the steps with silent speed. I lag behind, punctuating each step with a squeak from my brace. I resent my dependence upon Lester. He steals my lady, causes tension between Count and me, and now I have to rely on his talents to gain the advantage over Mathis and Strobe. My only solace is that it's temporary.

The differences between us are obvious. I must appear to be his gimp, and I must be taking too long, because Lester comes back down the stairs to where I am at, puts his arm around my waist, and begins to walk me up the steps. He supports me with only one arm, yet I feel weightless. But that weightlessness quickly gives way to a feeling of helplessness. I think back for a moment to the young me, that child recently crippled by polio, and the first time I climbed a set of stairs without the help of an orderly. When I made it to the top, breathless, my lungs hurt more than my leg. I looked down a floor below at my father. He wasn't smiling. "Well, you finally made it," he said. "It took a while, but you did it yourself. Remember that. Always remember that."

I doubt Lester has ever experienced the pain of physical limitations. I admit that I'm jealous of him, but my envy has already begun to evaporate as I wield the flashlight while Lester works the lock like a virtuoso with his pocketknife and an unfurled paperclip and opens the door of the agents' office. "Got it," he whispers.

I enter first and he follows. As we pass the threshold, Lester pushes me up against the wall. It's dark, but the whites of his eyes are disturbingly visible.

"When this is over," says Lester, "You and me are even." He only has his finger poking my chest, but I feel as if I'm glued to the wall. "Okay?"

I don't say anything. I'm afraid, but I feel a certain amount of relief. The big, dumb, and innocent act was getting old.

"Okay?" he repeats.

"Sure, Lester . . . even."

"Good," he says smiling, but I still don't move. "What you want me to do, Mr. Estem?"

I watch his face. The rage he tapped into starts to dissipate slowly. Eventually, that fog, dense and benign, makes its return.

"Watch the hall, Lester," I say as I take the flashlight and walk over to the file cabinet in the corner. Surprisingly, it isn't locked. I open the drawer. There are photographs of an old guitar taken from different angles, a cluttered room with Civil War–era daguerreotypes, and the schematics of a house with four red stickers, each with the phrase "Mic Here" written on them. I also see a file on Count—Reginald "Count" Glover, that is. It details his whole operation, the gambling, the sex, everything. I almost feel guilty for bringing this kind of scrutiny upon him. He ran a successful illegal enterprise for years without incident. Then I came along with my friends from the government.

There's a great deal of information in this cabinet, but I begin to doubt if I have enough time to find something useful—and then I see it. Yes, inside the drawer, there are many files. However, one intrigues me in particular: the file labeled JEST-0468. I pull out the folder to reveal its contents, which include memoranda and photos. At first, I do not pay much attention to them. I assume they are of random individuals whose importance is only known to Mathis and Strobe. It's still dark in here—only my flashlight offers some brightness. But then I look closer at the photos and realize that they are pictures of me. Pictures of me walking into Count's, talking in a phone booth, driving my new Cadillac off the lot. But it's the last photo that is the most telling. It is a picture of me in front of the bank where I foolishly cashed that SCLC check. But this picture was taken *before* I cashed the check. They were watching me from the beginning:

BUREAU BRIEFING: After an exhaustive search for a cooperative individual within the Southern Christian Leadership Conference (SCLC), we have secured SCLC accountant John Estem.

Andrew Young, Jesse Jackson, Stokely Carmichael were initially considered. However, the potential for rejection and exposure posed too great a risk.

While not an influential member in the SCLC, John Estem possesses the appropriate psychological profile suitable for information-gathering duties that require a great capacity for duplicity:

1. Frantic efforts to avoid real or imagined abandonment
2. A pattern of unstable and intense interpersonal relationships characterized by alternating between extremes of idealization and devaluation
3. Impulsivity in the areas of spending and sexual relations

This will hurt later, I know it. But I can't stop reading, like it's some torrid piece of Hollywood gossip—only this time, I'm the subject.

In a traditional context, these attributes would be barriers. However, given that these characteristics of his personality have, to some extent, marginalized him at the SCLC, it creates the opportunity to foster in him a certain degree of loyalty to the Bureau.

Among the other files, I see the letter sent to Martin, the one that caused such dread that day at the office:

King,
In view of your low grade I will not dignify your name with either a Reverend or Mr. or a doctor and your last name calls to mind only the type of King such as King Henry VIII.

King, look into your heart. You know you are a complete fraud and a great liability to all of us Negroes. White people in this country have enough frauds of their own. And I am sure they do not have one at this time that is anywhere near your equal. You are no clergyman and you know it. I repeat, you are a colossal fraud and an evil vicious one at that. You could not believe in God, clearly you do not believe in any personal moral principle.

King, like all frauds, your end is approaching. You could have been our greatest leader. You even at an early age have turned out to be not a leader, but a dissolute, abnormal, immoral imbecile. You will now have to depend on our older leaders, like Wilkins, a man of character and thank God we have others like him. But you are done.

Your honorary degrees, your Nobel Prize—what a grim farce—and other awards, will not save you.

King, I repeat, you are done. No person can overcome facts, not even a fraud like yourself. I repeat, no person can argue successfully against facts.

You are finished.

And some of them pretend to be the ministers of the Gospel, Satan could not be more? What incredible evilness! King, you are done. The American public, the church organizations that have been helping, Protestants and Catholics and Jews, will know you for what you are, an evil abnormal beast. So will others who have backed you. You are done. King, there is only one thing left for you to do, you know what it is.

There is but one way out for you. You better take it before your filthy, abnormal, fraudulent self is bared to the nation.

Long before I broke into his office, the agents crept into my mind. I cringe knowing that I failed to hear their footsteps as they surveyed my thoughts. Martin would also blanch at how much they know. They think that they've summed us up and figured us out. It's strange how they've handed down two divergent verdicts for the same offense: What they condemn in him they acquit in me. My only solace is that I know him better than they do. They've said nothing worse than what he has already said to himself. His embrace of the movement's most dangerous demands and his personal insistence on being a public ascetic are evidence of a desire for absolution—forgiveness through suffering. In his selfless contribution to this country, we are witnessing a grand display of self-flagellation. But the pain that follows can only be quelled by an amorous salve. This letter won't end with the result they seek. It will only encourage the behavior they so cravenly rebuke and so eagerly record.

I'm done here. I've had enough. I take pictures with my miniature camera of what I've seen, and then I tell Lester it's time to wrap it up.

Voices. One male, the other female. They exchange those loud whispers that are amplified by alcohol. The office across the hall softly brightens with a dim light, followed by loud, over-the-top laughter. I've never seen anyone in here before except Mathis and Strobe and the old janitor. Lester stands in the shadows, big and silent, like a tree in the forest at night. "Let's go," he whispers.

"Wait a minute," I respond.

The laughter diminishes to giggles, then to sighs, and finally to fairly consistent moaning, accompanied by the sound of furniture being scooted across the room inch by inch.

"Now," I say.

We walk out of the office leaving everything as we've found it. Of course, Lester is at the bottom of the steps very quickly. Me, I have to take my time. I time my steps to each passionate thrust coming from the other office, until I reach the last step and head out the door.

Lester doesn't say anything when we get into the cab, and neither do I. He seems smarter to me all of a sudden. He made some foolish and dangerous associates back in LA, and I am just one more. But he's already learning. He knew enough to draw the line and say what he would and would not tolerate before he got in too deep. I do not have his wisdom.

He drives me home, and I get out of the car without offering any parting words. I walk in and don't even bother turning on the lights. I just lie on my bed fully dressed, thinking about all that I've seen in the agents' office, trying to make sense of it. The money . . . all this time I thought it was the money that had pushed me into the agents' line of sight, but it was no such thing. Mathis and Strobe knew the choices I would make even before I did. For them, it was only a matter of time before I did something that would allow them to gain leverage over me. The mole thrives in darkness and secrecy; they saw it in my personality. Samantha saw it too—it was there early on, before Martin, before Gant, before Count. He sees it too. This is not new—it's only new to me. And here I thought being handicapped and Negro was a procryptic combination. Now, as I burrow deeper, blindly creating a hidden labyrinth in which only I am lost, how obvious is it? Like oracles in the temple, the agents anticipated my actions before I'd made them; as they set their gaze upon the glistening viscera, what does it reveal of me now?

33

Layer by layer, my true self was revealed to me in that dark office, and it has left me excoriated. Now, at work, I feel vulnerable and exposed. Even more so than before, I characterize the looks my coworkers send my way as silent judgments and the space between us as calculated attempts at distance. Despite the many times I may have disparaged them quietly, there are no fools at the SCLC—or so I thought.

Gant taps on my door, pokes his head in, and asks to see me in his office, thankfully saving me from being alone with myself.

"Make sure it's locked," he says as I close the office door.

"What can I do for you, Mr. Gant?"

"Estem, I'm going to tell you something, and it's very important that you keep it between the two of us. Can you keep a secret, Estem?"

"Of course I can."

"I received this letter today."

I open it, making sure to impose a shocked and horrified look on my face. I could do the right thing, tell him to ignore it and let Count think all is well. Yes, I could do that, but as I reach the end of the letter, I see that the bottom has been torn off—the part that contained the threat of exposing Gant as a homosexual entangled with Martin. Gant has obviously removed it. He didn't want me to see it.

"What has Martin said about this?" I ask, handing the letter back to him.

"He hasn't seen it. No one's seen it except you. It was sent directly to me."

"Why do you think that is?"

"I don't know," he says. For the first time since I've known him, he appears ashamed of himself. "Maybe they figured that since I handled the money I could persuade Martin to pay."

"Is that what you're going to do?"

"I don't know. I was thinking about it . . ."

"But you seem hesitant."

"He doesn't need the pressure, especially with everything that's going on."

"Well, what's going on, sir?"

"The Negro and the white woman that were killed. . . . Young feels it time for Martin to say something publicly about it and criticize the FBI more aggressively for their lax protection of civil rights workers. He's making some statements to the press this afternoon. I don't want to add to the scrutiny he's already placing himself under."

"I see. I hadn't heard about any planned statements."

"Of course you haven't. Why would you? I only found out moments ago myself. Why should I burden him? I think I should handle the situation independently. I mean these crackpots are getting crazier by the day. Maybe it's best to send a little cash their way and see if that doesn't make them disappear."

"Maybe. Or you could send a little taste their way, and it could just make them hungrier."

"It could Estem, it could. My, don't you sound savvy . . ."

"Sometimes I can be, sir. It depends on the situation and the circumstances."

"I see. And in these circumstances, what would you suggest?"

"In this situation, sir, I would suggest that you follow your instincts—your gut. This isn't an intellectual exercise."

"No, it isn't. So you think I should convince Young and Abernathy to pay?"

"I'm not saying that . . ."

"Are you saying that I should use some of the surplus money to pay this?"

"I haven't said that either, sir."

"Then what are you saying?"

"Well, I guess I'm saying that you should do what you think is best, and that you should be confident that whatever decision you make, you made it in the best interest of Martin and the SCLC."

"So if I tell Abernathy and Young . . ."

"They'll probably tell you to ignore it."

"And being ignored might just infuriate this crackpot, and he'll come back with something even more horrific."

"Yes, that's possible."

"Or I could pay, and just hope that he goes away."

"You could."

"And if he doesn't? If he doesn't, Estem? What then?"

"I don't know. Maybe you find out who he is and make certain he goes away."

Gant turns around and looks at the shelf behind his chair. There's a photo of Ralph Bunche and him shaking hands. Placing the photo facedown, he reveals a silver flask hidden behind it. He takes two hard swallows that make him wince. He doesn't offer me any.

"The question is if I were to do it, how could I get the money out of here without anyone knowing?"

"Without who knowing, sir?"

"Anyone! Everyone!"

"Are you worried about them finding out about a transaction you might make?"

"Yes, goddamnit. Keep your voice down."

"I don't know, sir. How'd they find out about payments to the property manager, and the chartering companies, and the printer?"

"I told them, of course."

"Yes, sir, you told them."

"I see . . ." Gant takes another sip from his flask and then leans in. "I can't just put my name on a check, now, can I?" he whispers.

"No. Of course not, sir. That would be stupid."

"Yes, that would be."

"If only there were some way that the SCLC could make a legitimate payment to someone or some other entity that you had access to. . . . It might all make sense."

"Yes. I guess it would."

"But since you don't have access to those sorts of things, you might have to tell them—or at least think about it."

"Yes, I guess I will." He takes another sip from his flask. "Thank you, Estem. That will be all."

34

I don't know what move Gant will make, but it's surprising that he would want to hide something from me—as if my opinion matters to him. I've always wanted to be in a position where I was giving him advice and he was the attentive student, but not in this way. Gant and I have arrived at the masquerade. How many others will be attending? I'm just glad that I'm not alone—and that matters more now than ever.

I pour myself a glass of scotch and lie in bed. More Macallan. LA made me develop a taste for the good stuff. It's funny how the first sip is always the sweetest; the second offers clarity and brings the hidden remedies for your ailing life into clear view. Of course, it's the subsequent sips that dummy up your mind; but now, somewhere in the middle, I allow myself to think of Candy, to miss her and the little game we played. I thought I was retired from it, but I just needed to sit on the bench for a while. I gulp the drink and a flare shoots up my chest, but I know it's her, not the scotch. I'm not ready to miss her yet. There she is being blanketed in Lester's dark muscles, cringing at the secrets he whispers to her about me. As far as her appearance is concerned, I hope she's fading fast and spreading wide—she's too cruel to deserve that beauty.

I pour another . . .

And another . . .

Until my drink decides to drift into song, somehow becoming a guitar, and my bed a car driven by a white woman. She's attractive in a very plain and conventional sort of way. She smiles at me, "Play," she says. "Play more." I go back to work, plucking and strumming a blues song I've never heard, but her smile disappears when she looks in the rearview mirror. I look behind us and see a pickup truck gaining on us very fast. We're on a desolate stretch of road, just us and trees and the truck.

She looks at me with dread in her eyes, "Don't stop playing," she says.

I continue, even as the truck pulls up alongside us and reveals its occupants. Strobe drives with both hands at the wheel, never taking his eyes off the road, while Mathis aims his shotgun at us. When he pulls the trigger, I spill what's left of the scotch in my lap.

They were already in my life and in my head before I was even aware of it. Now they are in my dreams. I look around my place and begin to find its simplicity deceptive. I grab the lamp on the nightstand and run my hand along the inner circumference of the shade, unscrew the bulb and inspect the socket, then remove the felt from the bottom and look inside. Nothing. I remove the phone from its cradle and dismantle the receiver. I inspect the perplexing wires and magnets like a flummoxed caveman, and then when I realize there is nothing sinister inside, I put the casing back on. I feel foolish. I was so sure I'd find something.

"John?"

At first, the voice strikes me like that of God coming from a burning bush, then I come to the horrific realization that the agents have planted something in my head—some sort of transmitter while I was asleep. Then I leave that scary place and come back to reality, back to the reassembled phone still in my hand, and hear my name come from it once more.

"Hello," I say, placing it to my ear.

"John?"

"Yes."

"I hope I'm not interrupting you while you were reading your Bible . . ."

"No, you're not. I was just—"

He lets out a laugh. "Well, anyway, brother, I'm just calling to tell you I appreciated those suggestions you made regarding Chicago a while back. I've been meaning to tell you for some time now. Although you met some resistance in the room, I've been thinking about it myself, and I want to thank you for your commitment. Of course, some details need to be ironed out, but I am thinking about it ever so seriously. There's a lot of good we can do up there, and I am glad you made us aware of what our focus should be, and not just the politics. We sometimes get caught up in the mere strategy of things while ignoring our responsibility to humanity in general. So I just wanted to say thank you."

"You're welcome, Martin, of course."

"Well, that's that. I guess I'll let you get back to your Bible." He laughs again, says, "Bye, now," and hangs up.

Chicago? The word sounds foreign as it bounces around in my head, trying to adhere itself to a meaning—but then I remember. Chicago. The ideas of the old me, before I knew myself better.

35

After work, my Cadillac and the smoky smell of its leather interior usually offer a welcome retreat, but as I drive home, I only feel uncomfortable and conspicuous. Gant offered no tell of his decision—or that there was even one to be made—and his haughtiness had already returned.

"King Criticizes Hoover, FBI. Cites Lack of Negro Protection." Since Martin's criticisms of the FBI went public, everyone at the SCLC has been bracing themselves for the inevitable retaliation.

"One of the great problems we face with the FBI in the South," Martin said, "is that the agents are white Southerners who have been influenced by the mores of the community. If an FBI man agrees with segregation, he can't honestly and objectively investigate." Obviously, Mathis and Strobe are not Southerners, but I didn't bother to point that out. The tension has already prompted a meeting between Martin and Hoover, and I'm sure Hoover made Martin aware of his inaccuracies.

I pull up to my building and see a white man parked in front. I get out, and as I walk closer, I realize that it's Mathis. I didn't recognize him at first. He's not in his usual G-man suit and tie, but a plaid hunting shirt and denim pants. Why is he here? He should receive my photos soon—if he hasn't already.

"Hello, Mathis . . ."

"Get in, John," he says.

I don't move. I'm not sure what to make of his tone. I take a moment to read the potential consequences in his eyes. His poker face is excellent. "Get in," he says again.

We are both silent as he drives. I think of Martin and the night those policemen put him in the back of their car: how they wouldn't tell him where they were taking him once downtown Montgomery and its jail faded behind them; the fear he felt, *like the closest thing to death while living,* as the dark unfamiliar roads only promised the most sinister destinations; and the absurd relief he felt once the sign that read MONTGOMERY JAIL became visible, and he realized that they had been toying with him.

I think of the woods where I saw Pete and that burning cross: how dark they were, and how many Negroes have disappeared never to be seen again. I wrestle with asking him where we are going, but I don't really want to know. That would just make the ride even more intolerable.

I don't have to suffer long as we approach his office. He parks in back, and then we go inside.

"Have a seat," he says. I grab a chair, and he walks over to the file cabinet, reaches into the bottom drawer, and pulls out a bottle of liquor. "I guess we'll finally be having that drink," he says. Two tin cups, the kind used for camping, follow the liquor. He wipes the dust off the cups with his shirt, places them on his desk, and starts to pour.

"I hope rye's okay," he says.

"Yes, that's fine."

He hands me the cup, I take a swallow, and it quickly fills me with enough heat and courage to ask questions.

"What are we doing here, Mathis?"

He brings his seat closer to mine, and we sit face to face, only an arm's length apart. He looks down while cradling his cup in his palm. "How do you people do it?" he asks.

"I don't know what you mean, Mathis. Do what?"

"How do you people pursue what you want—every impulse—no matter what people think of you?"

I'm taken aback by his question. I'm not sure if it is a compliment or an insult. "I don't know how to answer that, Mathis. I rarely think of 'us' collectively—at least not in that sense."

"Well, look at you. You're an accountant, but . . ."

I take a sharp short breath, my shoulders tighten, and I sit up in my chair.

"And even King," he continues, "he's a preacher yet whenever he wants a woman—if she wants him—he just has her. Restraint. How do you people live without restraint?"

He's being sincere, but I still laugh. "I'm sorry, Mathis, but I can't get over a white man asking a Negro how we live without restraints."

He smiles slightly. "Don't make fun of me," he says. "When I think about Hoover and the rumors about him—and the life I think he would want to lead, but doesn't—part of me sees a hero. But then I think of the pain he must be under. The constant agony of not going after what he desires, then the other part of me thinks he's a fool."

"Maybe he is a fool," I say. "What is life without happiness?"

He lets out a short sigh. "You probably don't know what I'm getting at, but to hell with it. Nothing goes better with whiskey than a good secret. There were these rumors going around influential circles that Director Hoover was . . . a homosexual. Trusted agents were told to look into it and discredit the source. Some divorcee of a very wealthy man, a professional socialite essentially, told me that Hoover and Tolson, his assistant director, had attended an orgy in complete drag—dressed as women—demanding to be referred to only as 'Mary' and 'Alice,' and engaged in acts of sodomy. We had already known the woman was not credible, even before her interview—morphine addict, shock therapy, crazy stuff—so I let it pass. But then someone sends me this picture anonymously."

I take a quick, hard swallow of my drink.

"Photographs of Hoover and Tolson having sex—if you can call it that. Photos. This goes way beyond some crazy woman saying she saw Hoover prancing around some hotel room in a dress. There were multiple photos of the two of them on the beach. Granted, they were blurry, and you couldn't quite tell it was Hoover, but the mind sees what it wants to see, especially after I learned of my Southern assignment. I didn't say anything; a good agent knows when to keep his mouth shut. But I wanted it to be true, goddamnit. If he was weak enough to go after what he wanted, it would have lifted a burden off my shoulders. I wanted the details, but damn that photo was grainy. Not a concrete detail on it—just one vaguely masculine blur wrapped around another. Even now I think of that picture. I go over it in my mind, seeing if I missed some aspect that might give Hoover away."

I think of Mrs. Mathis in the backseat of Lester's cab, smelling of gin and lavender perfume and spilling Hoover's nasty little secret. Even I had heard, and disregarded, those rumors about Hoover, but Mrs. Mathis's drunken candor gave them a new validity.

It must have infuriated Hoover no end when he learned of Martin's sexual habits, not because of the presumed moral objections, but out of envy. I don't know him, but he seems like a frightened man, rigid and unwilling to act on his desires. He has created an image for himself and the FBI that is inextricable. To be risky, even momentarily, is to risk everything. So then, how does he explain Martin, a man he views as a nuisance, and with at least as much at stake?

Listening to those tapes with Martin and a woman exchanging sounds of pleasure like pocket-sized notes, Hoover must have been a motionless, yet attentive, audience. Rewinding the reel over and over again, he listens. He's uncertain at first, but then he listens closer: *Yes, that is him.* He listens to Martin acting impulsively, indulgently, like a beast—a child—a man. He must not know whether to scream or applaud. Tolson, always the supportive one, must have placed a comforting hand on Hoover's sloped shoulder.

Martin's critical assessment of the FBI prompted the meeting with Hoover. Since there was no press in the room, who knows if Martin and Abernathy are being truthful when they offer the occasional detail at the office. But the encounter must have been hard for the old man. While they exchanged niceties and words limited by the formality of the setting, Hoover in the back of his mind must have been adding a visual narrative to the secret tapes of Martin. *Those sexual things . . . and with white women.* Some part of him, I'm sure, must have wanted to seek counsel from the young Negro. How does one maintain a fulfilling private life separate from the public one without people knowing? But Hoover stops there when he realizes that he himself knows, and that alone is one person too many.

Even though Mathis talks about Hoover, this is really about the girl. He wants to gossip about the fairy so he won't have to talk about himself. Maybe I acted too harshly—the photographs may have been over the top. I'm not used to this, but I think he's reaching out to me. He's trying to connect. I'm no expert, but it seems that despite everything, he wants me to see him as human.

I don't add anything, I just nod knowingly. For some reason, that takes Mathis out of his conversational mood.

"It's funny," he says, "but you don't seem surprised. Why is that?"

"I guess I expected it," I say.

"How?" he asks quickly.

"After working with Gant I looked for signs, characteristics. Hoover seems a bit . . . foppish, don't you think?"

His face relaxes and he leans back in his chair. "Yeah, I guess it is noticeable if you know how to look. You do know that Hoover's going to go harder on him, right? And it's not just the comments in the press, and the women—he knows what King really thinks of him. That he's senile and too old and broken down to continue as director. That pressure should be put on the president to censure him."

"I've never heard Martin say anything like that."

"Maybe you haven't, but I have."

"Why bring me here and tell me all of this, Mathis? You don't have to do this. I *know* you don't want to do this. You still have a choice. Freedom or servitude. Instead of meeting in secrecy, we can get out of here and have a drink together in public. We're both caught up in some shit we're better than, Dick. Right now, we can be more than just the men we want to be; we can be the men that we are. Let's get out of here, you and me. I know a place where guys like us can have a good time."

"Guys like us? You think we're the same?"

"I know that we are."

For a moment, the creases of his brow disappear and I see acquiescence in his eyes, but then he goes over to that tape machine of his.

"There's another one, you know," he says. "He's at it again." I know he's not talking about one of the Kennedys.

I think about playing indignant, but then I see how this validates all of my actions. I was foolish to show him sympathy. The tape plays and I sit back and enjoy my drink.

36

My confidence soon fades after listening to Mathis's third tape of Martin. I have been exposed to many threats during my involvement with the agents, but never have I felt more vulnerable than I do now. This tape had an ominous quality—they all did, but this one especially so. Martin rarely spoke on this tape. So little, in fact, that it's startling when he does speak. But it's the woman on this tape that is so troubling. He engages her with familiarity and in an almost apologetic tone. She does sound forgiving, but she seems to see through him. Even though she is alone with him, I feel that she is aware of her audience, and—more disturbingly—that I am her audience. I know this woman. I feel crazy even thinking it, but this is the same woman from the second tape Mathis played. Beyond identifying her voice, I know this woman. The quality of this recording is poor, that's the only thing keeping me from lunging at Mathis and beating him with that bottle of whiskey.

Immediately, reality presents itself and starts to coalesce. I think of everything I've done and the madness of those actions nauseates me. I tell Mathis that I am leaving. I practically fall, stumbling down most of the steps and out onto the street. I find a cab, and it takes me home.

For the first time fear sets in. I have left a dangerous trail behind me, and it didn't matter before, as long as I didn't care about the outcome. Agents, gangsters, and preachers—my volatile mixture of associations begins to sink in.

———

I park across the street from the *Atlanta Gazette* and look at the small but powerful passenger riding next to me: an envelope with the pictures of the files I took at the agents' office. It's enough to expose everyone—including me—but maybe it will put a stop to this madness.

Sitting here, lost in a labyrinth of possible outcomes, I wonder how I will be perceived—as a hero or a villain? A tap on my window snaps me out of it.

I look out at Strobe and see myself reflected in his sunglasses, as he points at my rear door. I unlock it and he gets in, making himself comfortable in the roomy backseat.

"Looking to change careers, Estem?"

The lack of menace in his voice throws me off.

"What?"

"The newspaper. Why the sudden interest in journalism?"

"About to buy a classified." The lie comes to me easily. "Trying to unload the Cadillac." I watch him in the rearview mirror as he looks out of the window. I give a look at the envelope and push it down into the cavernous floor of the Caddy.

"So . . . you and Mathis have been meeting one-on-one a lot lately," he says.

Is this about jealousy? I almost laugh, but I keep quiet.

"What did you discuss?" asks Strobe.

"Mathis didn't tell you?"

The mirror cools from his icy stare.

"I'm asking you, Estem."

"Actually, Strobe, it was the usual stuff—Martin, segregation, communism, illicit sex. The rest was personal."

"Personal?"

"Personal."

Strobe removes his sunglasses and leans over the seat, close to my ear. "This is where you should be careful, Estem."

I feel his breath on the side of my face.

"Careful? You pay me to talk. So I talk. What's the problem?"

"The problem is that his relationship with you should remain professional."

"He's the boss, Strobe. Are you warning me or him?"

"Hoover's the boss, but it seems that you and I both have bosses that need to be reined in."

"What do you mean 'reined in'?"

"Look, John," he says relaxing back into the seat. "Mathis has a history of using his cases as a way to escape. Maybe it's something in his own life, but sometimes he can become too personally involved. There was a situation in New York. A Russian immigrant and grand-scale con man agreed to work with us and bring down the outfit he worked for. It was a big operation too. Both coasts *and* Europe. Mathis and the guy got pretty friendly. Fine. But then Mathis gets pretty friendly with the man's wife as well. A real sexy blond number, with more curves than the road to Ronda. Next thing you know, the Russian decides to keep his trap shut and disappears into the fog. Just like that, two years of work down the drain. And when the higher-ups gave Mathis a temporary suspension, he didn't even take responsibility. He saw it as retribution for the botched job he did on one of Hoover's special cases. After that, they assigned me to him—to keep an eye on him."

"Why are you telling me this? I'm not Russian, and I damn sure ain't blond. How would Mathis feel if I told him you were putting his business out in the street?"

"You won't, because you like his attention. You're flattered by it." He says it as if there is no way I could disagree. "And you're smart enough to know that his interest in you is a double-edged sword. He could turn on you with the same intensity. How would he feel if you embarrassed him with what I told you? What do you think he'd do? How would he react?"

I stay quiet for a moment and try to weigh what Strobe has said. A behavioral pattern is forming. Could it be true that Mathis is so lost? I don't say it out loud, but Strobe nods subtly as if reading my thoughts.

"Thanks for the chat, Strobe, but I'd better get going." I start the car to signal my desire for his departure.

"Your ad," he says, still anchored.

"What?"

"Your ad for the car."

I look at the envelope, regarding it as a covered cage with a snarling animal inside.

"Thanks," I say, looking in the mirror, and then turning off the car.

He's silent for a moment—obviously contemplating knocking me out and taking a look inside the envelope. But Strobe stays civil. He opens the rear door and gets out, then comes over to my window.

"The next time you call or Mathis sets up a meeting, you make sure to ask if I'll be there. Got it?"

"Like the measles . . ."

He leaves and I follow through with my lie and list the Caddy in the classifieds. I'll hold on to the envelope for now. Strobe's already gone, but I know he'll be watching from somewhere.

3

I went to the Royal after placing the ad, but I didn't see a movie. No, I took an unlikely journey to one of the viaducts behind the theater. Early in the century, when the automobile was becoming popular, there was a struggle for space between cars and trains. So they built viaducts that would allow trains to travel underneath and cars to travel above. But to create these passages they merely built a new city on top of the old one. The railways were abandoned long ago, but they have just rediscovered intact and forgotten buildings inside the tunnels of the viaduct. Tanneries, blacksmiths, barbershops, and saloons—there's an entire city underneath the one we occupy. I am not a historian, I only recently became aware of it, but to me the thought of an underground city is compelling. Two worlds coexisting—one hidden, one seen. Despite the progress and might of the living world, the buried one remains, waiting like lava to reemerge.

The next day, Count requests my presence at court. I've been avoiding the place intentionally. I did all I could with Gant, but I don't want the blame if Count's crude attempt at blackmail doesn't pay off.

Claudel and Otis show their usual level of warmth. "Count's in a meeting," Claudel says. "You need to wait out here."

They stare at me, silent. Otis sits hunched over the bar while Claudel sucks his teeth at me. His wounds are beginning to heal. Spots of black are starting to show in the pink webs on his cheeks.

I wait with them for a while, saying nothing, only measuring their gazes for a hint of harm. Finally, the door to Count's office opens and a paunchy middle-aged white man with receding hair walks out. A teen-age Negro girl follows him in her long floral-pattern dress, probably her Sunday best, and a white shawl-cape that clasps in the front. They both wear the same defeated expression, and the reason becomes clear as Count comes out right behind them.

"I wish you two the best of luck," he says slapping his palm with a thick piece of paper folded in half. "Lord knows you're gonna need it."

The man and the girl walk past Claudel, Otis, and me, trying not to make eye contact. The girl does look up as she walks out. I realize she is the one from room 21—the girl that I was with the night I was arrested. I feel a bit exposed seeing her in this context. She looks lovely—excited, and scared, like someone just released from prison, anxious for a fresh start. It's strange, I don't know the details yet, but as they leave, I have a nagging suspicion that she may be better off on the inside.

"C'mon in the office," Count says once they've gone.

"What's going on with those two?" I ask as we go inside.

"Love, little man. Can't you tell?"

"What do you mean?"

"Ol' Bob fell in love with our little Clarice after spending a lot of money on her these past months. Said he wanted to be with her, so he agreed to sell me his house for a trade. The house for the girl. I felt it was an easy choice. He gave me a good price."

"Where will they live?"

"Well, he couldn't live in that house with her, now could he? These crackers would kill them both. They'll probably head out west to California. But they'd better be careful out there too."

I give a soft nod.

"Ain't it strange what a man will do for a woman," says Count, smiling. "I mean look at that fool Lester. This ain't the first time he lost what little sense he's got over a woman. There was this girl used to work for me, Etta . . . that boy was crazy for her. But she was hooked on that stuff. Hero'n. When she OD'd, the motherfucker tried to blame me for it. Can you believe that?"

I don't respond. Instead, I think of a girl that used to be around

Count's. A while back, she offered me a good time when I was low on cash. I was grateful for the offer. I never saw her again after that. I hope it wasn't her. I don't push the topic further. Count looks like he wants to change the subject. His jaw angles and his cheeks narrow, like he has just tasted something foul and can't wait to spit it out.

"Look, most of this is my fault," he says. "Getting you involved in this fight-fixing shit was too much to ask. That was a mistake. Sometimes this kind of thing comes easy to people, sometimes it doesn't. Everybody isn't like me—I need to remember that. I didn't use your talents in the right areas. I fucked up. I admit it. But now I'm about to correct that."

I'm relieved to hear Count take responsibility for his actions, but that pleasure is short-lived. Now I know that the stakes will soon be raised. Whatever he has in mind will make me long for the smoky boxing venues and their smelly locker rooms. Negotiations with shady underworld figures will seem like a cakewalk.

"What I got planned is even bigger than fixing fights. Hell, I was just trying to prove a point to Lester, but I'm getting too old to be doing shit for bragging rights. You see what I mean?"

Not quite, but I nod anyway.

"I can sense that things are changing, and they're changing fast—and I need to be on the right side of it. I need to take advantage of it."

I nod again and look at Count above the rims of my glasses, hands clasped in front of me, as if I were listening to Gant relay the details of the budget.

"Remember that Bozley Park thing? It's ready to roll," he says. "I just got some property over there."

"How did you get a house in Bozley Park? It's still very segregated."

"I know," he says holding up the folded piece of paper. "But ol' Bob sure does love Clarice . . . so says the deed to his house. But I've already stopped wanting the house. Yeah, I just ate, but I'm hungry again. Now I want the whole neighborhood."

I raise my eyebrows. I'm not sure what he means.

"All those white people will want to move out when they see a bunch of colored folks moving in. When the white folks leave, all those

Negroes that want to buy will have to pay a premium if they want to get in. White folks will sell low to me, and Negroes will buy high from me. We'll come in there and buy up the whole damn block."

"Count, that sounds . . . compelling, but I don't see how I can help you. You do know that I'm an accountant, right? I don't know anything about real estate."

Count stares at me. The humor provided by this scheme has faded from his face. "I know exactly what you are—even better than you do."

"I guess you're flush with cash now, right?"

"Yeah, that's right. Claudel was the pickup man. The pansy went down to Buttermilk Bottom and left a present in a rusted-out Packard. Just like we told him. What? You want me to say thank you?"

So Gant gave in. I know the point was to persuade him, but part of me wanted his better senses to prevail.

There is an awkward tension between us, as I can't tell what his next move will be, but that passes as he smiles and continues with his plan.

"You can do this," he says. "You're good with the numbers. After you do this, little man, you and me are square. Consider your debt to me paid."

The thought of not owing Count anything is too enticing. I'd join the circus if he asked me to. Why am I so drawn to danger? I've just followed an FBI agent gallivanting around with a young girl, and now I am taking it upon myself to desegregate a neighborhood. I am appalled by my recklessness, but not slowed in the least. I just want to be free of Count, but I am not going to make myself vulnerable in the process.

38

Count's plan was far more effective than I could have anticipated. There was a lot of interest once the Negro community got word that there was a house available to colored buyers in Bozley Park. Professional Negroes were especially interested. I met the first couple at a makeshift office that Count set up for me above a pool hall. The husband was a dapper insurance salesman; his wife was irritable and pregnant. It was obvious to me that he had a few women on the side. I could tell by the way he never walked or stood next to her. Always a few paces behind, he would let her drift away and then, after considerable distance, respond to the tug of her imaginary string, as if she were a bloated kite. But they were eager for the symbols of successful domesticity, and it showed. The husband tried to play hardball with me and negotiate stubbornly. I only agreed with him in a very calculated way, and I paced, for no other reason than to showcase my limp. It must have worked, because he agreed to a down payment that was ten percent above what Count paid for the place in its entirety.

And how savagely predictable it was that when the Negro family moved in, it only took a few weeks for the evacuation of the white residents to begin. Sure, they tried the usual acts of intimidation like burning in effigy a life-size Negro doll in their front yard, but it wasn't effective—their hearts weren't in it. Ever since the passage of the Civil Rights Act, they seemed to behave as if they were on the losing team. Martin even condemned the deplorable acts to the press, without knowing of my involvement. The juggling act between my job at the SCLC and Count's scheme has been tiring, but the thought of independence spurs me on. Eight homes have been installed with Negro families, but there is one house that remains occupied. My many offers and solicitations to buy the house have gone ignored:

**You may have discovered that the house
on the corner has been bought by a Negro.
Whether you like it or not, integration has come
to Bozley Park. I don't mean to insult your
intelligence, but when undesirables enter
a neighborhood, property values drop.
But do not worry. I am here to help you!
I want to buy your property. Name your price,
and I'll try my best to match it!**

Here I am, back in Bozley Park, in front of the house built in the old cottage style. Something about this place strikes a sentimental chord—it even has a white picket fence. It makes me think of Candy and the life I hoped we'd share. Maybe there is still time for us. Maybe if there were no agents and no Lester and no Count, I could just focus on my certification. I'd become a CPA, and maybe then we could live the American dream in this house. I'll save the sentimentality for another time.

I decide to be bold and knock on the door. A man answers, and I'm surprised to see a familiar face. That dark night in the woods and its ghostly visions come toward me once again. Pete stares at me, filling up the doorway. I'm not sure if there's any recognition there.

"What do you want?" he asks.

I pause for a beat, giving him the opportunity to place my face. "I came to drop off a flyer, sir."

He takes it from me, looks it over, lets out a laugh, balls it up, and throws it at me. "Let me tell you something, boy. I just bought this house for me and my little girl. Cost me everything I had—everything. And I'll be damned if I let some niggers come in here and take it away from me. See what I mean?"

"Yes . . . Yes, sir, I do." I smile. Maybe now he will recognize me. I wish we had matching rings or a secret talisman worn around our necks that we could flash at each other to give the signal that we're brothers. But in the secret club that Pete and I belong to, there is nothing of the sort.

"Well—" I almost call him Pete. "Sir, you do realize that with Negroes moving in, the property values are likely to decrease."

His face becomes redder underneath the already ruddy color that dominates his skin. "Now listen, I already told you I'm not letting any coloreds take what I worked hard for. You have no idea what I've done to get this place."

I pity his lack of awareness. My expression must show that.

"Don't look at me like that. It's not that I hate the Negro—it's that I love myself. The Negro is always screaming about his rights. Hell, I ain't fighting against his rights, I'm fighting for my rights. White man's rights. I fight everyday for the right to choose who I live near and who my child goes to school with. Isn't a man supposed to be free in this country? Do your people get their freedom at the expense of mine?"

As he says that, a female voice calls from within the house. "Daddy, what's going on?"

"Nothing to concern yourself with, Lucinda. Go on and get occupied. This here's grown-up business. Nothing to do with little girls."

She emerges and walks toward the front. A little girl who isn't so little. In fact, she's all grown up. I recognize her too. Not only is this Pete's little girl, she is Mathis's as well. I've seen her from a distance. Even then her beauty was apparent, but up close it is even more so. I see the spell Mathis is under. It's the sweet contradiction of her face: her lips are innocent pouty ribbons, but her eyes are large almond-shaped pools of accomplished curiosity. Even with her redneck father standing here in front of me, I have to break racial protocol and take her in. Pete's forearm interrupts the moment, quickly presenting itself in the doorway and blocking my view of his daughter. "Are we done here, boy?"

"Of course . . . I'll just leave this flyer in case you change your mind. I'll place it right here in your mailbox."

"You can put it up your ass for all I care. Now go ahead and leave already."

I leave Pete's porch, hoping that he will stay. Hoping that he will be stubborn and unwavering, allowing himself to be overcome by well-to-do Negroes who don't shuck and jive, who are not shiftless and lazy. No, they are too busy working for the American dream to worry about the rants and rhetoric of racist Pete. He'll be powerless and alone. He'll be outnumbered and rendered ineffectual by his lower-class anxieties: an angry man in a city too busy to hate.

Seeing her and Pete kick-starts a narrative that fills in the gaps of how she and Mathis may have met. Mathis may have gone to meet Pete to find out what was happening at the next Klan rally. After Pete gives him the information, and Mathis hands him the padded envelope, Pete's daughter comes outside with a bucket of water to wash down the porch. Mathis sees the beautiful creature that Pete has been hiding in his cave. In that very moment, Mathis becomes infatuated. She's everything his wife was and is not. She's beautiful and young, and he's already devising a way to get close to her, alone with her. He sees his salvation in her. Immediately, he begins to plan.

"What do we have here?" Mathis says, making sure she sees and hears him.

She turns around and looks at him.

"Good day, ma'am," he says, tipping his hat, addressing her formally, making her feel all regal and special.

"Go on inside, Lucinda," Pete says.

She does as she is told.

"You take care, ma'am," Mathis makes sure to say. "Fine daughter you have there, Pete."

Pete probably looks at him with cold, knowing eyes—a flash of warning each time he blinks, but that doesn't deter Mathis; he's already on a mission. It must have been a cakewalk for him.

He follows her to school one day and waits. He spots her and approaches her as she's coming out. "Hey," he says. "Do you remember me? I met you the other day. I'm your father's friend."

I'm sure she's nervous and uncomfortable seeing this man here. Pete has warned her not to talk to strange men. But this time is different. She had already noticed him, even before Mathis decided to tip his hat at her. She peered through the curtains when her father met him. She watched the mysterious and stern man that her father—the symbol of strength in her life—deferred to. This man intrigues her. When she walks out to toss that bucket of water, she does it on purpose. She makes sure to wear her shorts from gym class, the ones that always elicit a whistle whenever the stray teenage boy catches a glimpse of her in them. Yes, she puts those on and runs out there pretending to toss that bucket of water, to get a better look at the strange man who wears wool suits in this heat. What will he say? What will he think when he sees her? When she sees the man in front of her high school, waiting for her, she realizes that all boys respond the same, no matter what age.

He asks to give her a ride. She agrees. Mathis must feel the need to make her comfortable. She appreciates that, but she already is. She tells him he has nice eyes. He likes her eyes too. What kind of music does she listen to? Who's her favorite singer? It's someone he has never heard of, so he just laughs. She realizes he's never heard of them, so she laughs too. They bond. They talk. He wants to go about this gradually, but he can't help but tell her how beautiful she is. She thanks him, but Mathis is already regretful. He feels he's coming on too strong and doesn't want to scare her. He is surprised when he sees that she is not scared or uncomfortable at all.

As they get closer to her house, Mathis wants to tell her that he must stop and let her out. He has an appointment. She's already aware of how it would seem to her father or anyone who sees her getting out of the car of an older man. So she tells him to stop here. She'll walk the rest of the way. Mathis was going to say it himself, but she beat him to it. That impresses and, to a certain degree, emboldens him. This is where Mathis's latent quixotic nature surfaces. He sees this as a sign of their connecting on a hidden level—the two of them speaking an intuitive language beyond the communication of words. He didn't even have to say anything. All of this is confirmed when she says, "You can pick me up from school at the same time from now on . . . if you want to."

Mathis probably feels like a teenager. He thinks about when he began courting his wife, after a first date that he thought was disastrous, and he had no chance of ever seeing her again. She saved him from a broken heart. *You can take me out again . . . if you want to.* This is the same kind of feeling that Lucinda has given him, but this time it is more profound. He is not a teenage boy; he's closer to death than he is to that boy. Yet here is this young girl reaching into the grave to save him.

Okay, he says and agrees to pick her up the next day. Who knows how long it took him to suggest the motel—maybe she did—but that's probably how it began. Just like that. I concede that I have no proof of this. The only way to know for certain is to hear it directly from Mathis himself, but something tells me he won't be so forthcoming.

39

The plan was to ruin Mathis as he has tried to ruin Martin; and now I have the means to do so. I look at the photos of Mathis and the girl—Pete's daughter, Lucinda—and their front seat fondling. I have it all here. I sent photos to Mrs. Mathis, but I suppose she ignored them. Maybe it was a common sight for her, something she'd seen before, something she was used to; but I know of another audience that won't be so forgiving. A father in rage is a dangerous animal. Pete will do to Mathis what I cannot.

But when I leave to send off the pictures, I encounter the vision of four little girls outside my apartment playing jump rope and rattling off the rhythmic tongue twisters that accompany the sport. Hopscotch squares drawn on the sidewalk are already used and abandoned by the many little footprints still visible in the chalk. Why have they chosen this street? I have never seen them before. They make me think of those four little girls killed by Klan members in that church bombing last year. No matter how much I want to hurt Mathis, I can't send these pictures to Pete. I have no guarantee that only Mathis will see harm. In this situation, who knows what will happen. Pete could blame poor Lucinda for being too alluring and too provocative, and since she didn't have the decency to say no, he may insist she's a whore and harm her physically in some horrible way. All of that could happen. Yes, I think of those little girls. I think of the twenty others that were injured, and the way that children get hurt when adults play rough. That kind of violence was perpetrated by Pete's kind of people—who knows what he's capable of? I don't know Lucinda, but I don't wish that upon her.

So, I guess they've won. I thought I was learning to play, but I am bad at this game. I don't have the ruthless skill set of Mathis and Strobe. I've learned there are actually some things I won't do. I can't say the same for the agents—and that's where they have the advantage.

Work. The SCLC has seen an increase in donations since Martin's Nobel nomination. Most of the lower-level staff are delighted to be associated with someone bestowed with such a prestigious honor, but Martin's executive staff has been walking around in a perpetual state of anxiety. They are smart enough to know that this honor brings attention, and that is always followed by scrutiny. They think someone is always plotting to make it all come tumbling down. They are more right than they know.

I feel sad as I prepare the contribution thank-you letters. In some way, they feel like coded Dear John letters: *This must end . . . it's me, not you.* Yes, this will all be over soon. Martin's indiscretions will be made public, and he'll only be remembered as a depraved charlatan. No one will remember how much he sacrificed and loved this country. Nor will they understand how the burdens of love and sacrifice can lead to such desperate behavior. I find a little comfort knowing that my contribution will be forgotten as well. And to think at one time I had the foolish notion of being a public figure. No, thank you, limelight—the shadows suit me fine.

Gant knocks on my door and pokes his head in. "Estem, can I talk to you in my office for a second?" He looks somber.

"Sure."

I follow him to his office and take a seat. He gets right to the point. "Estem, I won't be working here any longer. I have offered Martin my resignation, and he has accepted it."

I'm shocked, but strangely, the first thing that comes to mind is my apprenticeship. I haven't really thought about receiving my certification in so long. I am only a year away from completion. *Only a year away.* I think it and say it aloud. Gant appears unmoved.

"Don't worry. This won't affect you. You're very resourceful,

Estem. I'm sure you'll find some way to finish the requirement . . . if that is what you truly want. Is this what you really want? Can you envision yourself doing anything else? If the answer is no, well, maybe you should find the thing that drives you the most, occupies your thoughts, your desires, your hopes. I don't mean just for practical reasons, but for larger, *existential* ones. To find out who you truly are is a gift. What do you want out of this world, and what type of mark do you want to leave on it?"

I don't respond.

"This is just a reflex reaction," he continues. "I'd be surprised if you ever think about me when I'm gone." His arms are crossed, and I detect a slight smirk on his face. I want to tell him to go to hell, and I plan to, but when I open my mouth all that comes out is, "Don't go."

"Look," he says, "I've been offered a job at a prestigious accounting firm in New York. The doors are finally opening, if only just a crack. Isn't that what we're fighting for, equal opportunity? I think this is a good time for me to leave. It's best for Martin, and for the movement."

I suppose he's right, but that makes me think of all the other Negroes I'll have to compete against. My desire to join an elite club of one hundred or so Negro professionals won't mean as much now. It will be the first thousand, the first ten thousand, and so on.

I can't help feeling that he's doing this to me on purpose, leaving just as I am so close to accomplishing my lifelong dream. Maybe this is not a coincidence. Maybe this is a parting shot. He sets fire to my dreams—an arsonist of ambition—he burns my hopes to the ground and flees with the matches. But then I come to my senses and remember the blackmail. I never realized how much he loved the SCLC until he stole from it to remain a part of it.

"What's prompting the urgency? Why now?" I ask.

"They've sent photos this time, Estem."

"What sort of photos?" I have to think for a moment to be sure that it wasn't me. Photos. No demands for money. Would Mathis and Strobe show their hand so deliberately?

"Photos of me . . ." he says, "with other men."

His honesty and lack of shame impresses me. "I don't know what to say . . ."

"It's funny, Estem, but that's not the response I expected."

I'm silent.

"Did you know that I am a homosexual, John?"

"No . . ."

"The South is hard, but the world . . . the world is cruel. There were threats to expose me—to even lie and suggest that Martin and I are . . . involved."

"Who do you think is behind it? The same as before?"

Gant is silent, but his look speaks volumes. "I have my suspicions," he says finally. "I have to step down, John. I can't let them undo everything we have worked for. Threatening letters, vile recordings, it's all too much. I don't know how Martin puts up with it, but I can't continue to add to his burden. You can't imagine the toll it's taking on him. This has brought out the worst in me. I even had myself investigated by a private detective to see how much of my dirt someone could get their hands on if they so desired. It was less than I expected, but ample enough. That's why I'm stepping down."

I recall the day I watched a man in a wrinkled trench coat give Gant a gift in the punishing rain.

"They even think I'm a communist. Hell, I'm no communist. I did attend the occasional meeting, but that was to impress a beautiful dark-haired boy. He had the eyes of a Gypsy king. It's strange what we'll risk for those fleeting moments of pleasure."

Gant's airy-fairy reminiscing makes me look away.

"I apologize, Estem. I must be making you uncomfortable with all this lavender-scented talk."

"No, sir. Of course not." My shoulders shift in my suit. "Please go on."

"Puritans," Gant says. "The country is being overrun by puritans. This is what it comes down to, John—who are you fucking and who is fucking you."

I feel sad for Gant. He wants to seem seasoned and wise right now, but then I think of that photo, that alley, and the payoff. If with all of his wisdom he couldn't avoid being reckless, there is little hope for me.

He comes down from his soapbox and looks me over to assess the effect of his sermon. He squints his eyes and arches an eyebrow.

He must not like what he sees, because he turns his back on me and addresses me over his shoulder. "Know this, Estem. You are not trusted. People are suspicious of you—Martin is suspicious of you. And he isn't suspicious of anyone. Keep your hands clean. I won't be here to protect you."

Martin is suspicious of *me*? I'm used to the judgment of my co-workers, but I never would have guessed that Martin shared their way of thinking.

"Sir, I'm not sure what you mean."

"I won't be here to protect you . . . as I have been," he says, turning to face me again.

I'm made rigid by a sudden surge of indignation. Who is he to protect me? I taught him how to save his own hide. Mathis and Strobe reached out their hands and gave me Gant's life to do with as I pleased. You could have added that scene to the ceiling of the Sistine Chapel for its beauty and significance.

"Aaron, I need you to elaborate. I'm completely in the dark. I'm not sure what you're talking about, but I suspect—forgive me—that I should be offended."

"Estem, you don't have to pretend with me any longer. The new car, the new clothes—your tailor is an artist, by the way—all these things are signs to me. Flashing red stop signs. I know you're spying for them."

His words rattle me. For a moment, I want to kneel and beg for clemency, but I feel as if someone has just tugged at my spine. Can it be true that all this time Gant has been playing me for a fool? Even in my fear, I can admit that I am impressed, but I do not respond. Gant is obviously impressed with himself as well.

"It's hard out there, believe me, I know," he says. "There is a great deal of temptation competing with the level of sacrifice that we demand of you. So I don't blame you, brother. I'm disappointed, but I'm not going to judge you. The NAACP is a fine organization—longstanding—it's understandable that they would feel threatened by Martin and us. It's flattering that they think so much of us that they would pay you for information."

I'm up to my glasses in an alphabet soup of intrigue. First, the

SCLC, and then the FBI. I almost think that the NAACP is one of their subsidiaries. When I realize what he's saying, I have to smile.

"Some of the people in the office think you're an FBI informant, but I put an end to that talk. I said, 'Estem? Really? How ridiculous. He's too harmless and unimportant for the FBI to even be aware of.' Isn't that the funniest load of shit you've ever heard?"

At first, I feel my jaw flex and then tighten. I swallow just to keep my head from bursting. Then I start to tremble, and I know I've been doped with that intoxicating dose of stupidity and courage.

"It's funny that you would talk about people being suspicious of me, while you're cavorting with strange men . . . and embezzling money to save your ass," I say as I stand. "You can play the victim all you want, but I know you, Aaron. I know you better than anyone. You're an arrogant son of a bitch. Retiring, my ass. Martin fired you. Discretion, you say. You wouldn't know discretion if it sat on your face and shat. I see through you. You're a weak and troubled man, Aaron. You can pretend that you're doing Martin a favor by leaving, but we both know you're being pushed out—shown the door. You're a liability—you always have been. You didn't care how your homosexuality affected Martin, until they sent pictures. And you speak of discretion. If you're leaving, then leave. I'm not going to be your deferential audience so that you can feel superior. Not anymore."

I feel good after that, so I turn to go.

"Is that all, Estem? What's your point?" He walks over to me and gets very close. I feel his breath and smell his cologne. "Was it you? Since you know me so very well—was it you who sent those photos? You seem like the type that likes to watch. Did *you* blackmail me? You little sour-mouthed, crippled motherfucker. You're here because I allow you to be. When I resigned, Martin asked me, 'Are you taking Estem with you?'—like you were a piece of office furniture I was fond of. I said no, because an assistant is just a professional man's tool, like the tools any other workingman uses. I said, no, he stays. When a janitor leaves he doesn't take the mop, now, does he?"

"I think you know what you can do with your mop," I say. "Get creative. And by the way, I am not working for the NAACP."

"You don't have to worry about convincing me of anything, Estem."

I leave his office. But inside, I have conceded. I dreamed of having an advantage over him for so long. I thought I had it, but I was wrong. They threatened him with exposure, but such an unveiling was Gant's deliverance. Mathis and Strobe gave him the chance to be free, and he took it.

I'm on a belligerent high after my spat with Gant. I walk out of his office and into my own. I sit at my desk, tapping it with my pencil to the recent events playing in my head. The nerve of him. There is something positive that has come from all of this. I knew Gant's contempt for me was real, not imagined. This confirms it. But satisfaction only visits for a moment; then it's gone. He's definitely prodded my insecurities. I need to get out of here, head home. Maybe muster up enough courage to head to Count's—get myself a real drink like a real man, maybe a woman too. . . .

I gather myself and walk out into the hallway. As I approach the exit, I notice that the door to Martin's office is open and he's inside. I stand in the doorway, looking at him. He's seated, but looks so exhausted that he wishes the chair were a bed. He seems deep in thought, but then he becomes aware of my presence. My eyes must be still buzzing with anger because when he looks at me he says, "Don't look at me like that. I didn't force him out."

I only let out a short clipped breath in response.

"He could have stayed if he wanted. It was his choice." He brings his hand to his face and strokes his chin. "He wanted to make the sacrifice . . . make a stand. He wanted to protect the movement—and that wasn't a sacrifice I asked him to make."

I take my eyes off Martin to look in the hallway and see if anyone is coming. I take advantage of the cloak of his dark mood and step inside, closing the door behind me. He doesn't offer, but as I did on that night of our intimate conversation, I take a seat across from him.

"I didn't ask him to do it. And I'm not trying to claim any moral high ground here. I didn't ask him because I didn't want to deal with the burden and guilt of doing so . . . not again. I should've asked him—I would have been completely within my rights—but I didn't. I didn't want that feeling, that I betrayed him. I didn't want to carry that burden. I just couldn't do it."

I lean forward, prompting him. "Go on, Martin," I say.

He rests his chin on his clasped hands and sweat begins to bud on his brow. "I am not one to judge how men express themselves *sexually*. When it comes to the test of loyalty and friendship, I worry that I may have failed. I turned my back on a man who was like a brother to me. He helped me shape my mind when it was still a crude ball of clay. I betrayed him to protect my image. I am on the right path. I have chosen this path, but he was the one who presented the path to me in the first place. After reaching national prominence on the concepts that he introduced to me, I turned my back on him."

He won't say his name, but I know he's talking about Bayard. Bayard Rustin, noted pacifist of the Gandhian variety. Aide to A. Philip Randolph. Architect of the March on Washington. A man who was Martin's mentor. An elegant man. An excruciatingly intelligent man. But a homosexual man.

With slow, labored movements, he unbuttons his collar and loosens his tie. "When the competition got too hot, that's when I got the call. I got threatened, brother. They threatened to expose my indiscretions, but this wasn't anonymous—this was from a leader in the movement. He felt I was getting too big for my britches and I should call off plans for a protest that he didn't agree with. If I didn't back off, he said he'd tell everyone that my mentor and I were involved in some sort of . . . *entanglement*. I've never been more disgusted with myself than I was at that moment, but I caved. I've suffered beatings, arrests, and insults, but the assault on my masculinity, my vanity—brother, that was too much to bear. And I have been trying to correct myself, correct the flaw ever since. So no, I did not ask Gant to leave—he did it himself." With his elbow propped on the desk, Martin rests his head in his palm. He looks askance at the many papers covering his desk. With his free hand, he picks up a pen and twirls it absently. "The urge is strong," he says. "It can make you do so many things. The irony is that something so . . . *life-affirming* can be so destructive." His eyelids droop as if weighted by anchors.

I look at him, and I hear him. I feel an intense brightness blooming in my chest. I didn't take advantage of it during our previous conversation—I just sat there and let him do all the talking. I didn't even attempt to share any of myself. But now, this is an opportunity to rectify that.

"This urge—"

I jump in. "Yes, Martin. I know what you mean. Sometimes I feel this urge, this intense feeling comes over me and it turns into something like an animal propelled only by hunger and desire. I see the world through a different lens. The world is my hunting grounds, its inhabitants are my prey."

His eyes trail off from making contact with mine. I realize we are not talking about the same thing. He holds up his palm for me to stop. "Humanity, brother. Humanity. I am talking about the urge to serve humanity."

"Of course," I say. "Well, I guess I'll be going." I look at my watch and stand up at the same time. "You have a good night, Martin."

"You do the same, brother. Let me follow you out." He lets out a groan as he stands.

I should have left it at that, but for some reason I can't seem to keep my mouth shut today. I turn back and say, "Don't worry about Gant. I'm sure we'll get along fine without him."

He puts his hand on my shoulder, but the pain becomes so unbearable that I have to shrug him off. He looked exhausted before, but now he looks near death. He reaches out to me and grabs my shoulder again. "I just need a second," he says, then collapses in my arms. He's a heavy man and I am not that strong. All the weight is borne by my bad leg. I can feel the metal digging into my skin as I try to prop him up and keep both of us from falling on the ground. Within seconds, it becomes a mission not to fall down holding him. I want this image to be ingrained in everyone's mind when they recall the story. So I squat, putting his weight on my good leg and my lower back, and I immediately feel the pain. I call for help—someone—just as much for Martin's sake as my own. First, it's Gant—our fight seems to be long forgotten—then Abernathy and Young come on the scene and lift Martin off me. He is limp in their arms, too, as they carry him out of the building, Young with his hands under Martin's armpits and Abernathy supporting him by the ankles.

Out of the building and into Gant's Lincoln, Young and Abernathy are in the back with Martin, while Gant is in the driver's seat. Young looks at me as I stand there watching them, wondering what I should say or do. "Get in the goddamn car, man," Young screams at me, "What the hell are you waiting for?" I get in the front seat. Martin's coming to and moaning softly. They offer him words of comfort as Gant runs stop signs and terrifies slow-footed pedestrians. I offer no such words; if Martin survives, their tactics will only grow more vicious and desperate.

40

The collapse was due to dehydration exacerbated by poor diet, insomnia, and extreme stress, the doctor informed us. Martin will be fine, but he must take it easy for a few days—but that's unlikely. Around midnight, a nurse brought a telephone to his bedside. Oslo was on the line: Martin had won the Nobel Peace Prize. He was immediately rejuvenated, and all evidence of his horrific fatigue was a distant memory—even the IV bag that floated above him glowed like a cartoon idea bulb.

"You're the first Negro to win a Nobel," Abernathy declared.

"No," Martin corrected him, "Ralph Bunche was the first. But I'm damn sure the prettiest!"

They all laughed, then Young added, "No, motherfucker, you're the *shortest!*" The laughter opened up to howls, but I didn't join in. I saw Coretta coming in with the children, and I used it as an opportunity to excuse myself to the waiting room.

After a while, among the uncomfortable wooden seats, the pea-green linoleum, and old copies of *Ebony* and *Jet* magazine—some of them even have Martin on the cover—I start to see the situation more clearly. The harm wished upon Martin has grown more sinister. They have sent him tapes and letters. Maybe, for his own sake, it's time for him to step down and give up the limelight.

I see Coretta leaving with the children, but I don't bother to acknowledge her, and she seems grateful. Somehow, I have come to that point where you can't tell the difference between bravery and foolishness.

I walk into Martin's room, where Young, Abernathy, and Gant are gathered around his bed. "There he is," Young says smiling. "*H-H-Help me! Somebody, help me!*" They laugh and Martin tells them to take it easy, then they look at me in astonishment as I just stand there trembling and speechless. They are waiting for me to say something, but no one tells me to get out. It's almost as if they know I have come to deliver some important news but they are not sure what—and neither am I. I open my mouth, and my lip and chin start to shake. All I can say is, "They're not going to stop. They won't ever stop."

In letting go, I feel a surge of relief and it's overwhelming. My eyes surge with heat and tears. How I must look to them. Abernathy looks down at Martin and grabs his hand. Young rubs his face and lets out a deep soulful sigh. And Gant only says my name.

"It's okay," Martin says. "It's okay. I know there are things out there. Forces, people who wish me and my family harm. Some of them feel they are doing God's work by praying for my demise. But I know I must stay calm." He pauses and points to his chest. "My scar here reminds me that I must be strong. It's no accident that the scar is cross-shaped. I know that the power of God is working through me. Throughout our struggle, I have asked him to remove any bitterness from my heart and replace it with the strength and courage to face any disaster that comes my way. I know that I have a Divine Companionship in this struggle. It may sound grandiose, but I know no other way to explain it. While all this turmoil is going on, God has given me an inner peace. He has given my family the strength to adjust to threats on my life, and threats of violence. I know the price I pay for a nonviolent movement. It doesn't mean that violence won't be inflicted upon me or anyone. But I am willing to allow myself to be a victim of violence, even though I will never inflict violence upon another. I live by the conviction that through my suffering, my cross bearing, the social situation for everyone may be redeemed or improved."

Abernathy offers an amen, and suddenly Martin is surrounded by congratulatory praise. "I know this son of a bitch didn't just give his Nobel address from a hospital bed," Young says. I could easily slip out of the room without being noticed. The love-in that has emerged does not move me. It's strange, but I have quickly shifted from guilty and apologetic to detached and cynical. In some shape or another, I have heard those words from Martin before, and I am tired of hearing them. He talks of God for his public strength, while I know of his private weakness. When the problems of life become too difficult to bear, he and I try to escape to the same place, preferably between the arms and legs of a woman. I am sure the others in this room are acquainted with the dirty details as well as I, yet they eat up this sermon like spoon-fed oatmeal. Haven't they grown tired of the sermonizing? I don't want reassurance; I want a tutorial. How does one maintain such a sterling image to others and to himself while his private life continues to corrode? Mathis asked me that question in so many words, and I didn't have an answer then either.

I'm ready to see her. I didn't realize it until after the craziness of the other night, and I didn't have anyone to share it with, anyone who could understand.

I park down the street from Candy's place—Candy and Lester's place—and wait for him to leave for work. When he does, I knock on her door. She looks different, no makeup. She has two spots, freckles, on her left cheek that I've never noticed before.

"Hello, John," she says. I can't tell how she feels about seeing me or if she feels anything at all.

"How are you?" I ask.

"Fine."

"Haven't heard from you in a while . . ."

"I know. I'm sorry."

"Don't apologize. I don't like it when women apologize to me. It makes me nervous."

She sees me looking at the piles of clothes waiting to be washed, too much of it to belong to just the two of them. "You think Count would let us live without paying a price?" she asks. "He took most of what I had to leave us alone. It's driving poor Lester crazy. I'm doing folks' laundry just to make ends meet. You ever feel like life is running away from you? And you're not living for yourself?"

Yes, with every heartbeat. "I'm not sure what you mean," I say, before lighting a cigarette.

"I thought being with him would help, but it didn't. He let me believe he was helping me, giving me what I wanted. I didn't even know what I wanted. Even though the man never jokes, I know he was laughing at me. I judged you, and I shouldn't have. I can admit that now. I pitied you for wanting to be like them—for wanting their power so much. But I was just like you. I felt small and wanted to lash out against the world, but now I see that on the inside nobody is smaller than them. Nobody hates themselves more than they do. I just didn't see it then, and now I do."

"Who's *they*?"

"Never mind."

I take a long drag from my cigarette and hand it to her. "I'll talk to him, if you want me to. Maybe get some of your money back."

She responds by folding a freshly ironed shirt. Smoke disappears into the fabric. "I know how to get it back if I need to. Well, look at you. You've sure come up in the world. Now you're his right-hand man."

I take an envelope from my coat pocket and place it between her and some socks that need darning. "There's a thousand dollars inside."

She looks at me, but I know she doesn't see me as before. "Whatever I need from a man, Lester can give me."

"I'll just leave it. Cab driver's a tough racket. It don't pay as well as gangster."

I drive home, but I don't get out of the car. I just lean back and listen to the radio. For so long she was the woman I wanted, but that dream girl is gone. This happens to a lot of men. In order to get over the heartbreakers, we have to imagine them dead in a strange way, only a ghostlike shell of her former self. Lester wasn't exposed to the full strength of her allure long enough to miss it, and Count is disturbingly indifferent to her absence. Even Mathis has a soft pretty thing. I've been good for a while, cautious of those Peeping Toms posing as agents, but seeing her reminds me of how much I need a woman.

42

I walk into Count's and see Joe Tex gyrating onstage in a gold lamé jumpsuit. The place is packed tonight. Everyone is drunk but exhilarated. Count holds court over in his usual corner booth. I spot him and make my way over. For the first time, I can say that he seems truly happy to see me. Pete remains, but financially the real estate scheme is working out.

"Hey, little man. How you doin'? Take a seat."

I sit down in the booth, and Count casually drapes his arm around me. His breath and smile tell me how drunk he is. Claudel stands at the table with his hands clasped in front of him. He keeps his eyes on me as Count pulls me in closer.

"Where's the other one?" I ask Count while looking at Claudel.

"Early retirement. This life ain't for everybody," Count says, then quickly changes the subject. "What can I do for you? Just ask me . . . anything," he says.

"I've been thinking about what you said—about Martin—and I think you're right."

His mood changes and his arm snakes off my shoulder. "Is that so?"

"Yeah, I got Gant to pay, so why not Martin? I've invited him over, but I need a couple of girls to come to my apartment." He can tell that I am lying, but I don't care, and he doesn't seem to either.

"You need two girls, huh?"

"Yeah, obviously I can't have them here, so I thought it would be safer to have them come back to my place." He just looks at me and

I feel pitiful. He says whatever I want is mine, but that's his angle: whatever I want must have the potential to benefit him.

"Two, huh?" He looks over at two girls with two smiling men at the bar. One is petite with a very light complexion; the other is statuesque with dark skin like polished ebony. Count motions for them to come over. They leave behind four unfinished drinks and two unhappy men.

"This here's one of my best customers," Count says when they arrive at the table. "Forget customer—this here is one of my best friends."

The two girls look at each other, and then they give me pained smiles.

"You two give him whatever he wants," Count says. "I don't want no problems."

The girls give each other a concerned look, then again they force their smiles at me. They introduce themselves. The tall dark one calls herself Ruby; the little light one goes by Gladys.

"My car's out front," I tell them. They don't seem to care as they turn and head to the exit. I get up to follow them, but Claudel steps in front of me. He says something, but I can't make it out. "What's that you say, Claudel? I can't hear you . . . music's too loud." His face is healing nicely, but even years from now some of the scars will still be visible—dark raised lines, like some sort of tribal markings.

He leans in close and puts his mouth to my ear. "I said I'm gonna do my best to kill you."

I lift my head and look him in the eye. "Good luck with that," I say as I step past him to walk out.

I put the girls in my car and drive home. They don't know what kind of show to expect, so I let them in on tonight's special guest and that seems to put them at ease. But when we arrive at my apartment, the girls look disappointed.

"I thought you said Dr. King was gonna be here," says Ruby. I had a plan, raw and carnal, but I think it has already faded. Now I just want their company. "Ain't he in the hospital or somethin'?"

"He said he'd be here," I tell them, "and if he doesn't come, then you won't have to do anything."

"You got anything to drink in here?" asks Gladys.

"Just scotch whiskey," I say.

Gladys makes a sour face.

"Don't worry about it, Gladys. I brought a little something." Ruby reaches into her purse and pulls out a reefer. "You got matches, don't you?"

"Yes, I say."

"Good. You want some?"

"Sure, why not . . ."

Hours later, I tell them about my unrequited love for Candy. Gladys is curled up on my sofa like a sleeping kitten, while Ruby and I lie together on the floor. She strokes my brace with her free hand, a joint in the other. She asks me if she can take it off and try it on. There's a pungent sweetness in the air that I like. She passes me the reefer. The smoke twists and turns, giving the illusion of clouds moving against a nighttime sky. It's beautiful. She sighs. She sees it too. She strokes my hair tenderly, and I turn to look at her. Something glimmers: a star twinkling in the darkness under the sofa. I reach over her and into the pitch. I can feel it in my hand. I'm stunned by my find as I bring it to my face for closer inspection: a small microphone about the size of a nickel.

"What is it?" she asks.

"Nothing. Just something I lost."

She tilts her head and shrugs her shoulders until one of them touches her ear. "Guess Dr. King ain't coming," she says with a laugh.

No, Martin isn't coming. And I couldn't be more relieved.

43

Morning. The sun sneaks through the curtains, casting its shaming light on all that has transpired. We yawn and stretch and look at each other with foggy, bleary-eyed regret. I still feel a bit out of it myself, and I am anxious to see them leave. The knock on my door makes us sharp and sober.

It's my mother. I am embarrassed to have her see me like this. So much has gone on here. But when I dare to look her in the eye, to my surprise, I see a glimpse of that woman my father knew before. The kind of woman that's used to seeing a man at his worst.

The ladies push past my mother. Her eyes follow them as they rush into the street, struggling with their shoes and grappling with their sweaters.

"Hello, Mama," I say. She's dressed for church, even though it's not Sunday. She has food with her. I know just by the smell that it's pork chops smothered in gravy. She walks in and looks around my place as if her gaze were a white-gloved finger inspecting the place for dirt. Then her gaze falls on me.

"I'd be dishonest," she says, "if I said I wasn't disappointed, son."

"I know, Mama, I'm sorry."

"And I'd be a goddamn liar if I said I didn't want to smack you in the face."

I'm hurt and offended by that, but I recover quickly, and it immediately toughens me up. "I'm a grown man, Mama. I can do what I damn well please in my own house."

She only squints in response. "I'm mad, son—really mad. I'm

mad because this means he was right about you. When you got sick, I blamed myself—any mother would—but he begged me not to. He said blaming myself would only make you weak. And the whole point of having a child, sick or healthy, was to make him strong, and dammit, he was right. But I blamed myself anyway. You've known that for a while, haven't you?"

I don't say anything. I notice that my pants are undone, and I zip my fly.

"You don't know how I fought in that house to protect you. A man doesn't look at his wife in the same way when she's the mother of a crippled child. He pities her or resents her, and for him that ruins her. I guess I ruined you too. You're father was right. You don't know how much that angers me to say, but I look around and you got whores in here—in your own home. I realize you are not much of a man at all. You never learned how to be a man. You never learned how to take care of yourself—how to take care of a woman. You're lying with whores in here. You're still a boy. Still a child. You expect to be coddled. And you talk about that girl Candice not wanting you. I used to think it was her loss, but now I see just how smart she really is. I've said what I had to. But now I don't know who to be more mad at—your father, me, you, or God."

She leaves and doesn't bother closing the door behind her.

44

Maybe the old man is right. Maybe she did more harm than good. Yeah, she blamed herself for the polio, but wasn't all the coddling for her benefit and not mine? Aren't I the victim in all of this?

There's no time to deal with my mother—she'll come around eventually. I head to work, but I don't even stop when I approach the office, I just keep driving. I don't feel like being there right now. I need a place to clear my mind, and Candy's not an option, especially after being verbally castrated, so I settle on the Royal.

I watch a couple of movies and pass the time, and then I head home. It's night by now. A whole day lost to the darkness of the theater.

There's a knock at my door. I answer it and see her there looking beautiful in that red dress. Her sunglasses make her look like a melancholy heiress or a rich man's trophy. We don't greet each other, I just step aside so that she can enter. I stay silent, only listening to the whisper of the fabric as she walks. She places her pocketbook down with a sigh and removes her big sunglasses. There's a bruise on her right cheek.

"Candy, what happened?"

"Lester found the envelope of money."

A pang of guilt hits me in my stomach. I reach out to her. I want to pull her close, but she just waves me away. She wants to continue her story without me touching her.

"He doesn't think it's you, though," she says. "Thought it was Count. He thought that money meant that I was leaving him. That Count still had control of me. He said I was still Count's whore."

Lester has done a lot for me up to this point. Maybe in some way I owe him, but I've never wished harm on a person more than I do now. Despite his size, his training as a professional fighter, if Lester were in front of me right now I'd try my best to kill him.

"Just sit down. Let's talk about it." I lead her to my bed and sit next to her.

"I don't have any place to go, John. I can't go back to Count."

"Well, you can stay here," I say. "You'll stay here and I'll take care of you." Our eyes tangle in shared gaze. For the first time, I think she understands what I mean. She smiles, wipes away a tear, and nods, "Okay."

I brushed back a strand of her hair that's fallen over the cheek bruised by Lester. I think about how this could all be different. This whole ordeal has generated a newfound understanding of my life and the world. I want to share that with her. All the mistakes I've made in the past will be forgotten. My new chapter with Candy begins now.

My phone rings. Reluctantly, I pull away from Candy to answer it. "Hello?"

He seems frantic and desperate in a way that I've never heard him before. He says he wants to see me—an urgent matter. It snaps me out of my love lust. He wants to meet at his house—his house, for God's sake. I don't even tell him I have company. "I'm on my way."

45

I told her to make herself at home, lie down in my bed and rest a bit, and I'd be back very soon to take care of her. She said she understood, that I should do what I had to do and not to worry about her.

When I arrive at his house, I wait inside my car for a moment, staring at the brick portico. I take a deep breath before I get out and make my way to his front door.

"Come in," he says. "Coretta and the children are not here. It's just the two of us."

They let him out of the hospital at his insistence. He looks a bit feverish, but I can't tell if it's because of whatever's troubling him or a preexisting condition. I enter and he gives two quick looks outside to the left and right before closing the door. I look over his home methodically, making sure to take in everything: the wallpaper in his living room with its baroque roses and endlessly swirling leaves, the nicked and scratched but well-polished wood of his piano, the yellowing sheets of "Amazing Grace" on the music rest, the modest dining room with a portrait of Gandhi above the dining table, which has now been turned into a desk that he's been putting to use. Books sit in stacks—Niebuhr, Gandhi, Whitman, a book about the Korean War—next to a well-used ashtray, a legal pad, and a few balls of crumpled paper. All of this, and just a few days out of the hospital. I look over at the pad and try to make out what's written on it without appearing intrusive. Something about the Vietnam conflict . . . poverty . . . peace.

I was blinded by the excitement of being in his home. I didn't see that everything is in disarray: shades removed from their lamps, the sofa, now separated from its cushions and their exposed stuffing, drawers overturned, papers and clothes on the floor, tables with their legs in the air like road kill.

This is only the aftermath, but I know the kind of fear that prompts such frenzied panic.

"John, are you listening to me?"

I snap out of it. "I'm sorry, Martin. What did you say?"

"This. This is what I found. Do you know what this is?"

I open my palm and he drops a small metal cylinder in my hand. It seems dented, like he tried to smash it. I know exactly what it is, but I ask him to identify it for me anyway.

"It's a listening device," he says. "They're bugging my home. They've gotten inside, John. I called you because you seem like you'd understand. I think I can talk to you. Some people at the SCLC . . . I don't know if I could trust them anymore."

That word "trust" makes me uncomfortable. Was Gant being truthful when he said that Martin was suspicious of me?

"Wait," he says. "They could be listening." Stepping over the wreckage, Martin goes over to his phonograph, removes the vinyl from its sleeve, and Mahalia Jackson's booming voice fills the house.

When you walk through a storm, hold your head up high. And don't be afraid of the dark . . .

He returns and gets very close to me as if preparing to tell a secret. "They think I'm losing my mind. Paranoid. Going insane. Yes, I'm under a great deal of pressure. But I'm no fool—this is more than just some lousy mercenaries who work for Hoover."

I think about all the bugs in this house that Martin has not found, and what Mathis and Strobe will think of being called mercenaries.

"I think somebody on the staff is working for the FBI. To get this close to my home? It may sound crazy, but I've known jealousy from my own people before. Especially in the leadership. The higher up people are, the more envious they become. You should have seen what I had to deal with during Montgomery. All the backbiting and backstabbing— and now Wilkins at the NAACP. I feel there are so few people I can trust. They don't know that I'm aware of it, but there is a plot to replace me—have me step down with my sanity intact . . ."

I watch his face for a tell. Nothing. If he is toying with me, then he's more persuasive than anyone could presume, and Hoover is outmatched.

"Martin, what do you want me to do?"

"I want you to keep your ears open at the SCLC. Let me know what you hear. They're getting too close to me. They know too much. They know more about me than my own wife. We need to look closer at who we allow to volunteer. Can you do that for me, brother? Can you help me?"

"Of course, Martin. I'd do anything you'd ask."

"I've got to be more careful about who I associate with. How well do you know that girl you were with in Los Angeles? Candice, I believe it was . . ."

"Candy? I know her very well." Our eyes collide and send off brief knowing sparks. "But she has nothing to do with this."

"No, of course not. I'm sorry, John. It just seems that after Los Angeles, a torrent of venom has descended upon us."

I panicked that night at the hospital. I didn't make my case as I'd planned, and the tension has been building up inside me. I want to tell him everything, even though I know it's selfish of me to do so; I want to free myself of the burden and let him deal with it. He's obviously a stronger man than I am. I'll reassure him that no one would judge him if he chose to turn his back on the movement in order to save it from embarrassment.

"Martin, have you ever thought about stepping down? You've given practically a decade of your life, your marriage, your family, all sacrificed to the movement. You've won a Nobel, for heaven's sake. Haven't you done enough?"

Walk on through the storm. Walk on through the rain. Though your dream be tossed and blown . . .

He looks at me with those eyes that were once filled with dread—now filled with anger, irritation, and contempt. "Step down from what? I'm not the executive of an insurance company or the manager of a department store. Do you know what's going on out there? I am just a soldier. God is the general. How do you turn your back on a revolution? Not you too, brother. Not you. Don't start with that nonsense.

This is bigger than being uncomfortable or inconvenienced. There are sacrifices we all had to put up with when we signed on. I know human frailty is a reality. I just need you to help me."

"Where do you think this is headed, Martin? This won't end happily."

Walk on, walk on with hope in your heart. And you'll never walk alone. You'll never walk alone . . .

"I've asked you to help me. This is how you can do it." He gives me a dismissive look. He's said what he had to. Our conversation is over.

46

It's time for me to go. I see that now. I wish my confrontation with Gant were so irreparably damaging that it would be impossible for me to return to work in the morning. I can't work there any longer. God knows what would happen if I left, but being free of that place might do me some good. I wouldn't have to deal with the pressure of managing all these secrets. And the agents—the agents would find me useless.

It surprises me, even as the idea warms up my brain, but LA sounds good to me now. Despite all the disappointment I suffered there, you've got to love a city that lets you down so often you stick it out just to see if your luck changes. Palm trees and sunshine, Candy in a bathing suit. I haven't a clue what I'd do there, but I'd make it work.

The door to my apartment is ajar. I call out Candy's name and reach for the light switch, but darkness persists. I slowly head toward the kitchen, which I can find thanks to the light from the streetlamp outside. I slip and fall to the floor. At first, I blame the goddamn brace, but then I feel wetness permeating my pants. I feel around. There is a puddle of warm liquid everywhere. I wipe my hands on my shirt and struggle to get up, but fall again. I get up once more and make my way over to the lamp. When I switch it on, I see that my floor is covered in blood, and so am I.

I see her there. Candice. What's left of her face is badly beaten. No, not Count or one of his goons—it's obviously the work of a skilled fighter. I reel back, trembling.

Lester.

Candice. I should have done more to protect her. I should have done more to protect her—from me, from the rest of us. I'm not sure what to do. Police are not an option. Then I see all the blood and shift from sadness to panic. Someone needs to help me with her, and someone needs to kill Lester. I hate to call him, but I don't have much choice.

I didn't give him any details over the phone. I just said that Candy's in trouble. He must have known by my voice what that meant.

Count touches Candice's forehead with a tenderness I've never seen from him before.

"I blame you for this. I should never have trusted you with her."

I do feel responsible in some sense, but at the same time I'm sobered by the reality of a dead girl in my apartment—and Lester out there roaming free or planning a suicide that will rob Count and me of our retribution.

"I let her go with you to LA, and you ain't even man enough to hold on to her. You let some other motherfucker take her, and you ain't even man enough to protect her and see that she's safe."

"Count, I thought it was your job to protect her and see that she's safe. You could've put an end to Lester at anytime. You chose to allow your little game to continue. You blame *me*? No, motherfucker, I blame you!"

Count lunges at me. I try to avoid him but the brace won't budge. He grabs me by the throat. "I should've killed your ass a long time ago."

I grab the lamp and smash it across his forehead. His grip loosens. He goes inside his coat and under his arm and comes back with a gun.

"Just remember that Lester is still out there," I sputter out with my hands in front of my face.

Count blinks rapidly as blood runs from the cut on his forehead. I find satisfaction in knowing I caused it. He pushes me out of his way and goes for the door.

"Wait, damnit. Where are you going? What about her?"

He looks at her, then quickly turns away. "I'll take care of Lester.

You take care of her. Maybe you'll get it right this time," he says as he walks out.

Lester worked her over good. Probably nothing fancy, just a bunch of straights and hooks. She looks like an overripe fruit. Her face is sunken in places, like the bones underneath gave way. I guess at some point he had some mercy to offer: she's still recognizable.

Seeing her like this, I realize I haven't done her justice. While telling my own story, I neglected hers. It may be too late, I'm not sure that it is, but I feel that it's my duty—as a final gift—to give her a voice. "Nobody hates themselves like they do," she said to me. I can hear her now, but her voice isn't coming from her or that little place she shared with Lester. All I see are the spinning wheels of a tape machine. In fact, her voice now bombards my mind, but it doesn't sound real—it's muffled by the crackle and hiss of recording tape, but it's her. It's definitely her.

4

I still don't know what to do, but I don't have to worry about that as my door opens slowly and two dark figures appear. Mathis and Strobe walk in with their guns drawn. They must have heard everything.

"You really fucked up now," Mathis says while staring at Candice's body. "At least cover her up with a sheet, for Christ's sake."

I grab the blanket off my bed and do as instructed. I think about that recording device I found. I had destroyed it, but of course, there were others.

"Get the stuff out of the car," Mathis tells Strobe.

Strobe walks out and then returns a few moments later with peroxide, towels, and gloves. Mathis pours the peroxide wherever he sees blood. Pink, hissing foam appears, and the air is fouled by a putrid-sweet metallic smell. The agents put on gloves, get on their knees, and begin to wipe frantically with the towels. I stand there marveling at the image of the two of them cleaning my floor.

They finish minutes later, covered in sweat.

"Got to get rid of that carpet," Strobe says, out of breath.

"I know," says Mathis. "We'll roll her up in it. Let's get her in the trunk."

Mathis looks at his watch then looks at Strobe. "We've been monitoring them all day. It'll fit. We can still make it," Mathis says to Strobe. "We've got plenty of time."

Strobe furrows his brow, "Are you out of your mind? Do you know what you're saying?"

"Yes," answers Mathis to both questions.

Strobe looks as if he were deciding whether or not to draw his pistol, but it soon passes, and they wrap up Candy in my rug and carry her out to their car.

I look around my apartment. The agents did a good job. It's as if nothing has happened—as if the only crime committed was that my rug was stolen. I can get over losing the rug. I can move on like none of this ever happened. I think about my new life, and I decide to start now, but then Mathis returns. He startles me. For some reason when he walked out, I thought I'd never see him again. "Get yourself together," he says. "Let's go."

As the city lights recede behind us, I know that we are headed for the woods. It's the perfect place to get rid of Candice—and me—but I don't panic. I know that I am outmatched, and I have accepted it. I'll accept whatever else this night has to offer. Everything that's happened has brought about a hypervigilance, and I notice Mathis struggling to speak softly to Strobe.

"Strobe, you can't get soft on me now," Mathis says as he drives. "We have to do this. This isn't about him, it's about *us*. If it ever got out that one of our informants had a dead girl found in his apartment, we'd be lucky if Hoover let us clean the toilets in a field office in Alaska."

"I get it, Mathis. Stop trying to sell it, for Christ's sake."

"If you get it, then act like it and stop sulking."

Mathis takes a dirt road that leads us through a densely wooded area that gives way to an open field. There is nothing but field, night sky, and a large but decaying old house.

"Don't want to get too close. Now, we just wait," Mathis says, staring through the windshield. Strobe turns to him and slowly shakes his head with a sigh.

I think of Candice in the trunk, wrapped in a rug stained with her blood. I tremble and sob softly.

"There they are," Mathis says. Two white men leave the house. "Just on time. They're headed for the rally. The tall one's Billingsley. We've got to be quick. I don't know when they'll be back."

Tall and gaunt, Billingsley is all sinew, like a wiry scarecrow come to life. Even though he's short, Cullworth is all rounded muscle. My bet is that he inflicted most of the damage to that couple.

"Let's just bury her in the woods," Strobe says. "What's the fucking difference at this point?"

"No. We have to try to make this right. Take a good look at their faces, boys. Think about that couple they killed, and how Billingsley and Cullworth would have hurt that girl in the trunk."

"Candice," I say. "Her name is Candice."

"Candice," Mathis says. "Think about how much they would have loved hurting her."

With Candice in the trunk and the ominous silence of the woods, my mind is unraveling. I can't stand waiting in the car any longer. The agents have already broken into the home of Billingsley and Cullworth, so I get out and find them. Inside, there are copies of the "If I Go to Jail" speech by L. G. Maddox and other segregationist pamphlets, scattered on a hand-me-down chest of drawers, too old and weathered to be considered antique. License tags with the Confederate flag and several "Goldwater '64" bumper stickers adorn the walls. Their idea of decorating, I guess. Even cans of the novelty Gold-Water soft drink rest in a milk crate. Strobe mutters "Goddamnit" as he trips over an axe handle with no axe: the defiant symbol of segregation made popular, once again, by L. G. Maddox.

Mathis tears the place apart, throwing clothes and knocking pictures of horse-mounted Confederates and old white people of the Grant Wood variety off the wall.

"I don't see anything incriminating, at least not any evidence," Strobe says, peeking under a shirt with his foot. "What are we looking for, exactly?"

Mathis turns to him. "Don't do this to me now. Not right now. Do you need me to tell you how to be an agent? We've got two murderers on our hands. They killed two people—a couple—and that poor girl in our trunk. Do you really need me to tell you what we're looking for? We need the guitar that Pete said Cullworth couldn't part with," says Mathis.

"Mathis, what the hell is happening to you? We've got a dead colored girl in our trunk and you're looking for a goddamn guitar? He probably pawned the fucking thing already."

A calm washes over his face. Mathis becomes still. "Man, you are one dimwitted bastard. I've been listening to him try and play that thing for weeks now. If he sold it, I would know. It's in here somewhere. I already took pictures of it when I miked the place."

That's when I realize I've been in this room before, or at least seen this room before—in photographs—the night I broke into the agents' office, but my flashlight was only to able to reveal so much.

"So that's why you need the guitar?" I ask. "Because it will be easier to pin one murder on them if you can pin two?"

"Who's *really* the agent in here?" Mathis asks as he turns his back on Strobe and begins to search the closets.

Strobe watches Mathis, down on his knees and banging at the baseboards, "Funny," Strobe says, "I was thinking the same thing."

Mathis's frenzied movements stop abruptly. "Got it," he says.

The guitar: a blues man's weapon and companion. This one looks like it could have belonged to Robert Johnson—like it can summon the devil and make him long for heaven. "Look at that," he says as he carelessly plucks a string. "Like the hunter who keeps the antlers of a deer." Again, he plucks a string, this time with intent. There's a look on his face, frustration, I guess, like there's a song in him that he wishes he had the talent and skill to express.

"Careful, Mathis," says Strobe. "Haven't you ever heard that it's bad luck to play a dead man's instrument?"

"Well, somebody should've told Cullworth," Mathis says.

"Shouldn't that have been in a dusty evidence room already?" I ask.

"It will be. Soon enough." His eyes wander up to the tuners and then to the fret board and puts it upright. "You see that?" he asks, pointing to the neck. I look closer at the faux-pearl chord marks and then I see it—a haze of rust brown splattering. Dried blood.

"I know I'm not much of an agent," Strobe says, "but the guitar doesn't connect to the girl in our trunk."

Mathis goes over to the dresser and opens a cigar box filled with tarnished medals and old coins. After searching through it for a while, he withdraws a horseshoe-shaped ring—faded gold, and an empty setting where the fake diamonds used to be. He walks it outside. I hear the trunk squeak open like a steel casket. When he returns, the ring has blood on it. He places it in the cigar box and gently closes the top. "Let's go," Mathis says.

"My God," says Strobe.

48

The crowd is full of white men, sun-punished and sweaty. Someone holds up a Confederate flag. Another man waves a sign:

**Senator, we DEMAND
that WHITE people
keep THEIR CIVIL RIGHTS!**

There is a man on stage in a black suit, speaking with the menace and warning of a tent pole revivalist. "If Lucifer Coon Jr. thinks he can stir up the niggers, then I promise we can stir up the white race to defend what's rightfully ours."

They clap. The few women who are here chew gum and kiss their mates on the cheek. Mathis slams the door behind us. They all turn and stare silently. Pete, sitting in a corner, sees us and begins to stand. Mathis subtly shakes his head.

"Listen up everyone. My friend here," Mathis places a hand on my shoulder, "says he saw two white men kill a colored girl." Mathis scans the crowd. Billingsley and Cullworth sit up front. "Do you see them?" Mathis asks me.

I pause, conflicted, relishing the opportunity to issue a death sentence on these maniacs, but regretting my proximity to the deed. There must be a better way than bloodying my own hand. *There must be a better way.* I actually repeat those words to myself over Mathis's question.

"Do you see them?" he asks again.

"That's them," I shout, pointing at Billingsley and Cullworth.

Cullworth springs to his feet. "That nigger's lying," he pleads. "We ain't got nothin' to do with no colored girl."

The crowd watches, sweaty and silent. Mathis looks at Cullworth and smiles. "You see, that's a lie. Don't say you don't have anything to do with a colored girl, because I know that you do. I know you do." Mathis casually reaches into his jacket, as if going for his lighter, but reveals his pistol.

The weathered, desiccated orator interrupts, "What kind of white man are you? You come into our gathering with your nigger, pointing fingers. Where is your loyalty?"

"You can shove your loyalty right up your ass. My grandfather was a Jew."

"Who here can vouch for the whereabouts of these two men tonight?" asks the orator. Almost in unison, pleas of "*I will!*" and "*I can!*" come from the crowd.

Mathis raises his hand above the shouts. "Billingsley, Cullworth, say good-bye to your friends. You boys are under arrest."

"Goddamnit," Billingsley stands and kicks over the chair he was sitting in. "We didn't do nothin'!"

Mathis puts the pistol to his own head and scratches at his temple with the barrel. "Now, that's another lie. We found the guitar, boys."

Billingsley throws a hateful look at Cullworth. Then they look at the door behind the podium and make a run for it.

"You see that," Mathis says addressing the crowd. "They're running. You saw with your own eyes. I suggested evidence and they ran." He motions Strobe and me toward the door. "Let's go."

I slow down the pursuit, but we get in the car and quickly catch up to them on the dirt road.

"Stop," Strobe screams to them out of the window. They keep running. Lit by the headlights, they appear to be running in place against a backdrop of blackness.

"Freeze, goddamnit," Mathis shoots at them with one hand on the steering wheel. "Start shooting," he says to Strobe.

Strobe just looks at him.

"Strobe, shoot, for Christ's sake. We're in this together."

Strobe is still silent, but then starts to aim his pistol out the window.

Nothing but the roaring engine, the clamor of gunfire, and the two men trying to run away from it.

Billingsley, constantly looking over his shoulder to gauge our proximity, looks one last time before his skull pops open like a squeezed plum.

A black geyser spews from Cullworth's leg.

Mathis stops the car, gets out, and walks over to Cullworth with his pistol cocked. Bleeding and sobbing, Cullworth attempts to crawl to his escape. On his belly, legs kicking in the red dirt, clawing and scratching toward the black night, he shouts, "Please."

"Please," he says once more as Mathis fires two shots into his back.

49

It was impressive when the police and the press showed up. Mathis and Strobe were astonishingly professional. They prevented the press from photographing me, making sure to cover my head so that they couldn't get a good picture. They put Candy's body by a tree near the Billingsley and Cullworth place, being sure to locate the particular item that would tie them to her murder. Mathis and Strobe. They dazzled the small-time police officers with the kind of confidence and air of authority that only an FBI agent can get away with. They declined having their pictures taken. Only Candy's was necessary. And seemingly, in a flash, it was over. But as they drive me home, I've yet to feel any relief.

Mathis stops in front of my apartment, but Strobe gets out before I do. "I'll walk the rest of the way," he tells Mathis. "I'm feeling sick." Mathis and I watch him walk down the street until he disappears into the darkness.

I move to get out, but Mathis motions for me to wait. "I am sorry about your loss," he says. "But don't feel bad. Something new is right around the corner. Soon you'll forget it ever happened. In fact, I suggest that you do that as quickly as possible."

I think about Candice, and how she fit so easily into the trunk.

"She left," he says. "My wife left me and I didn't even ask why. I was just glad to see her go. The funny thing is I'm not sure if I'm sad about it. I do feel liberated in a sense. Like I'm not burdened with the weight of guilt. Now I can see her in a way that I never could. I love her—so much so that I can't even be sad about my wife leaving. It's as if she gave Lucinda to me as a final gift, allowing me to have the new one in order to forget the old one. I feel this is the time when I could just run away. Please, John, tell me, is this a punishment or a gift?"

It's both. The gift of punishment, I think to myself. He's talked about his wife and for the first time referred to Lucinda by name, but he hasn't said anything about the photographs. He says he's fine with his wife leaving, but I don't see relief in his eyes. No man is okay with his wife leaving, even if the mistress stays. The point is to have them both. I'm outmatched. I know that. Mathis could wipe me out like a bloodstain on a floor. I'm not much more to him than that. "Thank you for your help, Mathis," I say as I get out of the car.

50

I stand in front of my door and wait for Mathis to drive off. He takes his time but finally does. I want to rest, but I don't want to go in. I look around frantically, like a child who's suddenly found himself alone. That doesn't last too long, as the door seemingly opens on its own.

"Couldn't find Lester," Count says, "but I'm sure he'll turn up . . ."

I just stand there.

"Well, what the hell are you waiting for? Come in, dammit."

I walk in and sit on the edge of my bed. Count pulls up a chair and sits across from me. He reaches into his pocket and offers me a cigarette. I accept and he lights up for us both.

"Let me tell you a story," he says, sending smoke from his nostrils. "One night, after my place got raided, two white men come in to see me. FBI. They say they know everything about me, and they ain't lyin'— they do. They list my rap sheet and tell me they got enough to shut me down, but it don't have to happen that way. All I got to do is cooperate. They want information about that nigger preacher. They want the good stuff. And since I already know someone working for him, it should be easy. They started explaining how this was in my best interest. I didn't say it at the time, but they were right. I thought, 'Damn, this could be a fruitful relationship.' I know it seems like that's why I kept you around, but that's not it. You grew on me, little man. We're more alike than you realize. I guess I didn't realize just how much until tonight. I decided to wait a minute before going after Lester, just to clear my head, but then I see that you and me have mutual friends. The same two white men—FBI—come to see you. I always suspected it. They got to me way too easily, and your ass gets rescued way too often. You and me are square. I mean that, so I'll let you live. But you're into some heavy shit. You brought me nothing but trouble since I met you." He takes a long draw from his cigarette and holds it for a beat before sending it out above us. "This is the last time we'll share a smoke. It pains me to say it, but you've got a black cloud over your head. And now, I'm asking you kindly to stay the fuck out of my life." He drops his cigarette on my floor, stands, and then grinds it out with his foot.

I look at the remnants of the cigarette: a smudge of black ash, an ember flickers before dying out.

"Okay, Count. I think that's for the best."

"Yeah, I think so too." He goes to leave but stops himself. "By the way," says Count. "The preacher is in trouble. They've already tried to embarrass him. They've tried to scare him. Now they're trying to ruin him—and you know what's coming next."

5

Count leaves and I immediately want to go running after him. I don't want to be alone in here. I made a mistake coming back. I look at the place where I found her, but there are no haunting visions of her body or her blood, just her voice drifting from that reel-to-reel. Even before she died, the whir of the tape reel had already become a permanent presence in my ears, in my sleep, even while driving. I am still listening . . . but I don't want to hear it. *You're a preacher. You shouldn't be doing this.* Almost a whisper. When I first heard it, I thought she was being coy, but she said it without a hint of irony. That sadness in her voice is too familiar to me. I know that voice. I know that woman. Or at least I thought I did.

Morning. I've seen many nights bleed away into daylight, but I never saw the new day as a gift. I do now. I spent the night in my car. I did not sleep. But now, I am truly awake. A new day, a new beginning. In all my life, I have never been so grateful for a sunrise.

I'll be a better man, and I'll start by being a better accountant. I get in the front seat and drive to work. I don't bother going inside to change and freshen up. I probably should have stayed home, but today is Gant's last day at the SCLC. It would look suspicious if I do not show. I must continue as if nothing has happened.

My euphoria has already faded by the time I reach the office. I look at the front door with a feeling of dread. I can't go back to my apartment yet; the image of her body on my floor is making a vivid return.

So I go in anyway. The office rats are mercilessly scrutinizing, even more than usual. They are silent, except for the occasional gasp, and are nervously avoidant. I enter my office, and all I can think of is the sight of her body and that tree.

The paper on my desk would suggest that I am crazy, or suffering from some sort of brain trauma, had I not witnessed the mastery of Mathis and Strobe. According to this bundle of newsprint, nothing happened as I experienced it last night. It was some sort of macabre hallucination:

Agents Gun Down Killers of Woman and Two Negroes

In a daring display of courage and heroism (gifted to society by Hoover's FBI) agents killed two men responsible for the death of a woman and a Negro male. . . . While the agents should be applauded, it is disappointing that these men were not stopped before they killed again. Another woman, Negro, was found dead and badly beaten, not far from the killers' home. Cannot something be done to rein in the hateful butchery of radical Klan types? Their madness only provides fodder for the malignant imagination of Martin Luther King and his ilk. . . .

Some of the ink has rubbed off on my fingertips. I put the paper down, and notice a brown-red spot on my wrist. I scratch at it—dried blood and dirt—a sad reminder of the night before. There is also a bit on my sleeve. This annoys me. I give myself a look-over and realize that it's not limited to my sleeve. My tie, my shirt, my suit—all of it covered in the scarlet stain of desiccated blood.

My equilibrium is assaulted. My vision seems as if it were placed on a seesaw.

Gant walks in. "John?" he says reaching out to me. I push past him and stumble out of my office into the hall, narrowed by the enclosure of stares. I don't try to run, that will only make the situation more memorable when they try to recall it days, weeks, *years* from now. No, I'll stay calm, gather myself, and stroll out. Gant walks beside me. "What happened, John?"

"Nothing."

"You can tell me, John. Let me help you."

"It's nothing, Aaron. I just had an accident, that's all. I'll be fine but, obviously, I think I should take some time off."

"John . . ."

Strange, until now I had considered my limp manageable while at the office—hidden with a graceful bob and bounce—but as I make my escape, the leg feels deadened. I might as well be dragging a slaughtered hog behind me. It doesn't help matters that as I pass his office, the disappointment and horror on Martin's face are the last thing I see.

52

It's been three days since I last saw Candice. Though my apartment isn't big enough to hide from her ghost, I am fearful of what awaits me outside. Three days of wrestling with the image of her on my floor— and the mess, cleaned up so well by Mathis and Strobe. I anticipated havoc and chaos, but it has been painfully silent. No one is looking for me. No one wants to find me.

Then the phone rings.

"There are going to be some changes," Strobe says on the other end. "We're wrapping this up. I don't think the operation will be continuing much longer. I'm obligated to let you know."

I know he anticipates my curiosity, even protest, but he must not be counting on my sheer relief. He hasn't specified what he means by "changes," but it does sound nice—an alluring oasis, palm trees and everything.

"Say something, dammit."

I grab a cigarette and light up, squinting as smoke curls toward my eyes. "I'm sorry, Strobe. I'm just used to dealing with Mathis."

"I understand . . . but Mathis is gone. Early retirement. If this thing starts up again there will be a new agent in charge. I'll keep you on file, but I can't promise that they'll use you."

"That's fine, Strobe. I'm looking forward to not being used. Is Hoover pulling the plug?"

"After the other night, does it have to be Hoover to pull the plug? I've seen some crazy stuff," he says. "I expected it—but this is not what I signed up for."

"Retirement, you say? At whose suggestion, his or Hoover's?"

"Look, I know you and Mathis had some kind of . . . friendship, but he had to be reined in. This couldn't continue. I won't allow it to."

"Rein in Mathis, huh? Good luck with that."

"No, John, keep that luck for yourself. You may need it someday."

Strobe hangs up, but I just let the receiver lie on my chest as I lean back into the sofa. I thought I had changed, but I haven't. It's over. Here's my chance to run. I can leave now, but I don't move. Eventually, the dial starts its staccato wail and I hang up.

There's a knock at the door. Police?

"Who is it?" I call from the sofa.

"Mr. Estem? I'm a friend of your neighbor's. The Porters. I'm interested in buying your Cadillac."

I didn't know I had neighbors called Porter—but then I remember the ad I placed in the classifieds. "It's not for sale!" I'm not ready to get rid of Black Beauty yet. I'll need her to make my escape when it's time.

"She's a fine automobile," says the man outside. "I'll give you ten grand for her. Cash."

I walk to the window and peer through the curtain. He's a large white man with a pot belly, a short-sleeved striped shirt, and sunglasses. I open the door, "Ten grand, huh? I guess you'll be wanting a test drive?"

"No, that won't be necessary," he says. "You seem like a guy I can trust." His right hand goes behind him and comes back with a pistol. "Open up."

I back up and he kicks the door closed. He keeps the gun on me. With his free hand, he reaches under his shirt and tosses a pillow— that used to be his belly—on the floor. The hat and sunglasses follow too. Pete just stares at me with his mouth open and jaw jutting forward. "I want to know if you've seen my daughter," his lips barely move.

"I have no idea where she is. We can talk, but you don't need that," I say motioning to the gun.

"You're right," he says and places the gun on the table, still closer to him than to me. He then walks over and punches me hard in the chest. I let out a blast of air and stumble backward. My throat feels drinking-straw-narrow. It hurts like hell, but I'm still standing.

Pete frees a deep breath as I search for my own. "See, that's the problem with niggers," he says. "When they try to get smart they just get dumb." He clenches his fists. "It took me a while but I figured it out. I didn't recognize you when you came to my doorstep that day, but when you showed up with Mathis the other night, it all came back to me. I thought something was strange about you, and when all those coloreds started moving into the neighborhood, you were all I could think about. And then I get this picture," he pulls the photo from his pocket, unfolds it, then tosses it at me. It's Mathis with Lucinda. "So I did some digging in the public records to find out who was buying up all the houses and selling them to niggers. That's right, I found out about that fancy nigger and that coon's nest you hang out at. And it didn't take much effort. I went there and asked some spook with a cut-up face if he'd ever seen you before, and he gladly told me where you live. So here I am. Now, where's my daughter?"

Finally, I catch my breath. "How the hell should I know?"

"Did you send me that picture?"

I take a moment, searching for the answer that won't get me killed. I thought the better part of me prevailed that day, and I saved a young girl from harm. But I was only deluding myself; no such part exits.

"Goddamnit! Did you send me the picture?"

"No . . . I don't know. "

"Start talkin'. Where is she?"

"I'm tired of playing this game. I don't know where she is, but we both know who she's with."

"He kidnapped her? Goddamnit, she's just a child! That crazy son of a bitch. Where is he?"

"I don't know. He's taken her away, and I honestly don't know where to. Back to New York, maybe. He says that they are in love."

"In love? Oh, really? He confessed all this to you? Everything? Even him lusting after my daughter? He confided in *you*? I bet his dirty little stories got your top spinning, listening to him talk about her like she's some sailor's whore. He told you all his secrets? Did he, nigger?"

"Listen, you stupid bastard. You've been done a favor. Someone let you know a man was screwing your daughter, and you did nothing. You sat on your hands, and now she's gone. You've been helped enough already."

He goes over to the table and picks up his pistol. "Well, I guess you'll have to give it another shot. You find out where Mathis has taken my daughter. I give you till tomorrow."

"How the hell can I do that? I've already told you everything I know. If you want to find your daughter, she's with Mathis. Where's Mathis? I don't know. The man is an FBI agent. I'll leave it up to you to track him down."

"You tell me where she is. The man who took those photos knows how to find what he's looking for. Twenty-four hours. One minute later and I start telling folks that you're the reason my daughter's gone missing."

53

I pack my things, which doesn't take much time. Just the essentials, like clothes and money—the rest can stay. A dead girl, a crazy Klansman, and the amazing unraveling agent—I should have been long gone by now. I get in my car and drive. Within moments, I realize I have nowhere to go. I've dreamt of escaping to many places, but now, as I try to leave this city behind, they seem like fading dreams, distant and fanciful. I turn back around once I reach the city limits.

Once I'm deep into the city, her voice returns. It's already lost that ghostly quality, but it reminds me of the business I've left unfinished. I stop by my parents' house, but I don't go in. I just watch their silhouettes flicker behind the curtained window.

When the polio first struck and I was still hospitalized, I would pretend to be asleep when my parents came to visit. The nurse would keep the curtain that surrounded my bed drawn. I could see their outlines through the gauzy fabric, and I would watch them, undetected, waiting to see what secrets they might reveal.

Candy's dance record rests in the passenger's seat. I hold it, looking at her face as it once was—that's when I notice the note folded inside:

John,
By now, you know the truth of what happened. I never meant any harm to you or such a great man, but Count promised me a lot of money—too much to turn down no matter how bad I knew it would make me feel later. Of course, he never paid because of Lester. He

even took more than he promised me. I guess that's why Lester got so mad. When he saw that envelope full of money he lost it. I never should have come here. I love him and I'll go back to him. Lester has a gentle soul. He just needs some time to cool off. I know you hate it when women apologize, so I'll just write it so that you'll never have to hear it again . . .

I am sorry if I hurt you.

Love,
Candy

Hadn't I known it all along? How many times have I watched her strut across the stage? That swaying rhythm, just as much a part of me as my own pulse. I knew it in LA as I watched her leave Martin's room— no blond wig could hide it. No, she never had me fooled. I knew her too well. I should be angry with Martin, but I'm not. Didn't I bring them together? Didn't I want him to be envious of me for once? But I didn't do this alone. Count's jeweled hand guided me at every step. Now, with that hand withdrawn, I know exactly what I need to do.

I fold Candy's letter, force it back into the record sleeve, and drive downtown. I get a room at the Fauntleroy, one of the few hotels in Atlanta that is friendly to Negroes. After getting settled, I step out for a bite. I haven't eaten much in the last few days, so I get a well-done steak with lots of butter. After the steak, I head to the pawnshop and buy a gun.

54

At first, the image is murky. Many glossy black shapes moving around. Then these shapes sharpen and coalesce, and I realize that they are glass bottles with silver tops, arranged side by side and filled with a dark liquid. Now I see that they are labeled. Each bottle says the same thing: MARTIN LUTHER KING: TYPE O. For some reason, as I sit at the table across from these bottles they begin to inch toward me. Now they are not just many bottles, but hundreds, thousands of them, coming at me like shiny black beetles. They surround me, filling all the negative space in the room, until they are no longer bottles, but people, marching, and I am no longer in the room, but on a dirt road. These people, millions of them, walk right over me. I hold up my hands for them to stop, but they keep coming, trampling me as I cover my face until the weight of their footsteps fades, and there is no one there except Martin in a hospital bed, IV in his arm, tube from his nose, and a large bandage on his chest. I reach out to him, and then I see that it is not Martin, but me in that bed. Then I feel it—the rough itch of rope scratches and snakes around my neck, growing tighter and tighter . . .

I open my eyes.

There it is. The ringing. I used to think of it as some sort of internal alarm, but now I know that it's a siren. A rescue call, screaming to the aid of a helpless man.

I roll over and hear the rustle of the hotel's coarse bedsheets.

I've been at the Fauntleroy for two days.

Two days since I last saw Lester . . . and Count.

"Negro Nightclub Owner and Two Others Found Dead"

That's what the paper said. How can a few words capture such a fucked-up situation?

I came here as soon as I left Count's. Hiding seemed like the only thing that made sense.

The burden of it all anchors me back to sleep.

It's strange how relieved I felt, when it became clear that I didn't have to take the reins. In some way, I think it absolves me for what was about to happen. Yes, I brought my gun, and I intended to use it, but Count's blood is not on my hands. I empathized with him, but that won't bring Candy back. Someone had to pay. I've been fooled by his moments of compassion before, but I feel he did not love her. His oppression of her had to be met with some sort of retribution. I just wasn't the right man to deliver it.

As soon as I walked in, Claudel approached me, only inches away, with a rigid jaw. "Don't even think about it," I said to him. "I've got something for you." I opened my jacket and showed him the heater I had bought at the pawnshop. "You look surprised to see me . . . learn to keep your mouth shut." Count's office door was open. "I'm here to see Count," I said loud enough for him to hear.

"Let him through, Claudel," he called out.

I inched past Claudel and went inside. Count leaned forward as I took the seat across from his desk.

"I meant it when I said I didn't want to see you anymore, little man, but you got a nervous look on your face, so I guess it's important. But this is the last time. After this, it won't matter that I don't want to see you, 'cause you damn sure won't want to see me."

"I won't take long, Count. I just came to tell you a story, and then I'll be on my way."

He leans back and lets out a sigh. "What the fuck are you talking about?"

"Let me tell you a story about someone I know who gets into trouble with some government types. These government types force him into making secret tapes of a reverend of prominence. He does it, of course. He likes his life on the outside. But there is a girl involved. His girl. A girl he says he loves. He puts her up to it—to seduce the reverend. Now she's on the tapes. He tells her she has to do it to get him out of trouble. So she does it. But then she meets a man, and she falls in love—for real. Someone wants to take care of her, but the gangster can't take it. He's too humiliated. So even though his debt is paid to these government types, he tells her she has to do another tape. Then when she does, that is still not enough, because now he just wants to humiliate her. And then she winds up dead. The end. What do you think of that story, Count?"

"Well, you've got a wild imagination, I'll give you that, but I think you should stick to accounting." He looked me over, loosely interlaced his fingers, and let out an uneasy smile. "I don't know anything about no secret tapes, man. I was told to facilitate a fucking introduction, and that's all I did. They just wanted me to throw pussy at the preacher until he gave in. Who knew it'd be so easy?"

"So why the blackmail scheme?"

"The situation wasn't profitable for me—and you know that's a problem. If the feds get dirt on King, so what? How does that help me? But I wasn't about to step on the government's toes."

"But it was your plan. You laid the whole thing out for me, twice."

"Yes and no. It was my idea, but your plan. You was my consultant. I said let's hit King, and you said no way, it won't work. But then I said what about the queer, and you found a way to pull it off."

"I don't care how you spin it, this is your fault," I said.

"I get it. Realizin' how fucked up you are is a hard pill to swallow, but once it goes down, you get numb."

"She's dead because of you, Count. You could have sent any girl that works to LA. Then Lester would never have laid eyes on her."

"*Please*. She jumped at the chance to be with him. What woman wouldn't screw a man on the cover of *Time* magazine? I didn't have to convince her—she volunteered."

"It's your fault she's dead. *You* brought Lester into it, not the agents."

"Well, you were supposed to be busy with Lester while she was busy with the preacher. But somehow *you* found a way to give that stupid motherfucker quality time with *my* woman."

"No. You're responsible. You didn't have to let her stay with Lester. You knew how crazy he was. You saw the way he came in here like some one-man army. You could have killed him where he stood. But you didn't, because you wanted to teach her a lesson . . . and so did I."

The way he looked at his palms, touching as if praying. "You've already gone too far. You need to stop."

"Every day that you kept her caged, she died a little. You pushed her. She had to escape. You made it impossible to live. Why'd you let it go so far, Count? Why didn't you stop us?"

He shook his head, smiling, then snapped into a rage, "Because she hurt me." The crystal ashtray, carved in the shape of an elephant's head, hints of silver for the eyes, went whizzing past my head, smashing into the wall behind me. I made it a point to stay perfectly still. "No one hurts me without getting hurt back. After everything I'd done for her, she chose that dumb son of a bitch over me. She got what she deserved."

There was a ruckus outside his office—glass breaking, a gunshot, but no confession of pain. I had an idea who might be out there, but I didn't offer any theories. Count grabbed his gun, got up, and opened the door.

Claudel was already on the floor. His head seemed to be looking completely and grotesquely over his shoulder.

"Aw shit," said Count, running out into the bar with his gun drawn. He looked around. The front door of the place was wide open. He looked out to see if someone was running away, then came back in, closing the door behind him.

"What the fuck is going on? You trying to ambush me?"

"Not me, Count. Maybe it's Candy. Maybe you should go to wherever she is buried, find her, beg her—or get on your knees right now and do it, beg Candy for her forgiveness."

He put the gun to my forehead. "Just one more word. I dare you. I'll bury you down here, and no one will ever find you."

I only heard the sound of my breathing as I looked over Count's shoulder and saw Lester appear in the doorway, stealthily, like some jungle animal about to leap upon its prey. Candy never had a chance. Lester and I were involved in a strange kind of dance. I could see him, but I didn't give Count any physical tells. I was proud of myself in that moment—not so much now—because even as Lester raised his weapon, I showed no emotion. I maintained eye contact with Count, and he didn't suspect a thing.

As I told Count to go to hell, he cocked his pistol. I closed my eyes, but not before Lester brought down a lead pipe against the back of Count's head.

Count's body lay on the floor. Lester stood above him, chest heaving, breathing loud punches of air. He swung at Count a few more times. I didn't look. I only heard the sound that it made.

I stared at Count, lying there dead and defeated. The relief I thought would come did not. I feel pity for him to have fallen in such a way. Lester struck the blow. I did not bloody my hand, but I find solace in knowing that I outsmarted him. I wish I could briefly resurrect him, just to the edge of consciousness, so I could whisper in his ear, "I won. I beat you."

I looked at Lester and drew my pistol. I'd never used a gun before, and wondered if I could even pull the trigger. He had Count's gun in his hand, but was he pointing it at me or just holding it?

"Well, what now? Are you staying or going?" I asked him.

"Looks like I might need to stay."

"Just remember that gangsters get killed every day by other gangsters. You know you'll be in trouble after this, Lester. May not be any coming back."

"Yeah, I know."

"Yeah, Lester, it's going to be rough out there. Maybe you should just stay here."

"Yeah, that may be best," he said. "I still got to pay for Candy. I know Count already paid for the bigger things, but someone has to pay for the smaller things too. I think I'll stay here." Lester walked over to Count's desk, felt the leather of the chair, and sat his big frame in it. I remember how the chair let out an exasperated squeak as he spun around in it, like a little boy in a tire swing. When he stopped spinning, he faced me. He was filthy and smelled like week-old mushrooms. Hair wild and wooly, he looked like a madman.

"I been out there in the woods, hiding, and thinking about whether I should just end it all and kill myself. You know how much I loved her and didn't want no harm to come to her, but somehow, being out there in the brush, not hearing no other voices except the ones in my head—memories of what I used to sound like. Nobody telling me what to do. There's something about being out there . . . living how I guess an animal would live. Things started to make sense. I thought about everything, and I realize this ain't really my fault. I mean it is on one hand, but on the other it ain't."

I wasn't moved. I just kept the gun on him, wondering if it would even fire or if I could handle the recoil when I pulled the trigger.

"There was this envelope from Count, full of money. I know he gave it to her, but she just kept saying he didn't. So I kept saying don't lie to me, don't lie to me . . . but she just kept on lying. So I hit her in the mouth . . . just to get her to stop lying. I meant to hit her once, but I just kept hitting her and hitting her. Before I knew it, she wasn't lying no more, but she wasn't breathin' no more either. I'm sorry." He put Count's gun to his head. I knew what was coming next, so I just turned and walked away. I didn't want to see it. I heard the gunshot, and my neck jerked at the sound, then I heard the muted thud of Lester's head hitting the desk.

I didn't look at the outcome. I just walked out into the bar and stepped over Claudel. I looked down at his face. I was wrong for doing that to him. The number of bodies has become comical, but I needed this to happen. I guess Martin and I are alike in that way as well. We both depend on violence to get what we want. I'll never forget how hot it was as I walked out of Count's and into the soul-slowing oven of a day. No one acknowledged me or seemed to care what had just happened. I was just another shadow fighting the sun for existence.

It's sad that it ended this way.

I wake from another nightmare with the strong sensation that someone is watching me.

The room is dark. Only the light from a street lamp makes its way through the curtain. I taste the smoke before I see the glowing ember pierce the darkness, and I realize that it really isn't over. Not yet.

55

"You're a strange man, John. All this shit coming down around you and you're sleeping like a baby." The lights come on, revealing Mathis in a chair at the foot of the bed, a pistol in his hand. Unshaven, hair mussed, he smells of cheap liquor. He's still the self-respecting agent with his government gray suit, but it's wet and his shirt is dirty. It's only been a few days, and early retirement doesn't seem to be sitting well with him. "You've got to love these Negro hotels," he says, grinding out his cigarette. "A white man walks in and nobody asks any questions."

"Well, that's not what I'd call being inconspicuous, Agent Mathis."

"I'm the only one concerned about what happens to you. Trust me."

I toss back the covers and sit up. "So what now, Mathis?"

"I've got a problem."

"I'm all ears."

"Someone's been sending photos of me around."

"A spread in *Life* magazine? 'Your FBI at Work'?"

"Not those kind. The personal kind."

"Those are the worst. That's why we should always be careful. Never know who's watching."

"I hear ya', brother . . . boy, do I ever. But these photos aren't just of me. There's a little girl involved."

"That's a tough one. Little girls should never be involved."

"Yeah, but she doesn't deserve this. She's got a father who might get upset."

"Ain't that the trouble with little girls? They all got fathers." I see now that the bottoms of his pant legs are wet and muddy.

"Excuse my appearance," he says. "My wife left me. She used to do all the laundry . . ."

"It shows."

"And I've been working hard to get your accommodations in order."

"I think I'll stay right here."

"I knew you were watching me," he says, ignoring my statement. "Part of me wanted an audience—I'm glad that it was you. Tell me what you saw. Is she as beautiful as I think, or am I just a fool? When my wife left me, she left a present behind. Photos. I'm sure you know what they showed. I knew it would end eventually, but did you really think I'd let you get to my wife? Did you think I'd let you contaminate our marriage with your twisted mind—and let you just walk away? I was going to let you live, but the last straw was when you sent the same photos to Pete. You almost ruined everything for Lucinda and me," he says, bringing the barrel to his chest.

"Would it matter if I told you I didn't do it?"

"You're not as smart as you think you are," he says. "You're the kind of dummy that wears a wig and fake mustache when he wants to go unnoticed—sunglasses and trench coat with the collar up. The kind of dummy who thinks two niggers in a yellow taxi are inconspicuous."

"I'm an amateur. I know. Even Pete paid me a visit. He wants his daughter, Mathis."

"So now you're his messenger? You went through all of this to help him? Do you think he's some sort of honorable man? Do you know how we turned him? He sat by and watched Negro men and women get beaten and killed, and he did nothing. He saw men get lynched in the woods, and he did nothing. But you know how we flipped him? He asked his brothers in the Klan to loan him some money so that he could open an auto repair shop, and they refused. That irritated him. So he stole the money from them. He didn't leave. He didn't quit. He stole. That's how we got him. Maybe that's why you're so drawn to him. You two have so much in common."

"I didn't do it for Pete."

"For who then? For King? For that dead woman and her black buck? Who?"

"I did it for *me*, goddamnit!" I must lean forward with too much passion, because Mathis's pistol makes sure I stay in my place.

"You're a fool, Estem. Don't you know how I helped you? You and your people. Pete's blown. He's done for. Won't be long until they find out he's the one who gave us info. And you had the nerve to chastise me about two people. Two murders. That's *police* work. Live or die, the world keeps on turning, parks get built, and the mail gets delivered. We were trying to bring down the Klan—the entire organization—and we couldn't do that with just two murders. The whole Klan. Bringing in Billingsley and Cullworth too soon would have brought down the whole investigation—and it did. The two of you. You and Pete. Two informants connected to two murders? We had to wrap it up. Whoever picks up the ball will have to start from scratch. They'll have to find a new man inside."

"So if you're trying to bring down the Klan, what were you trying to do to Martin and the SCLC? I know you are not trying to equate the two."

"All agents are centurions, guardians hired to maintain and preserve stability in this country. That's what all of this is about. Anyone threatening the future success of this country is an enemy of this country."

"So as far as the status quo is concerned, a nigger hanging from a tree is just as dangerous as a nigger hanging 'round a lunch counter?"

"Ask the ancient Romans about integration. Everything was fine until the Goths wanted their civil rights. This wasn't a figment of Hoover's imagination. King is out there saying that we'll see a Negro president within a generation. Think about that, John. Think about the kind of devastating upheaval that would require. Sure, these things start out honorably, but then they go Cuban, and the next thing you know the Soviets are calling the shots."

"Listen to you, Mathis. Still toting the line after what they've turned you into."

"I was wrong. It wasn't them—I was the problem. I see that now. And it's liberating." He stands. "But I wasn't the enemy, John."

"So what are you now? Are you the enemy now, Mathis? What are you here for?"

"I'm still trying to help you. You're the problem—just like me—and I'm here to put you out of your misery." He points his pistol at me. "Let's go. We have to make this quick. I've got to go see about a girl. You first." Mathis and the gun watch me get out of bed and put on my pants. He makes sure that no one is in the hallway before following me out, about two steps behind with the gun at the small of my back. We leave the hotel room, and then he checks inside the elevator. "Get in," he says. He keeps the gun on me but glances at the buttons and presses the one for the service entrance. The elevator groans and begins its descent. I try to think of ways to get out of this.

"What about Pete? He's looking for you, Mathis. He wants his daughter, but he's looking for you."

"Let him come," Mathis says.

"The man doesn't know where his daughter is, Mathis."

He looks at me with his slightly rheumy eyes and smirks. He lifts his arm and points his gun at me, higher now, chest-level. "Is that such a bad thing? You've seen what type of person Pete is. Is she better off with him than with me? I saved her from him. We were tailing this kid in the Klan—dumb kid, about twenty. He was taking weapons across state lines into Mississippi. That's federal, but we thought we could turn him. When I pull the kid over, I see that he's got a trunk full of weapons, and a front seat full of beautiful."

"Lucinda."

"Yeah, Lucinda. I told the kid I'd give him a break. Georgia's off limits, you can go anywhere else, but the guns and the girl are coming with me. It's a long drive from Mississippi to Georgia, enough time to get to know someone. The crazy thing is, it felt like she already knew me. I told her about my wife, and she told me about Pete. She didn't have to say it, but I could tell the guy's a weasel. What type of example does that man set? He has a daughter who needs love, and he's running around in the woods burning crosses. The sad thing is, he's not even a man of conviction. If he was dedicated to this life—to these beliefs—as a man, you might respect him. A man who lives by principles, no matter how twisted they are, deserves some respect. But at the first sign of trouble, what does Pete do? He bends. He was even easier to turn than you."

"Mathis, maybe you're looking at it in the wrong way. Doesn't that redeem him? You threatened him with jail. If he had not turned, who would have taken care of Lucinda?"

"I'll always take care of her."

"You didn't know her then. Doesn't that count? Pete did it for her, Mathis."

"I think you're giving the man too much credit."

"Maybe so, but he is out there looking for his daughter. Some part of you must sympathize with that. Try to understand that man's fear—not knowing where his child is."

"You're sounding desperate, John. Stop it. You wear empathy like bad cologne. It stinks on you."

The elevator stops at the service entrance, and we enter the alley behind the hotel. Mathis's black sedan is waiting. The air is muggy, and the streets are glossy black from one of our copious summer rains.

"Get in the front. You're driving," he tells me. "Wouldn't want to look suspicious." The barrel pokes my lower back as I get in. Mathis keeps his gun on me while I drive. "Just keep driving. I'll tell you when to stop."

I drive through the city, slowly. Mathis has entered a quiet spell, but everything he doesn't say tells me where he's taking me. The woods. I realize that escape is not possible. When this car stops, so will I. No, my life has not flashed before my eyes. But the many missed opportunities of flight do. All my neglected, life-preserving decisions flutter in my mind, frame by frame, like a rapidly regressing film reel. And then I see it. The place that allowed me to make so many escapes. A sign? No. I am beyond invoking religion. It's just the natural course of my evolution. A creature of the shadows learns to see in the dark.

The streets are empty.

I make a sudden U-turn.

The car tilts and the tires scream.

"What the hell are you doing?"

"You'll kill me in those woods for sure, but I may survive a car crash."

I make another sharp turn as a gunshot pierces the windshield. I close my eyes, anchor my foot to the accelerator, and drive into the gilded doors of the Royal Theatre.

56

I don't remember the impact. After coming to, I check myself for injuries. My nose is busted and my shoulder feels like I've used it to pound pavement. I look in the backseat and see that Mathis is unconscious but breathing. I get out of the car and feel the ball of fire in my shoulder—then I see the head of a young man lying on the hood. A jolt of panic shoots through me, but I realize that it's the head of a pharaoh, and one of the sphinxes that adorn the building has been decapitated. I look for a place to run to. The door to the theater is locked. The car damaged it some, but it didn't do enough to break the bolt and chain that secure it. Mathis lets out a groan, and I make my way into the alley next to the theater. Trying my best to develop some speed, I look over my shoulder as those taillights grow faint, and I go behind a building and into an alley that parallels the viaduct. "Hey!" I hear someone shout behind me. I turn around and all I see is a man obscured by distance and shadow at the end of the alley. It's not Mathis, but it's too far away for me to make him out. I don't stop moving either way. I see some steps that lead down near the entrance of the tunnel. It's dark and the train tracks are barely visible. I think about resting down there, just catching my breath until sunlight. Maybe then, things will be different. Maybe Mathis will give up and go to that motel and see that little girl of his—Pete's little girl. But then I hear those desperate footsteps, and I know they have a bounty on me.

I stumble down the last of the steps and enter the dark tunnel, staying far to one side so that I can rely on the wall to guide me and keep me from tripping over the tracks.

Into the darkness, only the sound of the echoing voyage of water—runoff from the earlier rain—my brace, and those menacing footsteps behind me. He calls out my name. I stop, but then I tell myself to keep moving. Never stop, no matter what.

Mold, decay, and rust. The excavation has released the smells of a tomb. Darkness and more darkness. Darkness persists until I come upon a service light. It is only in that brief moment of illumination that I realize how far down I've gone. In front of an ancient general store, covered in a blanket of cobwebs and neglect are the bones of an abandoned animal. Possibly a dog or a pig, I don't know. How long did it wait down here before it realized no one was coming, and it had waited too long to escape?

Gunshot.

It echoes past me, and my shoulders spring to my ears.

Footsteps. And then nothing . . . except my own breathing.

"Estem!"

My name echoes throughout the tunnel, punctuated by another bullet that ricochets so close that I feel stone fragments hit my back. Then I see another service light and a platform of some sort. I hope it's not a dead end. I wait in the darkness. I hear the scratch of flint, and then I see a new source of light—a glowing orb approaches, casting a pistol-wielding shadow along the forgotten storefronts, seeking me out, inching toward me, closer and closer . . .

It is then that I step out into the light, trying my best to make it through to the other side before Mathis can get another shot at me. I am too slow. As I fall through the shaft of light, his bullet hits me in my already wounded shoulder. In that moment, awareness and acceptance crystallize from the pain. I'm not going to run anymore. He's going to kill me, but I won't give him the pleasure of fleeing like an animal. He'll have to look me in the eye. The squeak of my brace breaks the silence as I lie on the ground exhausted.

"Estem?" Mathis calls out into the darkness. "Stop hiding. For once in your life, show some courage." He steps into the light, sees me lying here, and I foolishly anticipate a bit of mercy. "Don't worry," he says, "it'll be all over soon. Get up." I know he intends to instill a sense of dread with that comment, but it only summons relief.

From somewhere behind Mathis, I hear the ominous preparation of a shotgun. Mathis turns when he hears it too. It's not my imagination.

"She's just a little girl," says a voice coming from the darkness.

Mathis points his pistol toward the shadows. "Who's there?" his head dances about, searching for the source.

"You know good and goddamn well who it is. She's just a little girl . . ."

"What the hell are you talking about?"

"Maybe there's more than one. Maybe you've got some sort of problem, fella. I guess Lucinda don't mean nothing to you—'cause there is just so many girls you done raped."

The word "rape" sobers me. I can't see him, but I know the routine.

"She's just a little girl," he says again. Finally, the man steps into the light. Pete, no longer cloaked, no longer hooded, points the barrel of his shotgun at Mathis. "What makes you think you have the right? Do you think you own me?" Pete thumps his chest, letting his gun drift. Mathis twitches at the opportunity, but Pete resets his aim. "Do you think you're entitled to take from me—to violate my child? As if she don't even belong to me no more. Like she's yours for the taking? Where is she?"

Mathis clasps the butt of his gun with both hands, raising it eye-level. "She's in a motel room in Macon. I told her to wait for me. She's safe. Pete, you're pointing a weapon at a federal agent. I'm completely within my rights to shoot you if you don't drop that gun by the time I count to five. One," counts Mathis.

"Go ahead and count all you want, son of a bitch. You'll be dead before five."

"Two. Drop the gun, Pete."

"That don't scare me none. If I talk to them boys up in Washington, and tell them how you been raping my little girl, they'll understand what I've done. Some of them got to have children of their own."

"Three."

"Goddamnit, stop counting."

"This isn't about you, Pete. It's about her. Killing you would make having her a whole lot easier. Four."

"Five." Pete pulls the trigger. The blood from Mathis's knee splatters my face. He doesn't scream. He only fires his pistol as what used to be his knee buckles. Pete gasps, grabbing his throat as blood pushes through his fingers. He drops the gun, his free hand reaching for Mathis as he falls.

Pete must have followed me to the hotel, just as Mathis followed me in here. Count was right—I was in control the whole time. They were just flies caught in a web I'd spun. I wait until the last sounds of life fade into the gloom, and then I stand. Mathis's wound, visible in the dim pool of light, looks as if it had been caused by some ravenous animal. I don't want to see it. I walk away from it, farther into the tunnel. I don't know how long I walk. It seems like days, but I won't give up now. I am determined to see the other side.

I reach another service light, and then I see them: chimeras—half shadows, half men—scattering and scurrying like monstrous rats. But what I thought were hallucinations are actually people, vagrants who have made this place a home. They run past me, but their foul odor stays behind. *Help!* I plead, but they keep running. Who knows if I only thought it and never said it aloud. Who knows what they'll think of me when they come upon Mathis and Pete. As I get closer to where they were sitting, I see the weapons of street life: Saturday-night specials, brass knuckles, ice picks and homemade shanks, the occasional pistol. The darkness seems to lose a layer of dismal, becoming lighter and less soulless. Then sounds of the abyss give way to the sounds of life: squealing tires, breaking glass, and pointless screams. I've found the way out. Thick overgrowth obscures the abandoned train tracks and the tunnel's opening. When I finally emerge, I see young men, Negroes, holding down their corners. The do-rags, the undershirts, the clench-jawed toothpicks—all turn and look at me in disbelief. I've just crawled out of the earth, so it's understandable. Then their faces shift from shock to menace. Now I realize why those weapons are down there. That's where they've hidden their cache from the police that patrol the area. I don't say anything. I just walk past them and onto the main street. After all I've been through, I think I've earned it.

Once again, the night has found something in me worth saving and granted me clemency. Few are so fortunate. I think of poor Lucinda, alone in that motel room. When her lover doesn't show up, she'll be expecting her daddy to come and save her. I walk through the night streets, clumsily trying to find my way home. Sounds, some unfamiliar, echo inside my head until I realize their source. When I was a child, some bullies made fun of my limp, so I made fun of their inability to read, halting stammer and all. They took me out to the creek behind the school and beat me badly. I was fine with the beating, I was used to that, but they took my brace and left me there, helpless. I cried for hours, but no one came for me. It was starting to get dark, so I had to find a way home. I crawled around on my belly like an animal until I found a fallen branch that was strong enough to support me, yet small enough to control. One step at a time, I made my way out of the creek and onto the city streets. Maybe that's how my brother did it. I was exhausted and it seemed like it took forever. It did. But all I could think about was how disappointed my father would be when he saw how someone got the best of me and how that would be the likely pattern of my life. When he opened the door, he looked at my swollen face and gimp leg covered in scrapes and scratches, but then he looked at the branch that I'd used as a crutch. He took it from me, held me up with one arm, and with the other, he held up the branch. "At least you made it home," he said, squeezing me tightly. "You made it home."

They are surprised to see me at this late hour, which turns to shock when they become aware of my horrific state. Immediately, my mother starts with the questions, but my father tells her to let me be. He sees the blood on my face and on my clothes. He sees the wound on my shoulder and tells me not to worry, the bullet only grazed me and he'll stitch it up himself. He sees that something has beaten me down and tried its best to kick the life out of me. He doesn't need to know what it is exactly. He just knows that after a rough night, I made it home. I survived. While running liquor, he must have seen many men come home like this. *He* must have come home like this. He doesn't ask me questions. He just sits next to me, silent, in that disciplined way of the bootlegger, while I lie in bed, grateful for life and eager for sleep.

57

I'm not much of a religious man. I guess I'm only a Christian out of habit and inheritance. So it's fitting that I had to escape from one hell only to find another one waiting for me.

California did not disappoint. Upon my arrival, Watts went up in flames. An inferno of pent-up anger and frustration, the sky seemed permanently black with smoke. Black bodies did their familiar dance of violence and despair. It felt appropriate, as if I had brought all that bad fortune with me. I did not participate but I welcomed it, foolishly thinking that my survival through the ordeal might bring me closer to redemption.

Was it the level of destruction or that strange connection we had? I don't know, but he decided to follow me. But what he offered they had no use for. Not here. That talk of peace and love was already a dead and forgotten language here. They laughed at him, challenged his wisdom, called him a fool, and sent him packing, back to his dreamed-up Utopia.

That negativity, that dark pall must have stayed with him, soaking into his clothes, his hair, his skin, because it soured everything he touched. Everyone he came around thought he was stale, a relic. He came back to chants of Black Power! It was more than a slogan—he had entered a world where cynicism reigned. Still, he did not give up. He actually went to Chicago, but despite his best efforts, that city too erupted. Little seedlings of hate blossomed wherever he went. His failures mounted to the point that he was forced to lead from the margins, crafting messages that were viewed as less than strategies and more like corny advertisements of love and tolerance. The rest of the country had caught wind of vengeance and disappointment. There were graveyards full of optimists.

I have been in hiding. Maybe the word "exile" is more appropriate. Something about LA drew me back to it. I'm sure it helped that it is a world away from the rest of the country. You can lose yourself here, and no one will ever find you . . . or so I thought.

I paid back the SCLC in anonymous donations, thanks to a little tax business I opened to help working-class Negroes file their returns. I see young orderlies, jaded garbagemen, and even the occasional colored nursing assistant, but I never thought I'd see a nearly middle-aged FBI agent.

"How goes it, old friend?" Strobe asks without smiling.

I offer him a seat, and he keeps his hat and sunglasses on.

"It's good to see you're doing well, John."

I look at him and nod.

"You left quite a mess back there in Atlanta, didn't you?"

"What do you want, Strobe?"

Strobe takes off his hat and sunglasses, puts the glasses inside the hat and rests them on his lap. He reaches into his pocket, then throws down a pack of those foreign cigarettes that Mathis introduced me to. He looks serious now. "Your friend the preacher is in trouble. I've heard through the grapevine that things could get ugly in Memphis." Martin is in Memphis supporting the sanitation workers' strike. It's been all over the news.

"What do you mean by '*ugly*'? Martin's seen more violence than some World War II veterans."

"I mean the kind of ugly I, you, or anyone shouldn't know about. The anti–Vietnam War talk is earning him some special enemies."

I smirk at him. "Could these enemies be any more dangerous than Hoover's boys in their gray suits and narrow ties?"

Strobe reaches over and retrieves one of the cigarettes. "Do you mind?" he asks.

"Go right ahead," I say as I push over the ashtray.

"I don't know about you, but I've never been okay about how things went back there. It pushed me to my limit. The good thing is it helped me to learn what kind of man I am, and what kind of man I am not. Mathis wasn't always that way. The job just got to him."

"What are you asking me to do, Strobe?"

"I'm not asking you to do anything. This time I am providing you with the information. Do with it what you will. I just think someone should talk to him, warn him, tell him to ease up a little. Obviously it can't be me."

"Can I ask you a question, Strobe?"

"Sure."

"Why did you send those photos to Pete?"

"Mathis was right—we were in it together. He needed to be reigned in, but you were right. I couldn't do it."

"Who wrote that letter to Martin? You or Mathis?"

Strobe stands and puts his glasses and hat on. The dark lenses reflect nothing. "Take care, John. I'll be seeing you around."

"Only if you want help with your taxes," I say as he walks out.

I look at the cigarette still burning in the ashtray. I was always aware of the threat Martin faced. I never warned him. I pretended that it was because I was protecting him, but really, I was protecting myself: warning him would incriminate me.

While I was away, I spun a narrative that would allow me to live with myself. Over time, however, it was not enough. When I left, I was primarily concerned with making things right—whatever that meant. I realize now that I cannot be right with myself unless I am right with him. I need him to know. Even if he doesn't understand, I need him to know. I need him to forgive.

It is a balmy night in Memphis when I arrive at the Mason Temple where he's giving a rousing sermon to a congregation that looks like a swaying mass of church fans and sweat. He is sweating as well, profusely in fact, as if it were some self-willed physiological display of empathy. The church is crowded and there are no vacant seats, so I stand in the back among a group of people who have also failed to find seating.

He walks the crowd through ancient Rome, the Renaissance period, and his battle with Bull Connor. He tells them of the demented woman that tried to kill him, and the broken tip of her blade that made the possibility of a sneeze a deadly threat. Then he sees me. I can't detect any bit of recognition. He continues with his speech. I begin to feel I may have made a mistake in coming here. I decide to wait until after his sermon to make any assumptions, but then he comes to a point in his speech where he says, "I'm not fearing any man," and he looks me right in the eye, as if the line is intended for me. I feel as if a dagger has been thrown at my heart. I have failed. His disappointment is irrevocable. He finishes his speech and leaves the podium. He almost collapses but is propped up by Abernathy. The church vibrates with shouts and cheers.

I understand now. I thought I understood then, but I didn't. Martin possessed an even greater courage than I realized. His struggle was already mythic—already dangerous—just in its conception. I read somewhere once that there is nothing more difficult, more dangerous, or more uncertain than to take the lead and introduce a new order of things. All those who have done well under the old conditions are enemies of the innovator, and he has only lukewarm support from those who may succeed under the new. This resistance comes from fear of the opponents—who have the laws on their side—and partly from the incredulity of men, who do not readily believe in new things until they have had a long experience with them. I thought that I was on his side, but I wasn't. I never was. And not because of my admittedly self-serving actions, but because of my cynicism. I never believed in humanity as he did.

It doesn't help that we are both staying at the same place, the Lorraine Motel. I see him the next day talking to Abernathy and Young, but I don't want them to see me, considering the state I was in the last time they saw me. I duck into a little diner next to the motel and order a cup of coffee to get my courage flowing. As soon as I reach the bottom of this cup, I'm going to apologize to him face to face. It's a good thing my father isn't alive to see this—the disgrace that will surely follow. I'm not sure if my apology will be a confession, or a warning, or a strange mixture of both, but for my own peace of mind, I need to tell him. I need to let him know that while I thought I was protecting him from the diabolic voyeurism of the FBI, I was jealous. Jealous of you, of the agents and how close they got to you. It seems they were always revealing some new detail about you to me, and I guess I foolishly believed that we had some sort of unspoken connection. I know it's ridiculous and I made too much of it, but you need to know I am apologizing now and—

A gunshot. Screams. From everyone. Everyone. I already know the answer, even before the young Negro woman runs in shaking horribly and screaming, "They shot Dr. King! They shot Dr. King!"

All the patrons run out to see what has happened, if what this young girl has said is true. They hope she's crazy. They pray she's a disturbed prankster. They hope she's a liar. If so, even though her joke is cruel, they'll thank her and forgive her. But she's not finished.

"It's over! It's over!" she screams. I have never seen this woman before now, but I know, at this moment, it's the most honest she has been in her life. "It's over," her tears flooding her face. She reaches for me and cries into my shoulder. I know I should be crying too, feeling what she's feeling. I want to but I am not. My heart races. I haven't thought about her in a while, I've tried not to, but the smell of this woman's hair brings Candy to mind. Maybe I'm holding this woman a little too tightly, but she doesn't seem to care.

It takes me a while to pry her away and make it outside. The screaming crowd and the crying sirens make a terrifying marriage of sounds. The bloody balcony is even visible from here. One foot pokes over the edge. Abernathy, Young, Jackson, they are all around him, kneeling over his body. Then suddenly, they stand, all of them, and point. I know they are not pointing in my direction, especially with all these people and the chaos, I am certain that they do not even know that I am here. But I can't help fearing that they are pointing at me. They aren't, but I can't stop seeing it that way. It seems that everything has gone abruptly silent. I feel as if the crowd has collectively turned their many eyes toward me. I swallow and step back. I'm getting that feeling I know all too well: the need to escape.

I push through the ever-expanding wall of people, moving as quickly as I can, hopping in the opposite direction past the people now filling the streets on word of the sad news. I run until my heart feels like a fist trying to punch through my chest. I stop on a corner far enough away to allow the sirens and screams to register only as a faint buzz. There is no one around. I am alone, and for the moment I feel relieved. I didn't have to go through with it. I didn't have to see the disappointment in his eyes, and he the shame in mine.

I close my eyes, but I do not cry. I do not cry because I have already mourned. Why the execution? Don't they know he'll no longer be a man but a legend, a practically deified eternal symbol of self-sacrifice? Of course they do. After all of this, what bleary-eyed fool, intolerant of the world's intolerances, would think himself worthy enough to fight against injustice? His death sentence began long ago—this was just the exclamation point. Savior, Sinner or Martyr, but never just a man—the sniper's bullet was the deathblow to some-one already suffering from the wounds of fragmentation.

I open my eyes with their plot seared on my brain, and like the burning cross that night in the woods, I only see its brilliance.

Eventually, I wander back to the motel. The fears of mob violence were misguided. The streets have succumbed to an eerie, defeated silence, yet the patrol cars continue their vigilant crawl.

There is nothing but a whispering chorus of television sets trans-mitting the tragic news through cracked doors and open windows. Accompanying all of this is the sinister sound of metal scraping against stone.

I look at the balcony above me. In between the open spaces of the railing and underneath room number 306 is an elderly Negro man, crouched and working feverishly at a spot on the walkway. His arm goes back and forth in a sawing motion, sending the sound of that horrible scraping into the night. He stops to mop his brow with the back of his hand and slowly stands up. His arthritic knees creak loudly. He holds a large putty knife in one hand and a mason jar filled with a dark liquid in the other. He looks at the jar and begins to cry. That is the spot where Martin last stood. His blood is in that jar. He leans over the railing, staring out into the dark. Nothing is out there. But then he sees me, and our eyes meet . . .

58

A picture comes to me in my dreams, clear and unaltered. President Johnson sits at his wooden desk and signs the Civil Rights Act of 1964. He hands the pen to Martin, patting him on the back and shoulders as Martin leans in to add his signature as well. Martin looks toward the cameras almost stupefied, amazed, and definitely grateful, but there is an element of disbelief in his eyes.

I try to place myself there, but it's hard. When I do so, the image fades in and out, losing clarity. I can now trace this effect to the deep fear of being on the wrong side of history. We wish and hope for great change, but few of us actually expect it. That is what triggers Martin's look of amazement—the shock that not all of us can see that change is inevitable. He knew that one day America would have to wrestle with itself to live up to its ideals and promises. He saw it. I did not. I am angry with myself for not having the vision or the faith to see it. I am angry for choosing the wrong side.

As the status quo expanded, some of us wanted to sneak under the fence, including me. However, he had a greater vision: one of change, one of hope, a vision that I aligned myself with, out of pure pragmatism—a desire to hedge my bets. Maybe I was fearful of appearing cynical, but the foresight belonged to him, not to me. That vision, that courage—it fills me with shame to think of myself on his side. Now I see I was on their side—the side scared of change. Count, Mathis, Strobe—all of us are on the side scared of change, all of us desperate for inclusion, to receive that pat on the back from the establishment.

It pains me to say it, but I feel I am part of an old breed of Negro that dreams inch by inch, while these new brothers and sisters dream in leaps and bounds.

When I think of the movement, it seems that the media has provided my memory. It's the same black-and-white photos and footage of marches and beatings that everyone associates with the time. And to the disappointment of the occasionally interested young person, I offer no insight on the era beyond the superficial. Although the other ghosts have faded, there is one image that continues to haunt me.

I still see that man on his knees, twenty years later. I have since read a book that a prominent historian had written about that time. Scholars consider it the preeminent account of that period: *The King Years.* (There are other works, but I never dared to read them, fearing what they told or didn't.) I read the pages with careful interest, though pretending to be indifferent to whether or not my name might pop up in a paragraph. I got halfway through the dense text before going to the index and taking a look. I was there. But not in a chapter dedicated to exposing me, or a section intent on condemnation. Just a simple but troubling line buried in the voluminous notes:

> John Estem was an informant for the FBI. Agents recruited the young SCLC accountant to obtain information regarding the activities of King. This turned out to be a very expensive mistake. Estem was not a member of King's trusted inner circle, and King barely knew him.

ACKNOWLEDGMENTS

This book—and so many other opportunities—would not have been possible without the peaceful crusade of Martin Luther King, Jr. I thank him, and his fellow patriots—both remembered and forgotten— for their vision, courage, and sacrifice.

My thanks and gratitude go out to the following:

Scott Mendel, for believing in my work and finding it a home.

Malaika Adero, for granting me a home, encouragement, and guidance. Todd Hunter and the hardworking folks at Atria.

The Public School Heroes: Ms. Taylor, Mrs. Poulet, Mrs. Thrower, Ms. Balton, Mrs. Mullen, and Mr. Drulias.

The invaluable books on the era by David Garrow, Taylor Branch, and Michael Eric Dyson.

The Jacob K. Javits Fellowship. Jonathan Ames. The New York University Creative Writing Program and my teachers: E. L. Doctorow, Nicholas Christopher, and Chuck Wachtel.

Charles Salzberg and the New York Writer's Workshop.

Samuel Maio, for believing early (even when I did not).

My family: Khadija El-Amin, Leroy Harrison, Sr., Pauline Harrison, Robert Avery, Sr., Dena Avery-DeGuzman, Butch DeGuzman, Alberta Finch, Sweetie Dean, Uncle Junior, Mildred, Earl, Latiah Hill, Wanda Thacker, John Harrison, Moses Gora, Larry Miller, Melissa, Megan, Jeffrey, Paula Mathis-Ellebie, Tom Ellebie, Steven and Vivian Myers, and all the other family and friends that I have failed to mention. Especially:

Eileen Miller-Myers, for your open-hearted generosity.

ACKNOWLEDGMENTS

Doris Avery, for your wisdom and love.

Roy Harrison, for introducing me to faith and imagination.

Debra Harrison, for your strength, for all you've endured, for me, for *everything*.

Jennifer Harrison, my partner, best friend, soul mate, and inspiration.